"What an

Hanna glanced o   ere he still sat on his blanket, watching

"I'm not laughing, I'm smiling," he answered, "because I wish I knew what makes you tick."

Her eyes hardened. "What's that supposed to mean?"

Now he stood up, too, retrieved his hat, set it on his head and began to gather up their blankets. "You're an enigma, Hanna Winters. You're prim and proper on the outside and all fire on the inside, only you hate for anyone to know it."

"That's absurd!"

"Is it?" His topaz eyes darkened passionately. "The woman I saw last night isn't the same woman I'm looking at this morning."

"You were supposed to forget about last night."

"That's right, I was, wasn't I? Sorry about that. Some things are hard to forget."

Dear Reader,

Our titles for September include a new novel from June Lund Shiplett, *Boston Renegade*. When spinster Hanna Winters inherits a ranch from her long-lost brother, her quiet world is suddenly turned upside down.

In *Bodie Bride,* by Isabel Whitfield, Margaret Warren is furious when her father brings home a live-in guest, especially one who's so good-natured about disrupting her well-ordered life.

Knight Dreams is a wonderful story from first-time author Suzanne Barclay. Lord Ruarke Sommerville was drunk when he rescued French noblewoman Gabrielle de Lauren and impulsively wed her. Now he must learn to live with the consequences.

Mary Daheim's *Gypsy Baron* is the author's third book for Harlequin Historicals. Set in England and Bohemia during the early years of the seventeenth century, it is the story of an English noblewoman and a mysterious half Gypsy who draws her into a web of political intrigue.

Look for all four novels from Harlequin Historicals each and every month at your favorite bookstore.

Sincerely,

Tracy Farrell
Senior Editor

Boston Renegade

June Lund Shiplett

Harlequin Books

TORONTO • NEW YORK • LONDON
AMSTERDAM • PARIS • SYDNEY • HAMBURG
STOCKHOLM • ATHENS • TOKYO • MILAN
MADRID • WARSAW • BUDAPEST • AUCKLAND

Harlequin Historicals first edition September 1992

ISBN 0-373-28739-9

BOSTON RENEGADE

Books by June Lund Shiplett

Harlequin Historicals

Sweet Vengeance #110
Boston Renegade #139

JUNE LUND SHIPLETT

The granddaughter of an old-time vaudevillian, June Lund Shiplett was born and raised in Ohio. She has been married to her husband, Charles, for more than thirty years, and they have lived in the city of Mentor-on-the-Lake for more than twenty-five years. She has four daughters and two grandchildren, and enjoys living an active outdoor life.

Chapter One

Boston April, 1872

Outside the run-down boardinghouse the sun was desperately trying to peek through lowering gray clouds, while inside, in one of the sparsely furnished rooms, Hanna Winters leaned back in her overstuffed chair and closed her eyes. Her hands were still trembling slightly and her insides were taut and fluttery as she rested the letter she'd been reading on her lap.

How had he found her after all these years? How long had it been, ten? No, eleven. The last she'd seen of Henry was when he walked out the front door of their parents' home and said he'd be damned if he'd fight for a bunch of old men who were sitting in Washington. If he was going to dodge bullets he'd do it for himself. No one had heard from him since, and now this.

Straightening apprehensively, she lifted the letter and looked at it again, letting the words really sink in this time.

Dear Hanna,

When you read this it will mean that I am dead. I know there was never any love lost between us, but you are my sister and the only kin I have left. I have known of our parents' deaths for some years now and I am sorry Father left you penniless. Perhaps I can make up for that as well as the humiliation you suffered when I ran off. I have done well over the years and what I have I leave to you with one warning. Never forget the days we spent as children in the east wing of the old house. If you remember this you will never have to worry about money again, but beware for there are those who would take it all from you.

I risked my life many times for what now belongs to you. Do not throw it away.

Your Brother,
Henry G. Winters

The letter had been accompanied by formal papers from a lawyer. Hanna glanced toward the table beside her bed where the papers lay and frowned. The papers stated that she'd inherited a ten thousand acre ranch from Henry Girard Winters, who had expired on the fifteenth day of the third month, in the year of our Lord, eighteen hundred and seventy-two.

No note as to how Henry had died or anything. Just the papers and the name of the attorney to contact when she arrived in town.

She drew her eyes from the papers and looked once more at the letter. It seemed strange hearing from Henry after all these years, and now only after he was dead.

He said there was never any love lost between them. Whose fault was that? She wasn't the one who'd always picked the quarrels. And she wasn't the one who'd defied their parents every chance he had, stealing from their father and running around with the wrong crowd.

Actually it had been no surprise when Henry'd walked out that day after their father had refused to give him enough money to pay someone else to go to war in his place. The only thing that was a surprise was that he'd stolen the money anyway. Still, he'd never returned, and Hanna was sure it had been her brother's disappearance that had broken their mother's heart and eventually caused her death.

Sighing wearily, she stood up, walked to the window and stared out. Suddenly there was a knock on the door.

"Hanna?" It was her landlady.

"Yes?"

"Did you forget the rent?"

Hanna hesitated, then slipped the letter into the pocket of her bustled skirt and headed for the door.

"I'm sorry, Mrs. Brady," she said as she opened it. "I'm afraid I've been rather distracted this afternoon and forgot it was the first Saturday of the month already."

Mrs. Brady stepped into her tenant's room and watched Hanna hurry to her handbag on the dresser and take something out. She turned again and handed Mrs. Brady the eight dollars owed her for the next month's rent. Eight dollars that included all her meals as well as her room and laundry.

The landlady frowned as she saw how Hanna's hands were trembling. "Are you all right, dear?" she asked.

Hanna hesitated. She was never one to confide in others, but Mrs. Brady was more than just a landlady. She was one of the few friends Hanna had.

"It's nothing, really. It's just that the letter I got in the mail today was rather a surprise."

"Not bad news, I hope."

"In a way, yes. Yet I'm not sure."

"If there's anything I can do to help..."

Hanna had lived at Elizabeth Brady's for eight years now, and during that time the two had slowly become close, although the landlady had never nosed into Hanna's private life unless asked.

"Maybe you could help a little," Hanna finally said, deciding she had to talk to someone. "Would you mind sitting down for a minute so we could talk?"

Elizabeth slipped the eight dollars into the pocket of her red wool dress, fluffed up the white ruffles of her fichu and walked to the overstuffed chair Hanna had been sitting in only moments before. Her dark eyes studied Hanna curiously.

Hanna Winters was one of Elizabeth's best tenants. Always on time with the rent, never noisy, not a hint of scandal. Not even any suitors, but then that was understandable since Hanna just wasn't the sort of woman men were attracted to. At twenty-nine, her hair, which had been coal black when she was younger, was prematurely white and she wore it long, twisted and set in a knot atop the back of her head.

Even her eyes were a strange color. Not blue, not gray, nor purple, but a faded lavender, with gold and silver flecks running through them. Her dark eyebrows were striking because they hadn't turned white like her hair, and they gave her a haunting, mysterious look.

However, there was nothing unusual about the rest of her face. Her nose was straight with a slight tilt at the end, and her lips, although exceptionally pink, were full with just a slight overbite.

Mrs. Brady, who was twenty years older than her tenant, watched Hanna closely as the younger woman strolled over to the window and stood looking out for a minute, then turned to face her.

As a teacher at a private girls' school, Hanna fit in well; as a seductive woman, she left much to be desired. Her lavender eyes focused on Elizabeth and Hanna put her hand in the pocket of her dark green skirt, pulling out the letter. Once more her hands were shaking.

"The letter I got was about my brother," she said, her voice anxious. "I haven't seen or heard from him in eleven years and I just got the news that he's dead."

"Oh, my, and I never even knew you had a brother."

"I might as well not have. He was three years older than I, and I'm afraid we never did get along. However, it seems since I'm his only kin I've become his sole heir."

"To what?"

"A cattle ranch somewhere near a place called Hangtown, Texas."

"A ranch?"

"That's why I'm so upset. I'm a schoolteacher, Mrs. Brady. I don't know anything about ranching, and besides, I've never been out of Boston in my life. I just don't know what to do.''

Elizabeth Brady frowned. "What do you want to do?''

"That's just it, I don't know."

Elizabeth looked thoughtful. "You could sell the place, I suppose.''

"I suppose." Hanna fingered the letter in her hands, remembering the last sentence Henry had written telling her not to throw it all away. "But then if I write back and tell the lawyer who wrote to me to sell it for me, how do I know whether he'd be honest enough to send me what the place might really be worth?''

"My, you do have a problem, don't you?''

Hanna reached up, fidgeting with the pointed collar of her tailored blouse, its pale green color contrasting with the darker green skirt she wore.

"What would you do if you were in my position?'' she asked, her other hand tightening on the letter until it felt clammy in her hand.

Elizabeth Brady stared at her young tenant, then felt a twinge of regret nudge her. "What would I do?'' she mused, surprised that Hanna had asked. "Oh, dear, I'm not really sure, but you know, I honestly think if I had a chance to get out of Boston I'd jump at it.''

"You would?'' Hanna was taken aback.

"Oh, my, yes. Especially if I were young like you. After all, what do you have here? A class full of pampered, spoiled young ladies who give you nothing but trouble all the time, and a lonely room to come home to.''

"But a ranch?''

Elizabeth's eyes lit up. "Why not a ranch? You can learn about cattle just as well as anyone else. You're not dumb, Hanna."

"No, but I'm not stupid enough to think I could run a ranch, either."

"Don't be ridiculous, dear." Mrs. Brady reached up, smoothing a strand of salt-and-pepper hair. "Running a ranch can't be much different from running a schoolroom. It's just that there are certain things that have to be done and you do them."

"You make it sound easy."

"Well, I imagine it'd be a lot easier than riding herd on a bunch of young girls. After all, cattle can't talk back."

Hanna frowned. "I just don't know."

"Think how exciting it'd be. My, what an adventure. I wish I had the chance—I'd go."

"Would you? Would you really?"

Elizabeth's eyes narrowed suspiciously. "What do you mean, would I really?"

"Just what you said." Hanna's frown creased deeper. "I could never go out there alone, but if I had someone with me..."

"Go with you? You want me to go with you?"

"Why not? You've always said you hated running the boardinghouse for your dead husband's uncle. Well, this is your chance. And you wouldn't have to spend any of your own money, either. The lawyer sent me a bank draft for enough to get me there, and with what I have saved it should be enough for both of us."

"But just to leave..."

"That's what I'll be doing. After all, you have nothing more to hold you here than I do, and we've always gotten along so well together."

Elizabeth's hand went to her mouth and she looked apprehensive. Her fingers tapped against her lips nervously. Hanna was right. She'd always hated her life here at the boardinghouse, but when Daniel passed away she'd been ill prepared to do anything else, and not being a young woman anymore, it was the only way she could take care of herself and not have to rely on other people. Besides, Daniel's uncle had needed someone to take care of the house for him at the time and it only seemed logical for her to accept his offer when he made it. But oh, how she hated it. Mostly because Uncle Ambrose was such a crabby old miser. But to do something so drastic, and at her age.

She sighed. "Oh, Hanna dear, you want an old lady like me with you? Surely you don't mean that."

"Oh, but I do." Hanna was sure now that the decision she'd just made was the right one. The solution was ideal. "And you're not old, either. Don't you see, it'll be a chance for both of us. Please, Mrs. Brady. I just can't go out there alone, and I really don't think I want to stay here. As you said, there's nothing for me here."

Elizabeth was speechless. She stared at Hanna for a moment, then finally straightened in the overstuffed chair, finding her voice. "I don't know what to say," she said, her voice eager and breathless, the light in her dark brown eyes filled with wonder. "I never thought . . . I've always been so sure I'd die here in Boston collecting rents from boarders."

Hanna smiled. "Then you'll go?"

Mrs. Brady shook her head and shrugged. "Like you said, I guess I don't have any reason to stay here, either. But oh, my dear Hanna, I never expected anything like this."

Hanna unfolded the letter in her hand and smoothed out the wrinkles. "Then it's settled," she said emphatically. "How long before you think you'll be able to leave?"

"Oh, my." Elizabeth looked thoughtful. "I suppose Uncle Ambrose will have to find someone else. And how about the school? Won't they have to find someone to replace you?"

"Shall we give them a week?"

"Only a week? That's not very long."

"Do you care? Do you really care?"

Elizabeth's jaw set stubbornly and she reached up, primping her hair. "You know, I really don't," she answered, her voice sharp and caustic. "Oh, my!" She clasped her hands, a smile softening her sharp features. "Isn't this exciting?"

"I hope so," Hanna said. She looked at the letter again, then at Mrs. Brady. "And I'm so glad you're coming with me," she went on, her lavender eyes crinkling excitedly. "Just think, Texas. Who would have dreamed . . ."

Later that evening Hanna stood in front of the window in her room and looked out across the front lawn of the boardinghouse. The clouds had won their battle with the sun just before dark, and now rain fell steadily, making it hard to see as the wind that had risen whipped at the trees lining the road.

Her years in Boston hadn't been all that bad, really, up until her father's death. It had only been then that life had started to disintegrate into everyday survival. If her father hadn't been so deeply in debt she might have been able to retain a semblance of respectability, but he'd owed everyone, and by the time the creditors were paid off she'd had no other choice but to find employment.

Thank God she'd always paid attention to her studies. However, she never had been happy teaching. Mrs. Brady was right, she dreaded every day spent at the Bryn Mawr Finishing School for Young Ladies.

But a Texas ranch? Just the thought was frightening. And she had absolutely no idea where the town of Hangtown might be. The letter from the lawyer said it was some few hundred miles west of Fort Worth. She didn't even know where Fort Worth was. It was undoubtedly a military post somewhere, but she was sure she'd never heard of it before.

She and Mrs. Brady had spent most of the afternoon making plans, and Hanna was glad now that she'd asked the landlady to join her. She'd always liked Mrs. Brady. Maybe because Hanna had never had any aunts and Mrs. Brady seemed to fill the void. The landlady was always concerned but never overbearing, and she seemed to have a zest for life lacking in all the other women Hanna knew.

Of course the other women Hanna knew were all teachers like herself. All except the librarian, who also boarded at Mrs. Brady's. But all of them, including the librarian, seemed quite happy with their lot.

She reached up, pulled the window shade down, then began unbuttoning the little pearl buttons on her green blouse. She was going to need some new clothes, that was for sure. She hadn't bought anything new for years. But then she'd had no reason to.

By the time she slipped into her plain cotton nightdress, brushed out her hair, then tucked it up into her lace nightcap, Hanna was already making a mental note of everything she'd have to take with her.

A week and a half to the day after Hanna received the letter from her brother's attorney, she and Mrs. Brady were standing on the train platform at the depot, waiting for their baggage to be loaded and the train to pull out.

Ambrose Brady had been furious with his nephew's widow for leaving him in the lurch, as he nastily put it, and the headmistress at Bryn Mawr had told Hanna she'd be too hard to replace and tried to get her to change her mind.

Hanna, however, had been emphatic. Now, as she watched the last of their luggage disappear into the baggage car and started to board the train, she knew more assuredly than ever that her decision had been the right one. She was finally getting out of Boston. Staid old Boston, where you weren't anyone unless you had money, and even with money you weren't anyone unless your background was the right one.

Well, her background had been the right one, but the loss of her father's wealth had changed all that. Too bad, she thought as she sat down in her seat in the coach and made room for Mrs. Brady beside her. There were other towns besides Boston, and she was determined to make a place for herself in one of them. Hanna watched with a fluttering stomach and new expectations as the train belched smoke, shooting sparks high into the sky. The city of Boston was soon left behind.

They had bought tickets for as far as Chicago. From there they'd change trains, heading for St. Louis, where they'd pick up the Kansas Pacific Railroad for the next few hundred miles and get off in Abilene. According to the ticket agent in Boston, they'd have to make different arrangements from Abilene south to Texas, since no railroads ran that way as yet. What arrangements he'd meant Hanna had no idea, although she had heard about the stagecoach lines that were common all through the west.

She had sent a letter to the attorney who'd written to her, telling him when she was coming, and now as she sat back in the stuffy coach and relaxed, watching the scenery go by, she tried to imagine what it was going to be like in Texas.

It didn't work. She knew absolutely nothing about the state except what she'd read occasionally in newspapers or books. Ah, well, she'd learn soon enough what she had got them into, and settling her hands in the lap of her dark blue traveling suit, she began to once more watch the scenery go by.

Three days later, tired and weary, Hanna stood beside the train in the dusty street of Abilene, Kansas, and turned to Mrs. Brady.

"Are we really here?" she asked, her gaze sweeping the length of the train, then stopping to watch the men from the baggage car unloading their luggage.

Mrs. Brady tried to smile, but she was just as tired as Hanna. They had slept on the train every night, and she felt as if all the dirt and grit in the world had settled on her.

"Well, the conductor did say Abilene," she answered. "We'd better get over there and make sure they have everything."

Both women had carried a carpetbag on the coach with them, and picking them up, they headed toward the far end of the train, where the baggage car was, to check that all their trunks had arrived with them.

Besides the bags they were carrying, each woman had two small trunks, only now Hanna wasn't quite sure what they were going to do with them because, unlike in Boston or even Chicago, there were no porters of any kind, only myriad people scurrying about the recently arrived train.

There were four men handling the baggage, and Hanna walked over, set down her carpetbag and tapped one on the arm.

"Excuse me, sir."

The man slid one of the trunks aside in the dusty street, then reached in his pocket and grabbed a big blue kerchief, wiping his brow.

"What can I do for you, ma'am?" he asked.

Hanna glanced at their baggage. "I'm afraid my friend and I are going to need some help with the trunks you've just unloaded," she said, turning to look at the man, who was quite big and brawny. "I was wondering if you could perhaps direct us to a hotel where we might stay, and to someone who could haul our trunks there for us."

The man finished wiping his brow, then straightened and looked off across the wide street filled with horses, carriages and people, put two fingers between his lips, and whistled so loudly that Hanna was startled.

A young man sitting in front of a huge three-storied building across the way jerked to attention, waved a hand and strolled over to where a horse and wagon were parked. Climbing into the driver's seat, he maneuvered the wagon across the street and alongside the baggage car. There wasn't even a platform for the passengers to step out onto here in Abilene, so the wagon could draw right up next to the train.

"This here's Leroy," the baggage handler announced as the young man began to climb down. "He can take you to a hotel, but I'll have to help him with the trunks."

"Then please do," Hanna urged him.

After watching the men load the trunks onto the wagon, which Leroy called a buckboard, Hanna and Mrs. Brady let Leroy help them onto the seat next to him, then the young man took the reins and turned to look at Hanna.

"Which hotel, ma'am?" he asked.

Hanna had no idea. From where they were she couldn't get a good look at the town. She could hear cattle bawling somewhere nearby, and with the bustle of people the place was frighteningly crude and noisy.

"Whichever's the best," she finally said. As she straightened stubbornly, the young man slapped the reins and the buckboard moved forward.

Moments later Leroy was pulling the horses to a halt in front of the building where he'd been relaxing. It was painted yellow with green trim, and there were venetian blinds at most of the windows. The place was huge, and Hanna could see that it had its own dining room.

"Here we are," he announced as he fastened the reins securely. "This is the best, the Drover's Cottage."

Hanna had to admit the place looked far better than anything else in town, but even at that it was awfully close to the stockyards they'd seen earlier from the train. It was probably just as plush inside as the fancy hotels in Boston. However, there were no porters or bellboys.

Hanna let Leroy help her and Mrs. Brady down, and while the two women went inside, the young man found a couple of men lounging around outside to help him with their trunks and they followed the women in.

By the time the men had all four trunks in the lobby, the women already had the keys to their rooms, only Hanna wasn't very happy.

"You're sure the stage south won't be in until Wednesday?" she asked again, wishing she could change the man's answer.

"Sorry, ma'am." The desk clerk was insistent. "The stage goes through here only twice a week, Wednesdays and Saturdays, like I said."

"Well, at least that'll give us a chance to clean up some." Elizabeth looked at Hanna, then at her own dirt-covered clothes before looking at Hanna again. "I think we both could use some soap and water and a change of clothes, don't you?"

Hanna knew how Mrs. Brady felt. It was as if the grit and filth had been ground right in.

"Yes, but I'd feel better if we didn't have to spend so much time here." Hanna glanced out the front window. "Two days in this godforsaken place. Goodness, we could be halfway to Fort Worth by then."

The desk clerk smiled. "That where you ladies are headed?"

Hanna nodded, the flower on her fancy little hat bobbing unceremoniously as she did. "That's only our first destination," she said, her unusual Boston accent out of place among the people in the lobby who were speaking in slow lazy drawls. "Eventually, we're headed for a place called Hangtown. Perhaps you've heard of it?"

"Nope, can't say that I have." The desk clerk glanced at the register where the women had signed, then looked at Hanna. "You want to leave them there trunks in the storeroom until the stage arrives?" he asked. "Ain't gonna be any too easy for anybody haulin' 'em up them stairs."

Hanna hefted the portmanteau she was carrying a little more securely in her hand, then smiled. Actually she had an extra change of clothes in it, as did Mrs. Brady in hers, but still they might need something more.

"It'd be nice if we could," she said, then frowned. "But what if we might need something from one of them?"

"Don't see why we can't let you get anything you might want."

"Good, then," she answered, thanking him, and a short while later both women were ensconced in their rooms enjoying nice warm baths.

The next two days went slowly and neither woman ventured far from the hotel. The quick glimpse of the town they'd had gave them the impression that it looked a little too raw and rough for them. They just weren't used to cattle towns, and finally, on Wednesday morning, Hanna and Mrs. Brady were once more ready to travel, waiting patiently near the hotel for the stage to be loaded.

All clean and well-groomed again, Hanna was in a deep purple suit, the bustle sporting bands of black velvet, the black velvet collared jacket fitting her slim waist like a glove. It was a decided contrast to her pale hair, and the purple hat with its fancy little black feathers gracing the brim matched the suit perfectly. It was one of the new outfits she'd bought just before leaving.

Mrs. Brady had on a new traveling suit of deep rust-colored poplin, the bustle higher in the back than usual, the neckline of the formfitting jacket dipping into a lower V in front than what she normally wore. And with the small straw hat, its cascade of orange and yellow flowers trailing down the back of her salt-and-pepper hair, she felt far younger than her years.

They stood a few feet from the steps of the hotel, watching the stage driver and some other men struggling desperately to get their trunks on board and get them tied down. Neither of them noticed a horse and rider heading their way from the other end of town.

Blake Morgan slumped low in the saddle as he neared the hotel, then let his gaze rest on the two women waiting beside the stage. His deep amber eyes narrowed as he whistled softly to the Appaloosa he was riding, then rubbed the two days' growth of deep chestnut beard on his chin.

"Well, looks like that's her," he whispered to the horse as he rode along, his eyes never leaving the two women. "Just like the orders said." Just to make sure, he reined Diablo in to a good spot from where he could watch, waited until the women had boarded the stage, then rode on to the hotel where he checked to see if Hanna Winters's name was on the register.

Satisfied she was the woman he'd been waiting for, he went outside, mounted the Appaloosa again and took off in the same direction the stage was traveling, but at a much slower pace.

Fort Worth was even dingier than Abilene had been, and Hanna and Mrs. Brady were far more the worse for wear when they got off the stage than they had been on leaving the train.

The stage route had taken them straight through Indian territory, and although some of the tribes in this area were fairly peaceful, there were always others who wouldn't conform, and twice they had to outrun raiding parties.

Even if there hadn't been any Indians, the stage was the most uncomfortable conveyance Hanna had ever been in, and between the constant dust and the jostling and bumping around, she'd never been so glad to arrive anyplace than she was when she'd stepped off the stage at Fort Worth.

Now, however, as she stood looking around her, there were tears close to the surface. "Oh, good heavens, what have I gotten us into, Mrs. Brady?" she said as she watched the driver and some men unloading their trunks. Fort Worth wasn't really a fort. It was more of a military camp set in the midst of a conglomeration of ramshackle buildings that looked as though they'd been very hastily erected.

Elizabeth smiled. "You didn't think it was going to be easy, did you?"

"I didn't know what it'd be like."

"Well, don't fret, my dear." Elizabeth Brady wasn't about to knuckle under. "The driver said we should be able to hire someone to take us to Hangtown without too much trouble."

"I'm not really sure now I want to go."

"Don't be ridiculous. You've come this far, haven't you?"

Hanna marveled at Mrs. Brady's courage. She sighed. "I know you're right, only I just hadn't expected it to be like this."

Mrs. Brady glanced around her, taking in everything she could in one quick look. "What did you expect?"

Hanna shrugged, then reached up, tucking a stray hair back beneath her little purple hat. "I don't know. I guess I thought the people out here would be more civilized."

"The people are civilized, my dear," Elizabeth offered, her dark brown eyes sparkling warmly. "It's the land that's not. Now, shall we find out from the driver how we locate someone to escort us the rest of the way, or are you going to just stand here while you try to convince yourself you made the right decision?"

Hanna looked at the older woman, now more than ever glad she'd brought her along. If she had her way right now, she'd probably turn tail and run, and deep down inside she knew if she did she'd regret it for the rest of her life.

"All right, let's go," she said and they both reached down, picked up their skirts and headed toward where the stage driver was busy helping unload the last trunk.

Despite the presence of the soldiers, there seemed to be the same rowdy element here that they had seen in Abilene, so neither Hanna nor Mrs. Brady were surprised at the stares they were getting as they questioned the stage driver.

"See that trading post over there?" the man said, pointing to a building on the other side of the street from where the stage had stopped. "Well, everybody who comes into town, civilians and military alike, ends up in there eventually. The man who runs the place is Sam Baker, and he can help if anybody can."

Hanna stared at the building. It didn't look any too inviting. The horns of some animal hung over the door, and part of the front window was covered with canvas where it was broken. But if that was where she had to go, that was where she had to go.

She looked at Mrs. Brady. "You stay here with the luggage and I'll be right back," she said as the driver headed toward the stage and climbed aboard. Shouting to the team, he slapped the reins vigorously. As the stage took off down the dusty road continuing on its route south toward San Antonio, Hanna straightened her shoulders and started walking toward the trading post.

The place was dim when she stepped inside, and she was glad because she knew she was flushing profusely from the looks she'd received from some men lounging on the porch out front. Men in Boston had never looked at her like that, nor had they made any of the remarks she couldn't help hearing from some of them, either. And Mrs. Brady said they were civilized, she thought.

Tilting her head up defiantly, she tried to forget their disrespect and stood for a minute letting her eyes adjust. When she could finally see, she walked briskly over to a man who looked like he'd be the proprietor.

"Excuse me, sir," she said in her most polite manner. "But the stage driver said you could help me."

Sam Baker had been putting some hardtack out on the counter when Hanna had walked in, and he'd paid little attention, figuring she was some elderly lady from the stage, but now that she was closer he could see that he'd been wrong. The woman standing before him was much younger than the white hair led the casual observer to believe, and he'd never before seen anyone with such strange, hypnotic eyes.

"Yes, ma'am?" he said, studying her appreciatively.

"He said you'd know where I could find someone to take me and my friend to a place called Hangtown."

"Hangtown?"

"You've never heard of it?"

"Oh, yeah, I know where it is, but it ain't gonna be that easy to find someone to take you that far."

"May I ask why?"

"You've seen the land out there. Indians, rattlers, outlaws, not to mention the weather."

Hanna frowned. "Then what do I do? We have to get to Hangtown."

"Well, now, I didn't say it was impossible," Sam said. "I'll have to ask around some, that's all."

"And how long will that take?"

He shrugged. "Who knows? An hour, a day, a week. All depends on who shows up."

"Oh, fine. And in the meantime?"

"In the meantime, lady, you could talk to me," Blake said as he stepped out from the shadows where he'd been standing watching Hanna ever since she entered the trading post.

Hanna whirled abruptly and found herself staring into a pair of intense, amber-colored eyes in a clean-shaven face that looked like it had been chiseled from granite. The man wasn't handsome by most standards, but there was something intriguingly rugged about him that caught Hanna by surprise.

"I beg your pardon?" she challenged.

"I said you could talk to me. I'd be willing to take you to Hangtown."

"Oh? You're headed that way?"

"Not really. I'm not headed any place in particular, but if the money's right . . ."

"Well, at least you're honest."

"A fault I rarely own up to."

Sam Baker hadn't seen the stranger come in, and now he studied him curiously. "You ain't from around these parts, are you, mister?" he asked.

Blake grinned. "I know my way around if that's what you're worried about."

Sam's scowl was deep enough to let anyone know he wasn't sure he believed the stranger. "You got a name?"

"Morgan, Blake Morgan."

Hanna was looking at Blake Morgan so she missed seeing the look of recognition in Sam Baker's eyes, although Sam said nothing. "Well, Mr. Morgan," Hanna said. "Just what would you consider the right price?"

"All depends." Blake glanced over at Sam. "You wouldn't happen to have a beer, would you?" he asked.

Sam moved to a keg behind the counter and drew off a mug of beer, then handed it to Blake, who tossed him a coin. The beer was frothy and warm, but Blake didn't seem to mind. He took a big gulp, licked his lips, then looked at Hanna.

"First of all, I have to know what's involved," he finally said.

Hanna clasped her hands, trying not to appear too nervous. "There are two of us, Mrs. Brady and myself," she answered, hoping to keep her voice steady. For some reason Blake Morgan made her all too aware of her inadequacies when it came to men. "We each have two trunks apiece as well as the portmanteaus we've carried with us."

"That's all?"

"I should think that would be enough." She inhaled, then straightened more confidently. "So, how much will you charge?"

"Well, let's see. We'll need a wagon and a team of horses."

"Good land, that'll cost a fortune!" Hanna was astounded. "It never dawned on me we'd need all that."

Blake eyed her apprehensively. "I hope you didn't expect to haul four trunks on the back of a horse."

She shook her head. "I guess I just didn't think about it."

Blake looked at Sam. "You know anybody's got a team and wagon for sale?"

Hanna looked flustered. "You mean I have to buy them?"

"Don't worry, you can sell them again when we reach Hangtown."

"I certainly hope so."

Blake addressed Sam again. "Well," he asked, "do you?"

Sam thought for a minute. "Only place I know of is the livery stables. Zeke's always got somethin' around he's tryin' to sell."

Blake downed the rest of his beer. "Shall we?" he asked, looking at Hanna while he handed the empty mug to Sam.

"But you didn't tell me how much you'll charge."

"And you didn't tell me your name, either," he shot back.

"Hanna, Miss Hanna Winters," she answered somewhat hesitantly.

"All right, Miss Winters, you buy the horses, wagon and supplies, and I'll charge you fifteen bucks on top of it, how's that?"

Hanna stared at him for a few minutes while she argued silently with herself. She probably shouldn't trust him, but she had to get to Hangtown, and she hated the thought of waiting around here like they had in Abilene. Besides, the accommodations here would probably be far worse than they had been at Abilene. She hadn't seen anything that even remotely resembled a hotel. "Done," she finally said, her lavender eyes deepening to a cool amethyst.

A few minutes later she and Blake Morgan left the trading post. She waved to Mrs. Brady, who was still guarding their luggage, while she and the man she'd just hired to take them to Hangtown headed toward the livery stables down the street.

Hanna had no idea so many supplies would be needed. However she tried not to complain as Blake Morgan had her buy potatoes, coffee, flour, hardtack and a number of other staples.

According to Morgan, Hangtown was approximately two hundred miles west of Fort Worth, not far from the Salt Fork River.

"I've been there a couple of times in my wanderings," he said as they loaded the things onto the old buckboard they'd bought from the liveryman. Blake had even bought an old water barrel and as Hanna watched him and one of the other men heft it onto the buckboard and fill it to the brim, she began to question just what she'd really gotten herself into.

Mrs. Brady wasn't helping matters. "Are you sure you can trust him?" she asked from where she stood next to Hanna. "After all, what do you know about him?" Her dark eyes studied the man intensely. "He doesn't look any too honest to me. Really, Hanna, don't you think you should have asked around a little more before hiring the first person who came along?"

"And taken the chance on having to stay here for days on end? I told you what the man in the trading post said."

Elizabeth's eyes narrowed as she continued to stare at Blake Morgan. "I just hope he doesn't get us out there in the wilderness somewhere, rob us and then leave us to die.''

''Mrs. Brady!''

''It's happened before to innocent travelers.''

''Not to us, it won't.'' Hanna was very emphatic. ''I made sure to warn him that we won't stand for any funny business, and he assured me he'd get us there safe and sound.''

''Oh, I see.'' Elizabeth sighed. ''I'm so glad you told him.'' Hanna was so naive. ''But I think I'll go see if I can buy some more positive assurance,'' and she started to walk away.

Hanna caught her arm. ''What do you mean, more positive assurance?''

''Nothing for you to worry about, dear,'' Elizabeth answered as she patted Hanna's hand where it rested on her sleeve. ''I'm just going to go see if I can buy us a gun.''

''A gun!''

''Shh. Do you want him to hear you?''

''But a gun?''

''It's the best assurance I know of,'' Elizabeth answered as she lifted Hanna's hand from her arm. ''Now, go back to what you were doing, and I'll be with you as soon as I can.'' And she strolled away, heading toward the trading post.

A scowl was deeply etched in Hanna's face as she watched Mrs. Brady walk away. A gun. Oh, dear, she thought, now I really wonder what I've gotten us into. But before she could decide to change her mind and try to get someone else to take them, someone perhaps recommended by the post commander or even Sam Baker, Blake Morgan called her to give him a hand. While she helped him sort through their staples, checking to make sure they had everything, she didn't have time to worry about Mrs. Brady and her gun.

The stage had arrived at Fort Worth a little after ten that morning, and by three in the afternoon the old weathered buckboard with Blake Morgan driving and Hanna and Mrs. Brady on board ambled down the street past the military encampment and headed west.

The seat of the buckboard was only big enough for two to be comfortable on, so Blake had confiscated an old chair from Sam Baker and nailed it to the bed of the wagon for Mrs. Brady. He'd also insisted that the ladies extricate their parasols from their trunks, and now as they rode along, Mrs. Brady rested the handle of hers on her shoulder while she sat on the chair and listened to the conversation that was going on behind her while she kept her eye on Morgan's Appaloosa, tied to the back of the buckboard, and watched the scenery go by.

"Just what kind of work do you do, Mr. Morgan?" Hanna asked as she held the parasol in front of her to keep off the hot afternoon sun. Mr. Morgan had been right, she'd have been burned to a crisp already without its shade.

He clicked to the horses plodding leisurely along. "Most anything comes along," he answered. "And you?"

"I'm a teacher. At least I was a teacher before coming out here."

"Where'd you teach?"

"At the Bryn Mawr Finishing School for Young Ladies in Boston."

"Ah, Boston. You're a long way from home then."

"I'm afraid it's not home anymore."

"What did you teach?"

"Etiquette and manners."

Elizabeth was sure she heard the man choke on that one.

"Etiquette?"

"That's right, etiquette."

"You mean they actually teach people things like that? I thought good manners just came naturally."

Hanna glanced at him. "It all depends on what you consider manners. I'm not just talking about greeting people, Mr. Morgan. In Boston one must know the proper way to hold eating utensils, the proper way to excuse oneself from the table, the correct way to address mail."

"You mean like holding your little pinky out when drinking tea like I've seen some ladies do?"

"Precisely." Hanna was pleased she'd found someone out here in this godforsaken country who understood.

"But that's a bunch of nonsense," he said, suddenly deflating her. "Who cares how the hell someone holds a teacup, or addresses mail for that matter, as long as it gets to where it's going?"

Blake saw her jaw clench angrily and knew he probably shouldn't have said it, but that didn't change the fact that he had.

Suddenly her eyes began to dance angrily. However, unlike most women who would have lashed out at him with a verbal attack meant to wilt the brawniest of men, she merely drew her eyes from him and stared straight ahead down the road.

"I guess I can't really expect you to understand," she said, her voice ringing loud and clear in the hot afternoon. "After all, from what I've seen of the populace out here so far, I doubt anyone within miles of here has ever even been taught about the finer things in life."

"That's what you think?"

"That's what I know."

"Well, I'll tell you, Miss Winters," Blake answered, his voice rough and unsympathetic. "I think you're going to find out that the populace out here are too busy trying to survive to worry about whether they've got their pinkies balanced just right on their teacups or not. Besides, we're coffee drinkers, and the stronger, the better."

"Fine, then I'll know what to expect, won't I?" and for the rest of the afternoon Elizabeth listened to them bantering back and forth about the differences between civilized and uncivilized humanity, and how it all could be improved, although she had to admit Hanna did most of the talking.

By the time Blake maneuvered the buckboard off the road toward a small oasis of trees where he announced they'd spend the night, they'd left a little over eight miles of hot, dusty road behind them and only had about a hundred and ninety some to go.

He fastened the reins, climbed down, then started to walk back to take care of his horse.

Hanna sat primly on the seat and cleared her throat. "Excuse me," she said quite loudly to make sure he'd hear.

Blake looked at Mrs. Brady. "What's wrong with her?"

"I believe she wants you to help her down," Elizabeth answered, and Blake's eyebrows rose.

"Really? I didn't know she was helpless." His eyes were crinkling slightly in the corners as he started toward the front of the wagon and he reached up to help Hanna down. "So sorry, Miss Winters," he said, apologizing. "I completely forgot about your lecture on manners and I certainly don't want to give you the wrong impression about mine."

Hanna was sure Blake had ignored her on purpose just to be ornery, but still she had to have help getting down. Her suit skirt was too cumbersome, and she wasn't used to such strange conveyances.

She took his hand, let him help her, then she stood looking about. "We'll have to sleep here?" she asked, her voice showing her consternation.

"Don't worry, I'll let you ladies sleep in the wagon," Blake assured her as he started walking back to help Mrs. Brady down. "I'm used to the ground."

"You mean there are no towns with hotels or inns on the way and we have to spend every night out in the open like this?"

Blake couldn't resist. "That's why we call it the wild west," he said as he lifted Elizabeth from the back and set her on her feet.

Elizabeth could see the mischievous gleam in his eyes and was suddenly certain she wouldn't need the extra assurance she'd bought at Fort Worth and stuffed into her handbag. Blake Morgan might look like a hardened drifter, but the warmth that crept into his eyes now and then gave him away.

The spot Blake had chosen for them to spend the night was off the road quite a distance and screened by bushes. After untying his horse and setting him to graze a short distance from the wagon, Blake turned his attention to the ladies, who didn't seem to be doing much of anything except gazing about.

"We're going to need some firewood, ladies," he said as he approached the wagon again. "Now, if you two head off over there—" he pointed toward some cottonwood trees and underbrush beyond the horse "—I think maybe you'll find some."

"And what of you?" Hanna looked displeased. "Aren't you going to help?"

He leaned an arm against the side of the wagon and stared at her. "Well, I figure it this way, Miss Winters. Since I'm sure you and Mrs. Brady don't know the first thing about unharnessing a team of horses that should be my job. But then if you want to try a hand at it yourself—"

Hanna was aghast. "Good heavens, no! I just thought..."

"I know what you thought. You thought I was going to sit back and watch the two of you do all the work, but don't worry, I'll earn my keep. Only I can't see where it'll hurt any for you ladies to help now and then instead of just sitting back on your duffs and letting me do everything. Can you?" He straightened and headed for the front of the wagon so he could get the team out of their harnesses for the night.

As Hanna watched him walk away she felt like a fool. They'd been talking all afternoon about the sorry state of affairs out here in the west and Hanna had decided it was because most people came out here expecting good fortune to just drop in their laps. They weren't willing to work for what they wanted. Then she had to act like one of the pampered little school-girls she'd left back in Boston.

Well, she'd show him. Manners were one thing, hard work another. Turning to gaze at the Appaloosa who was grazing contentedly, she picked up her skirts and marched toward the animal, heading for the underbrush at the edge of the grassy clearing.

Elizabeth watched Hanna stalk off and a smile tilted the corners of her mouth. She knew Hanna was fuming, and yet she also knew Blake was right. It wouldn't be fair to let him do it all, only that's just what Hanna'd been used to doing all her life. Letting other people do things for her.

Her meals were cooked for her, her clothes laundered for her. She'd never had to hitch up a buggy. About the only thing she ever did for herself was take care of her toilet and dress herself, and before her father had lost all his money she'd had maids to do even that for her.

Her world in Boston had consisted of Bryn Mawr, the boardinghouse and an occasional excursion to the museum or some other equally dull place with one of her fellow teachers. But work as most folks knew it was a rarity in her life.

This'll be good for Hanna, Elizabeth thought as she lifted her skirts and followed after her. One thing for certain, the trip was really starting to prove interesting.

It was almost dark by the time Blake dragged a couple of boxes from the wagon for the two women to sit on and they congregated around the fire to eat the meal Hanna had helped Mrs. Brady prepare.

Running a boardinghouse for a man as stingy as Ambrose had been meant that besides collecting the rents, Elizabeth Brady had cooked all the meals. She did all the cleaning and laundry as well, so when Blake had started dragging out the supplies he'd bought it had only been natural for her to take over.

Now, as they sat eating potato soup seasoned with salt pork and some hardtack washed down with black coffee, Hanna was again glad she'd asked her landlady to come along. The soup was delicious. Far different from the horrible-sounding concoction Mr. Morgan had been ready to prepare for them.

Blake stared across the fire to where the two women sat balancing themselves on the boxes, their food on another box between them. For himself he preferred the ground.

His golden brown eyes studied Hanna more appreciatively now than when they'd started out. Hanna Winters was far different from what he'd expected. After her long lecture most of the way on the finer things in life and how important it was not to forget social amenities and the common mores society dictated, it seemed strange to see her sitting with her hair all disheveled and messy and minus the perky little hat, her purple traveling suit dirty and stained from hauling wood and helping Mrs. Brady.

Even under these circumstances, however, she had a white handkerchief covering her lap in place of a napkin and was sipping her coffee daintily from the tin cup. The hardtack was also being nibbled at as if it were what he'd heard genteel ladies call hors d'oeuvres.

He studied her surreptitiously in the firelight as the night shadows deepened around them. Hanna wasn't a pretty woman, really. Not in the sense that men gawked at her beauty or anything like that, but there was a sensual quality about her that had surprised him when he'd first seen her up close in the trading post. A hauntingly lovely look that had suddenly made him glad he'd taken on this assignment, although he wished the circumstances of their meeting could have been different.

He watched her put the last bit of hardtack in her mouth, finish the last of her coffee, set the mug down, lift the white handkerchief and daintily wipe her lips, then slide sideways and start to get up from the box. Suddenly she hesitated and at the same time he saw the flames licking up the side of her skirt. She'd stepped too close to the fire.

"Look out!" he shouted, hoping to warn her as he bolted into action. Dropping his coffee cup, he jumped to his feet, leaped across the fire, grabbed Hanna by the shoulders and before she realized what he was doing he'd shoved her to the ground and began frantically rolling her back and forth, trying to put out the fire while she fought hysterically.

"What are you doing?" she screamed as she beat against his chest, then suddenly she realized what was happening and her eyes widened in horror. "Oh, my God! I'm on fire!"

"Not anymore, you're not!" he yelled, as he quit rolling her, letting her come to rest on her back while he knelt beside her in the grass, panting breathlessly. His eyes searched her face. "If you'll take time to check you'll discover the fire's out," he went on more calmly. "I didn't mean to scare you, but there wasn't time and it was the only thing I could think of to do."

Hanna inhaled as she stared up at him, the hard ground uncomfortable against her back, and she didn't know what to say. The smell of burning cloth was strong in her nostrils, and she could still feel the heat against her legs where the fire had been.

"I owe you an apology," she said as she started to move to get up, and he held out a hand to help her. "I've never had anything like that happen before in my life."

Elizabeth was beside her, and she knelt down, also giving her a hand. Hanna let them pull her to her feet, then stood looking at the burned skirt, still smoldering ominously here and there. Just to make sure it was out all the way, Elizabeth began to pat at it hurriedly.

"I was going to suggest both you ladies change anyway," Blake said as he saw Hanna staring at the ruined skirt. He knew how she must be feeling. "We've a long way to go yet. I know it's only April, but the weather here's nothing like it is back east and you'll be far more comfortable in something a little more simple." He looked at Mrs. Brady. "I don't suppose either of you has a riding skirt or anything," he suggested.

"Neither of us," Elizabeth answered. "However, I'm sure Hanna and I'll be able to come up with something more suitable in the morning. Come along, dear," she said, taking Hanna's arm. "Let's see just how much damage has been done," and she led Hanna toward the fire so she could get a better look.

The whole left side of Hanna's skirt from her thigh down was a charred ruin, and her petticoats were scorched and burned.

"Well, it could be worse," Elizabeth said. "Your leg could have been burned, too. But don't worry, in the morning we'll find something appropriate from the trunks. For tonight it won't hurt to sleep in it, if you can stand the burned smell, that is."

Hanna sighed. "It can't be much worse than any of the other smells out here," she mused and glanced toward where the horses were tied for the night.

Blake saw the look on her face and frowned. "Since you don't seem to like things out here, just why are you going to Hangtown, Miss Winters?" he asked as he started picking up the tin dishes that had been scattered in the confusion.

"Come to think of it, I didn't tell you, did I?" she said as she started to help him. She handed the things she'd picked up to Mrs. Brady as she went on. "I've inherited a ranch from my brother," she said. "Have you ever heard of the White Wind?"

"Can't say as I have," he lied convincingly.

"Well, it's supposed to be somewhere near Hangtown according to the lawyer who wrote to me."

"Then you're the new owner?"

"I guess you could say that."

He chuckled and she looked indignant.

"What are you laughing about?"

"You'll have to forgive me," he said as he also handed the things he'd picked up to Mrs. Brady, who headed toward a bucket of water with them. "You just don't seem like the type to be running a ranch, that's all."

"Oh? May I ask why?"

"Because you don't know a damn thing about it, that's why." He looked skeptical. "Are you sure you know just what the hell you're getting yourself into, Hanna Winters?" he asked. "Running a ranch isn't anything like teaching etiquette, you know."

"Well, it can't be that hard or so many people wouldn't be doing it," she answered, trying to convince herself that he was just trying to be hard to get along with. "After all, if my brother did it, so can I," and she lifted her head haughtily and started following Mrs. Brady.

Suddenly a shot rang out from somewhere in the darkness around them, and Hanna felt a sharp stinging sensation in her upper arm. Once more, Blake's hands were quickly sinking into her shoulders and he spun her around, pulling her to the ground with him.

"What on earth...!" she yelled as she lay beside him on the ground, staring into his dark topaz eyes. "Mr. Morgan, what in the world do you think you're doing now? I'm not on fire anymore."

"I know that," he said, his eyes boring into hers. "But take a look at your arm."

Hanna stared at him hard for a minute, then glanced down to the spot on her arm that was now suddenly very painful. Her eyes widened in horror.

"Oh, my gracious," she blurted, not wanting to believe what she was seeing. "I've been shot, haven't I?" And not giving him time to answer, Hanna Winters fainted dead away.

Chapter Two

Hanna was confused as she started to come to, but as soon as she opened her eyes and focused them on Blake everything came flooding back to her.

"Are you all right?" he asked when her eyes began to flutter open.

She inhaled sharply, then tried to raise her left arm. It hurt like the devil.

"Don't," he cautioned. "Mrs. Brady went to get something to clean it up with."

"But why?" she asked, finally finding her voice. "Why would anyone want to take potshots at me?"

"I was hoping you could tell me."

Blake reached out, helping her to sit up, and they both began examining her arm where blood was still spreading across a jagged hole in the material of her purple jacket.

Blake reached out and began tearing the hole in her sleeve.

"Hey!"

"Let's face it, Miss Winters, between the fire and this you might as well kiss your pretty purple suit goodbye."

Hanna watched his fingers separating the cloth from the wound, wincing as she saw that the bullet had ripped a sizable chunk of skin and flesh off just above her elbow.

Although it hurt, she was amazed that it didn't hurt more. Whenever she'd thought of anyone getting shot it always seemed like the worst thing that could happen to them. But then she had to remember this was probably what they'd call a flesh wound. Still, it was bad enough.

"Here, this is all I could find," Elizabeth said as she started to hand Blake a pan of water, a cloth and what looked like the remains of a petticoat she'd ripped up for bandages.

"No, you do it," Blake said as he straightened and stood up, his right hand drawing the Colt strapped to his hips. "I'll go check to see if our target shooter's still around," and he headed off into the darkness.

Hanna stared after Blake for a few minutes, then brought her attention to Mrs. Brady, who had already dropped to her knees beside her so she could tend the wound.

"Here, let me look at that." Elizabeth reached toward Hanna's arm, and as Hanna turned toward the firelight so Mrs. Brady could see it better, both women grimaced at the sight. "My Lord, what's this world coming to?" Elizabeth went on as she dipped the cloth in the pan of water and began to wash away the blood.

"Ow." Hanna flinched. "It hurts! Be careful."

Elizabeth's mouth pursed disgustedly. "I never heard of such a thing. Shooting a woman. What sort of animal would do this?"

"You're the one who told me it was only the land that wasn't civilized."

"Don't remind me." Elizabeth's eyes were fixed steadily on Hanna's arm. "I guess I just hadn't been here long enough to make a proper assessment, that's all," she said and she continued to clean the wound, then frowned, her fingers tightening on the wet cloth as she looked around thoughtfully. "I wish we had something to put on it."

"Like what?"

"Disinfectant, witch hazel, anything to keep it from getting infected." Her fingers were gentle as she concentrated once more on the wound and finished making sure it was as clean as she could get it. She was just about to start bandaging it when Blake emerged again from out of the darkness, holstering his gun as he came.

"Looks like whoever was out there's gone now," he said and walked over and stood looking down at Hanna. "How's it going?"

"It'd go a lot better if I had something to put on it." Elizabeth shook her head. "I'm worried that it might get infected."

"It should be all right till morning." He looked at Hanna, realizing she was taking the whole thing much better than he thought she would. Especially after having fainted. "Bandage it up for tonight, and maybe in the morning I can find something."

"Like what?" Hanna asked.

He watched Mrs. Brady start to wrap the strips of white cloth around Hanna's arm.

"Who knows? There's nothing in what we've brought with us, but the Indians have always been good at finding remedies for anything that might come along. I'll just do what they always do."

"What's that?"

"Improvise. There're all sorts of plants that could make a good antiseptic, only I don't intend to try to find one in the dark."

He watched Mrs. Brady tie the end of the bandage off, then he reached out and helped her to her feet. Once she was standing, they both helped Hanna up and as they did she glanced about fearfully.

"Don't worry, like I said, whoever it was is long gone." Blake held her hand a little longer than normal to make sure she was steady on her feet, then he studied her face closely.

"You sure you have no idea why someone would shoot at you?" he asked.

Hanna shook her head. "None."

"How about your brother? Maybe it has something to do with him."

"If it does, I don't know what it could be. It's been eleven years since I last saw Henry and he never even wrote in all that time."

Blake wondered if she was telling the truth. After all, Henry Winters could've been sending money back east to her all these years without anyone ever knowing. Still, it didn't seem logical. From what he'd learned of the man since his investigation started, Henry, or Hank, as most people called him, wasn't much on sentiment.

Besides, Blake wanted to believe her. He watched her reach for a few strands of hair that were brushing her face and push them away. In the firelight her hair looked more golden than white, and again he wished he'd met her under different circumstances.

"Well, there's nothing more we can do about it tonight," he said. "In the morning I'll take a look and see if our visitor left anything behind. And I'll also see if I can locate something to use on that wound." He glanced briefly at the bandage on her arm. "For now, if you want I'll help the two of you set up some sort of bed in the wagon."

While Mrs. Brady finished cleaning up the rest of their eating utensils and took care of the things she'd used to bandage Hanna's arm, Hanna and Blake climbed into the back of the wagon and proceeded to make up a couple of beds between the boxes and trunks, using some old blankets Blake had insisted they bring along.

When they were finished, Blake jumped off the wagon, then reached up to help Hanna down. His hands circled her slim waist and he felt her stiffen.

"Relax, I won't drop you," he said.

Her hands covered his as if she were about to rip them from her, then instead she moved her hands over his, feeling the weathered flesh beneath them. Blake's hands were as sinewy as the rest of him, the muscles hard, like rocks, and she knew she wouldn't be able to unclasp them from about her waist even if she tried, so she did as he said and relaxed, letting him lift her down and set her on the ground.

When he'd helped her down from the seat earlier, he'd only taken her hand. But now, as she stood level with his chest, then looked up into his face, she was very aware of the virile masculinity the man virtually exuded.

"Thank you," she half whispered.

He smiled then said, "All thanks kindly appreciated." But he still kept his hands on her waist.

"Where will you sleep?" she asked.

He nodded toward the fire. "Over there. But don't worry, I'll sleep with one eye open."

"You think that's necessary?"

"Maybe not, but we can't take any chances."

Again she thanked him, and this time he did release her waist, although reluctantly.

Hanna Winters was an enigma to Blake. Prim and proper, she was also provocatively sensual in a strange sort of way. If she'd been born and bred in Texas he imagined she'd never have seen the inside of a girls' finishing school and probably would have ended up in a saloon somewhere, or married with half a dozen kids by now. Funny how things like where people were born and raised could affect their personality. But then, maybe he was wrong. Maybe if she'd been born and bred in Texas, she'd have ended up in a convent. It was hard to tell whether her prim and proper attitude was strictly surface or built right in. He was inclined to think it was the former. Or maybe that was only wishful thinking on his part.

As he looked deep into her eyes, he suddenly saw a spark of something that made him wish he could tell her the truth about why he'd volunteered to take her to Hangtown. Yet he knew he couldn't. First he had to find out just how deeply she was involved, and that was going to take time.

"Shall we see if Mrs. Brady's ready to turn in?" he asked as he took her arm. Before she could answer he

was escorting her to one of the boxes where Elizabeth
had set up a pan to rinse off their dishes.

"So, how's the arm?" the older woman asked,
glancing at the makeshift bandage.

Hanna looked at it, too. "It could be worse, I guess.
Although it's really hurting now."

Elizabeth looked at Blake. "Are you sure you'll be
able to find something to put on it in the morning?"
she asked.

"Positive." Blake picked up his blankets from
where he'd tossed them when they'd first arrived and
began spreading them out on the other side of the fire.
"But now, I think since you've got the last of the
dishes done up for the night, we'd better turn in. You
ladies have had a long day and we've got a longer one
ahead of us." With that he straightened up, walked to
the pile of wood Hanna and Mrs. Brady had gathered
earlier, picked up a few pieces and plopped them onto
the fire.

Hanna watched him curiously. One thing she had to
admit, when Blake Morgan took on a job, he took on
the whole thing. You'd think he'd hired her and Mrs.
Brady the way he ran things. Or should she say, tried
to run things?

But then, he was right. It had been a long day. A
little too long. Hanna looked at her burned skirt, then
at her arm, before looking at Mrs. Brady.

"Are you ready?" she asked.

Elizabeth nodded. "As soon as I put these things
away." So while Mrs. Brady set the dishes in the boxes
for them to use in the morning, Blake waited, walked
back over with them, helped both women up onto the
wagon, then stood for a minute looking at them.

"Well, ladies, let's see if the beds are comfortable enough," he said, and as he watched, they began to settle down in their makeshift beds. After assurances from both women that the beds would do fine, he called out, "Sweet dreams," and returned to the fire.

Hanna wriggled, trying to get more comfortable beneath the brown blanket, her head on another blanket she'd rolled up to use as a pillow. Finally she lay quietly, listening to see if Mrs. Brady was moving around. She wasn't.

Slowly everything around Hanna grew quiet except for the various night sounds that made her all too aware of how wild the land was they were traveling through. She could hear a cricket chirping from somewhere beneath the wagon, and in a few minutes it was joined by a whole chorus of them, then an owl hooted nearby.

Although it had been hot during the day, the night was starting to cool down, and she reached out, pulling the blanket up a little higher over her shoulder against the chill. The blanket smelled musty and she wasn't sure which was worse, the smell or the cold. Deciding she could put up with the smell better than she could put up with goose bumps all night, she finally closed her eyes and tried to sleep.

She was just starting to drift off when suddenly the still night was shattered by a horrifying scream. She bolted upright, and her hair stood on end. Even Mrs. Brady was petrified.

"Mr. Morgan!" Hanna shrieked, her voice quivering.

"Don't worry, it's only a bobcat off somewhere in the woods," Blake yelled from where he lay next to the fire. "It's mating season and the cats like to prowl all night, that's all. He won't bother us."

"Oh, fine," Hanna mumbled and exhaled. She'd been holding her breath in fear of what might happen. "You're sure?" she called back.

"Positive!" he answered. "Now, good night."

Her good-night was lost on the breeze as one of the horses nickered, then grew quiet. Once more Hanna began to relax and settle down as did Mrs. Brady, but it was a long time before she finally fell asleep. It wasn't just the bobcat or her wound, it was everything, and once again, Hanna wondered if maybe she should have stayed in Boston.

But then, as the soft chirp of the crickets and quiet of the night began to envelop her, she told herself that in spite of everything, things would work out. She finally dozed off.

Dawn was just beginning to creep into the sky in the east as Hanna stirred, then lay quietly listening to the whistling. She opened her eyes and stared at the trunk next to her, then closed them again wishing it was all a mistake. It was still awfully dark out yet, and that had to be Blake whistling. How he could sound so cheerful at this hour of the morning she'd never know.

Pushing the blanket off her shoulders, she rolled over onto her back, looked up at the sky that was just beginning to get light, then stretched and sat up. My God, she was stiff and sore. It took a few minutes to get the kinks out, then she glanced over to where Mrs. Brady was sleeping, only no one was there. She might've known. The landlady was used to getting up with the birds, too.

Hanna quickly tossed the blanket aside, raised up the rest of the way, then straightened and stood next to her trunk, gazing about. The fire was kindled high and the smell of freshly brewed coffee was already beginning to replace all the unfamiliar smells that filled the morning air.

The sun wasn't up yet, but it was light enough so she could see Mrs. Brady and Blake fussing about the fire fixing breakfast.

Suddenly Blake glanced her way, and she stiffened as she saw him start toward her.

"Well, good morning," he said as he reached the back of the wagon. "Sleep well?"

She rubbed some sleep from her right eye, then stifled a yawn as he helped her down.

"You always get up this early?" she asked.

He pretended to look shocked. "Early? When did you get up in Boston, noon?"

"At least we waited for the sun."

"By the time it gets here we'll be on our way."

After a breakfast of dry biscuits, coffee and some fresh eggs Blake had insisted they stop and buy at a small ranch the afternoon before, Hanna and Mrs. Brady rummaged through the trunks for something more appropriate to wear. By the time the sun was just breaking through the trees overhead, they were settling down in the wagon for the long day's ride.

Hanna set the parasol down next to her feet as they got ready to start out, determined she wasn't going to use it until she had to. She was bareheaded this morning since all the hats she had were for show rather than to keep off the sun, but after the cooling night, the warmth of the sun felt good on her head.

The two women had changed clothes behind the wagon right after breakfast, while Blake found some leaves from a wild plant to brew so they'd have something to clean her wound with. Then, just before starting out, while Blake was putting the boxes back on the wagon ready to leave, Mrs. Brady rebandaged Hanna's arm, rinsing it thoroughly with the concoction Blake had cooked up.

Now, as Blake slapped the reins, moving the wagon from underneath the cottonwood trees and out toward the road again, Hanna looked at her left arm above the elbow where the bandage was hidden beneath the full sleeve of her white blouse. All morning she'd been racking her brain trying to make sense of the whole thing. She had no idea why anyone would want to shoot her.

For a while she'd thought maybe it was just a mistake, that the bullet had been meant for Blake, but after thinking it over she realized that wasn't logical. If the bullet had been meant for Blake whoever was shooting surely wouldn't have been that far off target. She'd been too far from Blake when the bullet hit.

She glanced at Blake, wondering what he must be thinking. Well, it was no business of his. After all, all she did was hire him to take them to Hangtown, she didn't hire him to fight her battles for her. Somehow, she'd find out what it was all about, but for now she was just glad whoever pulled the trigger had been a poor shot.

She was wearing a dark brown poplin skirt. The bustle was uncomfortable against the back of the wagon seat and she reached over and grabbed the side of the seat as the wagon hit a big bump and they bounced onto the road again.

"Are you all right, Mrs. Brady?" she called over her shoulder.

Elizabeth smiled as she leaned back again in her chair, her gaze on the road behind them. "I'm just fine, Hanna," she answered, opening her parasol and holding it up to keep the morning sun from her face.

Blake had been right the night before when he said they had a long day ahead of them and Hanna sighed disgustedly as the day wore on. At the pace the horses were moving they were making only three to four miles in an hour's time and she felt as if they'd never get there.

"Can't you make them go any faster?" she asked Blake as she watched the animals plodding along.

He stared straight ahead. "Oh, yeah, I can make them go faster," he answered. "Only they won't get you where you're going if I do." He glanced at her. "You can't run a horse into the ground and still expect him to do a good job. We don't have any relay stations like the stages do."

"Oh." Hanna realized how stupid her question had been, but that didn't make her not wish they couldn't go faster.

Shortly before the sun began to sink below the horizon they reached the Brazos River, and Blake was glad they were having a dry spring so the water level was lower than usual. Even with that, though, the crossing wasn't easy. The wheels kept slipping on the stones and sinking into the muddy river bottom, and the horses had to fight against the strong current all the way. But they finally made it without any mishaps, and once on the other side, Blake reined the wagon off the narrow road toward a small grove of trees and they made camp.

As they had the night before the women sat on their boxes to eat while Blake used the ground, then, after cleaning things up, they settled down, again using the same sleeping arrangements.

The next morning they were once more on the road before sunup, hoping to put as many miles behind them as they could.

It had been six days since they'd left Fort Worth. Six days of tedious monotony as they made their way through the inhospitable Texas countryside with its stark contrasts. The dust from the windswept plains would swirl up so thick at times they had to cover their faces with handkerchiefs, and ragged cliffs overlooked dry arroyos that lay desolate in the sun. Then occasionally the landscape would change abruptly and spring wildflowers would dot the sloping hills, splashing them with color, while groves of trees would herald a small stream or lake. Ranches and towns were few and far between, and Hanna was discouraged at seeing so little civilization.

They were making somewhere between twenty to thirty miles a day depending on how fast Blake urged the horses and the condition of the roads, which at times were nothing more than worn rutted tracks.

Now it was evening of the sixth day and they were getting ready to call it a night. Hanna finished helping Mrs. Brady get things ready for morning, then started toward the wagon where she'd already made up her bed. It was pitch dark and the thought of sleep was inviting. She turned suddenly at the sound of foot-steps behind her, then she relaxed. It was only Blake.

"How much longer do you think it'll take us?" she asked as he joined her. It was something she'd been wanting to ask all day.

"About three, maybe four days, barring any trouble."

"Trouble?"

"Let's face it," he said. "Just because no one's tried to take a potshot at you again doesn't mean they aren't still out there waiting for another chance." He glanced at her arm. Mrs. Brady had been taking care of it for her. "By the way, how's the arm?"

"Coming along nicely. Whatever that was you brewed up worked like a charm. It's even scabbed up already."

"The Indians call it yellow root. They use it for just about everything you can think of."

They reached the wagon and by the time Blake had helped her up into it, Mrs. Brady had joined them.

It was late already, so Blake helped Mrs. Brady up too, bid the ladies good-night, checked the fire to make sure it was high enough to keep the animals away, then climbed into his blankets.

Hanna was weary as she said good-night to Mrs. Brady and settled down into the makeshift bed, bunching the pillow blanket up beneath her head. She felt dirty as well as tired, but that was understandable. She'd had quick washups every morning before starting out. But her body hadn't been fully submerged in water since she and Mrs. Brady had left the Drover's Cottage in Abilene.

She was looking forward to tomorrow, because Blake said they'd probably be near enough to one of the towns they had to go through to spend the night, and if they did she was going to make sure she got a good hot bath.

Just the thought brought on a feeling of euphoria as she remembered what it was like to be submerged in warm, soapy liquid, and it wasn't long before Hanna was sound asleep.

Hours had gone by and it was well past midnight. Hanna had no idea what might have awakened her, but suddenly she lay tense, eyes open, frowning because she was so wide-awake.

She had learned quickly over the days to distinguish one sound from another once she was settled down for the night, so whatever had awakened her had to be something she wasn't used to.

She lay still, not moving, hardly even breathing, and strained her ears in the darkness. The full moon was high above the trees already, spreading a silvery glow over everything, and she stared at the trunk next to her, the metal clasps on it shining in the moonlight.

She was on her side, curled up, with the blanket beneath her chin, and she shivered slightly as she felt gooseflesh beginning to rise on her arms.

Then she heard it. Just a creak and a slight scraping and rustling, only the sounds weren't coming from where Mrs. Brady lay. They were coming from the rear of the wagon, as if someone had just climbed aboard.

Holding her breath, Hanna waited. Everything was quiet, then she heard the noise again and the hair at the nape of her neck stood on end. Someone or something was in the buckboard with them. She could even hear heavy breathing as whoever it was took a step so they were standing between her and Mrs. Brady.

As she stared hard toward the trunk she knew it was a man and not an animal because she could see the tall shadow where it fell across the top of the trunk, and her heart began to pound unmercifully.

Blake? No, it wouldn't be Blake. He'd have no reason. Besides, she could smell the distinct odor of strong tobacco, and Blake didn't smoke.

My God! What was she going to do? Evidently, whoever it was couldn't see her face and didn't know her eyes were open as he stood above her.

Well, she had to do something, that's for sure. Making a quick decision she began turning over so she could see who it was, only just as she did, the man raised his arm and Hanna caught sight of moonlight glittering off the knife just as it started to descend.

Having only a split second in which to react, she let out a piercing scream and rolled sideways just as the knife sliced by her ribs and stuck into the bed of the wagon.

The man wielding the knife tried to pull it out, but he'd slashed at her with such force that the knife was caught.

"Damn!" he cursed in a rough low voice.

Hanna reacted without thinking. Drawing her arm back, she belted her assailant as hard as she could, catching him by surprise, and he cursed again, fighting for balance. As Blake's voice filled the quiet night, yelling for him to stay put, the man, apparently realizing he wouldn't have time to retrieve his knife, leaped onto the trunk next to Hanna, jumped to the ground, half rolling, gained his feet again, and took off into the darkness while Blake fired some shots after him. A few seconds later the sound of hoofbeats could be heard off through the trees, then they faded away in the distance.

Inside the wagon, Hanna was breathing heavily as she relaxed onto her makeshift bed and lay there trembling. That was close. So close she could still feel the cold steel of the man's knife against her rib cage. My God! An inch or two more to the right and it would have gone clear through her.

She heard Blake's booted feet hit the floorboards of the wagon and the next thing she knew he was on his knees beside her.

"Hanna!"

"I'm all right." She groaned, struggling as she tried to pull out the knife. "But this stupid knife won't budge. It's got me pinned to the floor."

Blake holstered his gun, then reached out, pulling as hard as he could. The knife finally came loose.

"You're sure you weren't hurt?" he asked, his gaze studying the knife in the moonlight.

"Well, it did scratch the skin, I think, but not enough to hardly feel."

"What is it? What's happening?" Elizabeth asked from behind Blake. She was still a little dazed, having been jolted out of a sound sleep. "What's going on?"

"Somebody tried to use a knife on Miss Winters. Only they missed."

Hanna was still flat on her back and she stared at Blake, watching as he studied the knife in his hands. A few minutes ago he'd called her Hanna, now it was back to Miss Winters again.

"Are you all right?" Elizabeth, too, was staring at the knife. "My goodness, but that's a wicked looking thing."

"It's a bowie, a hunting knife."

Hanna shivered. "And he was hunting me."

"You sure you didn't hit him, Mr. Morgan?" Elizabeth asked. "I heard you get off a couple of shots."

"Afraid I missed. At least whoever it was kept right on going." He frowned, then sat back on his heels pondering thoughtfully as he looked at Hanna. "You have no idea who it was?"

"Me? I didn't even know he was there until I looked up in time to see the knife. And that's all I saw was the knife, really, except for his shadow."

"That's what I was afraid of." Blake hefted the knife in his hand, then tucked it into the waistband of his pants before looking at Hanna.

"Do you think you're going to be all right now?" he asked.

Hanna swallowed hard as she stared at him. "There's no way you can sleep in the wagon, too?"

He knew what she meant. It had taken him too long to get from the fire to the wagon. The next time, if there was a next time, he might not make it at all. He glanced toward the back of the wagon.

"You win," he said. "At least for tonight. I'll stretch out across the back, only I'll have to go get my blankets."

Blake straightened, then stood up and left the wagon, heading toward the fire.

"Hanna, are you sure there wasn't something in those papers the lawyer sent that could be a reason for someone trying to kill you?'' Elizabeth asked when Blake was out of earshot.

Hanna shook her head. ''No, nothing.'' She pulled the cover up, then let her fingers slip through the slits the knife had made just to prove she hadn't been dreaming. ''I've thought and thought. Why, I even got the papers out of my handbag the other evening and went through them, and found nothing.''

Elizabeth didn't like it. Not at all. People didn't kill other people without reason, and especially people they didn't know, and it was certain Hanna didn't know her assailant.

''Well, there has to be a reason somewhere, my dear,'' she said. ''Maybe we'll find out when we reach your brother's ranch.''

''Maybe.'' Hanna sighed. ''Now, though, since I survived again, I think maybe we'd better settle down and try to get through the rest of the night, don't you?''

Mrs. Brady nodded and moved back to her own makeshift bed a few feet away. Blake hefted himself onto the wagon, spread his blankets out across the back, then lay down after first making sure one more time that Hanna was all right.

Once he was settled in his blankets, he called out another good-night, and within minutes the camp was quiet again, only unlike earlier in the evening, Hanna was a long time in dropping off to sleep again.

It was morning. Hanna stirred, opened her eyes, then frowned as she felt the sun in her face. The sun? Her frown deepened and she rolled over, lifting herself onto her elbows as she looked to where Mrs. Brady usually slept. Her bed was empty. That was logical, though, because Mrs. Brady always got up before she did, but they'd always been up before the sun ever since starting their journey.

Tossing back the covers, Hanna got up just as Mrs. Brady appeared at the back of the buckboard.

"Good, I was just coming to wake you," Elizabeth said as she saw Hanna.

Hanna stared at her curiously. "But it's so late. Why'd you let me sleep so long?"

"Blake figured you needed the rest after last night."

Hanna folded her blanket up as she talked. "Oh, now it's Blake instead of Mr. Morgan, is it?"

"Well, like he said, it does seem ridiculous to keep calling him Mr. Morgan under the circumstances."

Hanna set the blanket aside with the one she used for a pillow, then joined Mrs. Brady at the back of the wagon. "What circumstances is that?" she asked.

"You know very well what he meant," Elizabeth answered. "In fact, it might be nice if you started calling me Elizabeth, too, instead of Mrs. Brady all the time. After all, I'm not your landlady anymore now, Hanna."

Hanna stared at her curiously, then shook her head. "Oh, I couldn't do that. It just wouldn't seem right. Besides, you'll always be Mrs. Brady to me. It has nothing to do with whether you're my landlady or not. It's just that I think of you as Mrs. Brady."

Elizabeth smiled, suddenly realizing what Hanna meant. To Hanna, the name was a term of endearment, giving Elizabeth a special place in Hanna's life. It had nothing to do with landladies or proprieties or stations in life.

"Well, if you're sure," Elizabeth said. She reached up and helped Hanna sit on the back of the wagon, then Hanna hopped to the ground.

"I'm positive," Hanna answered. "Now, since you were on your way to wake me, I assume breakfast is ready, right?"

While they walked over to where Blake was waiting Hanna showed Elizabeth the slits in her blouse where the knife had gone through. By the time they reached the fire, the fear that Hanna had managed to squelch the night before was beginning to emerge again, but she tried to ignore it.

As usual they were on their way shortly after breakfast. As they rode away from the campsite Hanna eagerly searched the road up ahead, wondering what more could happen before they reached Hangtown.

The day went well. A little slower than usual due to the hilly terrain, but as darkness neared they began to see houses and barns here and there, and shortly before dark they rode into the town of Hubbard Creek.

As with most of the towns they'd been through, the place was isolated and lonely looking out here on the plains, with the ever present dust, heat and wind.

A piano could be heard as they rode past one of the saloons, but few people were about. Blake reined up in front of one of the buildings without a facade and brought the horses to a halt.

"I know it doesn't look like much," he said as he fastened the reins securely, "but the couple who own it came here from France and they do try to give good service."

Hanna glanced at the sign outside the hotel. "The Chez Pari?" she questioned, frowning.

"From what I've heard, he wanted a gaming house, she wanted a hotel, so they combined the two. Gambling downstairs, sleeping upstairs. But I've been here before and it's better than the hotel down the street," and he nodded toward a dilapidated building with a bunch of drifters lounging around outside.

Hanna had to agree, especially when they were greeted at the desk a few minutes later by a charming woman with dark hair and bright blue eyes. Her heavily accented English was interspersed here and there with little French phrases, and she seemed only too eager to please.

"You'll have to forgive my Francois," she exclaimed after promising to see that water was sent to their rooms so they could all bathe. "He usually tends to such things for our guests himself, but since it's late, and he's dealing already, I will see to it myself, but it will take a little time. You will be patient?"

Hanna nodded. "Perhaps we could find someplace to eat in the meantime." She turned to look at Blake. "I am terribly hungry."

After showing them their rooms, the little Frenchwoman, who told them her name was Yvette, promised to have their baths waiting for them by the time they returned, for an extra fee of course, then Blake escorted both Hanna and Elizabeth down the street to what looked like the only eating place in town.

While Hanna enjoyed her really first good meal in days, home fries, steak and raisin pie, Blake once more asked if she could think of some reason for the attempts on her life, but Hanna could come up with nothing.

When they finally returned to the hotel, it was dark outside and the gaming tables were in full swing.

"Where do they all come from?" Hanna asked as they passed the gambling room and headed for the desk.

Blake took a quick peek at the tables. "Most are drifters, some work on nearby ranches and the rest probably live in town."

Mrs. Brady smiled. "At least they seem to be enjoying themselves."

Blake had to agree. Men always loved to gamble, even out here, and if there wasn't a poker game to be had they'd bet on how far they could spit. When they reached the desk the little Frenchwoman was all in a dither.

"Oh, mademoiselles, m'sieur, you are just in time. I had to hunt about, but we managed to find three tubs and the men just finished filling them. I was afraid the water would get cold before you returned."

"Not a chance," said Blake. "We've been looking forward to this too much, haven't we, ladies?"

Hanna and Elizabeth both agreed, the Frenchwoman gave them the keys to their rooms, and the three went upstairs.

Hanna's room was the first on the left, Blake's was across from it and Mrs. Brady's was farther on at the end of the hall. Blake unlocked the doors for both women, then handed each of them their key, reminding them not to forget to tell the proprietor's wife when they were through so the tubs could be removed. This done, he disappeared into his own room.

Hanna shut the door to her room, then stood taking it in. It was about the same size as the room she'd lived in at the boardinghouse, and the tub was set up halfway between the bed and the dresser.

Before going to eat Hanna had brought her carpetbag up, set out her nightclothes and turned back the covers on the bed. Since it had been almost dark she'd lit the lamp on the dresser, and now its golden glow made the room look inviting.

Warm water, she thought as she stared at the narrow copper tub. A genuine bath. Anxious to feel the wonderful sensation of being clean again, she began unbuttoning her blouse.

Unfortunately the only clean clothes she would have to put on in the morning would be the underdrawers she'd been carrying in her portmanteau along with her nightclothes. That's one thing she had been doing. She had six pair of underdrawers and every time they'd make camp near water of any kind she'd wash the dirty ones, spread them out on bushes to dry overnight and pack them away again in the morning. But the rest of her clothes, her skirt, petticoats and blouse, were still filled with the dust and dirt of the trail. And that's all it was most of the time, a lonesome trail leading off ahead on the horizon for what looked like endless miles.

The last vestige of clothing left her body. Hanna tossed the clothes onto a chair near the dresser, then walked to the tub where she stood wondering whether she should wash, or do her hair first?

Realizing that too much soap wouldn't be good for her hair, she took out her hairpins, set them on the dresser, then knelt down beside the tub and washed her hair first. She rinsed it as best she could and toweled it dry. This done she grabbed a brush from her portmanteau, stroked her hair enough to get it to behave some, then fastened it back haphazardly with a ribbon she'd found in her carpetbag instead of securing it in its usual knot.

After tying the ribbon, she reached down and felt the water. It was still warm, thank goodness. Straightening expectantly, she finally stepped into the tub. What luxury. The old copper tub was battered and beatup, with green corrosion along the upper rim, but all she could see was the soothing water as she eased herself down in it with a sigh.

Never before in her life had Hanna ever realized how luxurious a bath could really feel, and she wriggled her toes, letting the water swish between them.

After spending almost half an hour enjoying the feel of the warm water, she finally realized it was starting to cool off. If she wanted to get clean before it got completely cold, she'd better get started.

By the time she'd scrubbed every inch, the water was not only cold, but a scum was settling on top from all the soap and dirt. Grabbing the sides of the narrow tub, she pulled herself up, stepped from the water, reached over to the bed and grabbed the big towel that had accompanied the cloth and soap.

Once dried off, she wrapped the towel around her, then started toward the chair to get into her street clothes, figuring she wouldn't put her nightclothes on until after they'd taken away the tub.

Suddenly she stopped, hesitating, her gaze moving from her clothes on the chair to her nightclothes spread out on the bed near where the towel had been.

A frown creased her forehead. She squinted, straining her eyes. Something had moved. She'd caught the movement out of the corner of her eye when she'd started for her clothes. But what could it be? Cautiously, her hands gripping the top of the towel, she moved toward the bed instead of the chair, only she didn't see anything, not at first. Then, when she was only a few feet from the big four-poster, she caught the movement again, and this time she let out a startled shriek and froze motionless, staring.

Across the hall, Blake has just finished shaving and was wiping his chin with the towel. The bath had felt good, but not wanting to linger too long, he'd hurried through it, then slipped on his pants and boots, but not his shirt because he decided he needed a shave.

He looked in the mirror, studying the clean-shaven face that stared back at him. Hardly handsome, that's for sure, and the wind and weather had played havoc on what once had been tender, youthful skin. God, he was getting old. At thirty-five he felt ancient already.

He was just about to toss the towel aside to put on his shirt when Hanna's startled scream brought him up short. After everything the woman had been through already, he didn't even wait to see if she'd scream again. Instead he bolted for the door, and seconds later flung the door to Hanna's room open. Blake stepped inside quickly, then stopped, standing transfixed at the scene before him.

At first he didn't see the snake. But damn, he could hear it. The sidewinder's rattles were vibrating and echoing loudly off the walls of the otherwise quiet room.

"Where is it?" he asked, his eyes intent on Hanna's motionless figure as she clutched the towel frantically around her.

Her voice when she answered was barely a whisper. "On the bed next to my nightclothes."

Slowly, deliberately moving only a fraction of an inch at a time, Blake began to ease himself farther into the room until he was finally standing next to Hanna. Now he could not only hear the snake, but see it, too.

It had evidently slithered out from under her nightgown and was coiling up only inches from it, its head drawn back, rattles a blur they were moving so fast, and all Blake had with him was the towel. He hadn't put on his gun belt after his bath, and for the first time in years he was going to have to find a way out of a jam without relying on his Colt.

His hands tightened on the towel he held in his hands, then he inhaled determinedly. "Don't move. Don't even hardly breathe," he whispered between barely open lips. "If he decides to strike he can hit you easily right where you are."

The only way Blake knew Hanna had heard him was the low, half-strangled groan that came from her throat. Not only wasn't she moving, but he hadn't even seen her blink since he'd stepped into the room.

Tensing hesitantly, he finally knew there was only one thing he could do, and slowly positioning the towel in front of him, he eased closer to the bed, trying desperately to put himself between Hanna and the diamondback.

When the rattling became louder he'd freeze, then when the snake would quiet down some he'd move again. Finally he stopped altogether when he'd gotten as close as he felt the snake would allow. His insides crawled feverishly and sweat dampened the back of his neck.

He was going to have one chance and one chance only and he knew it. "When I throw the towel I want you to run to the other side of the room as fast as you can," he said, his voice a low monotone.

He heard a strangled sob from behind him.

"You understand?" He waited for her answer. When it came it sounded like a strangled gasp.

"Yes."

"Good." His voice was still hushed and low. "Now I'm going to count to three. On three you go. One...two...three!" As he uttered the word, the towel left his hands, the snake struck out at it, and Hanna ran. Blake's hand shot out, hitting the back of the towel where he figured the snake's head wouldn't be, and with one movement he scooped the snake off the bed and onto the floor, then brought his boot heel down where he could already see the snake's fangs puncturing the towel.

Over and over again he ground his heel into the towel until blood began to seep through it, then finally, after one last crunching blow, he stepped back and stood breathing deeply, keeping his eyes on the towel.

Hanna cringed against the far wall staring at the towel, her heart in her throat, hands trembling.

"Is it dead?" she finally asked, her gaze moving from the bloodied towel to Blake's tension-filled face.

Blake didn't answer because he wasn't sure himself. In spite of all the blood, the towel was still moving. Blake knew snakes didn't always quit moving right away even when they were dead, but he was still hesitant.

Very cautiously he reached down, lifted one end of the towel, then quickly dropped it into place again.

"His rattling days are over," he finally said, looking directly at Hanna for the first time since entering the room.

She was leaning against the wall, clutching the top of the towel, her face pale, eyes closed. He assumed in relief. Then, as he watched, she apparently tried to compose herself, her eyes opened and she took a deep breath, then straightened. That was when he realized that her hair was falling loose instead of twisted into its severe bun, and with the flickering light on it from the lamp it looked all golden and soft. So different from the stark whiteness it usually was in the sun.

Even her eyes looked different somehow tonight as she looked at him, conveying her relief and thanks for what he'd done. They had deepened to a grayish purple hue with what looked like little flecks of silver running through them.

"Are you all right?" he asked, realizing he had to say something.

She nodded. "I've never been so petrified in all my life," she answered, her voice breathless and barely under control.

Suddenly he saw her legs start to give way and he hurried over, grabbing her by the arms to help her stay up.

"I'm all right, please," she murmured. Summoning all the strength she could, she finally forced the muscles in her legs to stop quivering, then looked into his face. "Thank you," she said.

His hands eased on her arms, but he still didn't let go. "You're sure you're all right?"

"Yes. I'm fine."

Blake stared at her, suddenly very aware that Hanna Winters seemed to have lost her prim and proper manner, and it had been replaced with a warm, sensual vulnerability. A quality new to her. Funny, he'd never quite thought of her as being vulnerable before. And yet, as he stood staring into her beautiful eyes, his hands still on her shoulders, he had the distinct feeling that if he bent down and kissed her she wouldn't resist.

Hanna swallowed hard as she stared into Blake's face. Something was wrong and it had nothing to do with the snake. It had to do with Blake.

Her eyes were on his and she felt a weird stirring deep inside. A sensation she'd felt more than once when he'd been around, but stronger now than it had ever been before, and frightening. As frightening as the sight of the snake had been.

All too aware of his hands still holding her arms, Hanna felt her once pale face suddenly grow hot and she wanted to die from embarrassment because she was sure he knew exactly what she was thinking. And right now what she was thinking was something Hanna hadn't thought of in years.

Blake's hands moved up her arms until they reached her shoulders and he touched her long pale hair, sifting it through his fingers.

"It looks nice loose like this," he said, his voice husky in the quiet room.

Hanna's gaze moved from his clean-shaven face to his hairy chest. She didn't know what to say. The smell of his shaving soap was strong and she breathed it in deeply. The sensation made her jaws tighten and her insides quiver.

"It's . . . it's too unruly to leave loose during the day," she answered for something to say.

His fingers on the bare flesh of her shoulders were exceptionally soft, and every place they touched they sent little shocks running through her. Now they were moving up her neck toward her face and she swallowed hard. Was he going to kiss her?

Blake started to bend forward, her hypnotic eyes mesmerizing him, the feel of her soft flesh beneath his fingers tantalizing him until there was no way he could stop, and as their lips met, he knew she'd been waiting for it.

Hanna moaned under the pressure of Blake's lips, not from passion, but from fear. She had wanted this, yes. While she stood staring up at him she'd wondered what it would be like to be kissed again, really kissed, this time for what she was, not what she had. Only now that it was happening, it was almost more than she could bear because she knew it was arousing feelings in her she'd buried years before.

Feelings that had no part in the life of Hanna Winters. Feelings she'd sworn never to give in to again, yet here she was not only giving in to them, but letting them get the upper hand.

Suddenly forcing herself back to the real world, she began to struggle.

"Please, Mr. Morgan!" Her voice was raspy and broke on the words as she pulled her mouth from his, her eyes widening indignantly.

Blake shuddered inside, trying to bring his emotions under control, his eyes boring into hers as he straightened, catching his breath.

"Sorry," he apologized, his voice hoarse. His eyes hardened forcefully. "My mistake," and as he continued staring at her he could once more see the prim and proper Hanna Winters starting to emerge and he frowned. Damn! He hadn't wanted to do that. He couldn't afford to let his feelings get tangled up in his work. Taking her cue, he released her, then watched her hands quickly grip the top of the towel as if it had been ready to fall.

Hanna was breathing erratically and she knew it. And she also knew that for a brief few minutes she had kissed Morgan back. However, that couldn't be helped now. He'd caught her off guard, that was all.

Lifting her chin stiffly, she stepped back, acknowledging his apology. "I'm sorry, too," she said, her voice harsher than she meant it to be. Still she went on. "And yes, it was a mistake. One I'm sure will never happen again, will it?" She flicked her head, tossing her hair off her shoulder as she avoided his eyes and looked toward the towel, which had finally quit moving. "I presume it was just the excitement of the moment, that's all. Shall we forget it?"

Blake could sense that she was as unnerved by what had happened as he was, and yet she was putting on a good show of bravado.

"Why not?" he answered, feigning indifference over the whole thing, then he turned his attention to the creature that had brought him to her room. Forcing his gaze from her unsettled face, he straightened stubbornly, walked over and took one more quick look under the towel just to make sure, then scooped the whole mess up so the dead rattler was inside the towel, and he headed for the door that was still standing open.

"Where are you going?" she asked as she watched the powerful muscles rippling across his broad back. He didn't even have a shirt on yet.

"To see Madam Yvette," he answered, his amber eyes snapping angrily as he turned briefly to face her. "Snakes don't climb in through hotel windows, Miss Winters," he went on. "And I'm going to go find out who put it there and why." As he went out, he slammed the door shut behind him, leaving her standing in the middle of her room staring after him, her hands gripping the towel to her like a shield, a strange, curiously bewildered look on her face.

Chapter Three

Blake was oblivious of his bare chest as he made his way down the steps toward the lobby. In fact, he was oblivious of just about everything except that somehow he had to forget what had occurred in Hanna's hotel room. All he needed right now was to get tangled up emotionally with Hanna Winters.

Reaching the lobby, he marched over to the desk, deposited the bloody towel on top of it and stared hard at the woman behind it.

"M'sieur?" Yvette asked, her gaze moving from his face to the towel, then to his face again. "Something, she is wrong?"

"You're damned right something she is wrong," he mimicked her. "Maybe you can tell me where the hell that thing came from."

She shrugged, looking perplexed. "What is it, m'sieur?"

He took one corner of the towel and pulled it back so she could get a good look, then he watched her eyes widen with horror. "But it is a snake, m'sieur."

"That's right, and a rattler, too. It was in Miss Winters's room, curled up on her bed next to her clothes."

"Oh, but no." Yvette shook her head. "But how could something like that happen? And why?"

"That's what I came down here for." Blake covered the dead snake again, then his eyes darkened ominously. "Evidently someone put it there earlier while we were gone."

Yvette frowned. "But who would do such a thing?"

"Who filled the tubs?"

Yvette's gaze moved from Blake's face to the other side of the lobby and she held up her hand, beckoning toward a man who'd just stepped in through the front door.

"M'sieur Bandy, come here," she yelled, then looked at Blake. "M'sieur Bandy was in charge of getting the tubs filled."

The man Madam Yvette called Bandy was obviously the handyman about the place, only he didn't seem to know anything about the snake, either.

"Lessin' it was that stranger what give me and Geezer a hand," he said, his weathered face screwed up in thought.

Blake eyed him dubiously. "What stranger?"

"The one what helped us carry up some of the water." Bandy hesitated for a second, then went on. "Come to think of it, he did ask which room the lady was usin'. Said he didn't want to get her water too hot."

"There were two ladies," Blake reminded him.

"I know." He nodded. "That's why I'm sure it musta been him, caused he asked specifically for the lady with the white hair."

"What did he look like?"

"About my size, give or take a few inches. Sorta wizened up, though, and shriveled from the sun with a mustache that sat tight on his upper lip as if it was drawn on."

Blake's eyes narrowed. "He still around?"

"Don't think so. Iffen I remember right, I ain't seen him since we come back downstairs."

Madam Yvette continued to shake her head. "I am so sorry, M'sieur Morgan. If I had known... But why would someone want to harm your Mademoiselle Winters?"

Blake straightened, his gaze resting on the bloody towel. "If I knew that, madam, I wouldn't be down here asking questions."

"Ah, yes, *oui*, I understand."

Blake could tell the woman was upset as she instructed the handyman to get rid of the snake, then she looked at Blake and her eyes moved from their perusal of his face to his hairy chest and he suddenly realized he'd come down without his shirt on.

"You'll have to excuse me," he said, clearing his throat self-consciously. "My only thought was how close Miss Winters came to being bitten."

"Then she's all right?"

"Thankfully, yes. Only I think perhaps I'll accompany your Mr. Bandy and his friend, what is it, Geezer, when they go after the tubs, just to make sure?" And a short time later, he was following behind Bandy and another man, who seemed just as friendly as Bandy, while they removed the tubs from the rooms, starting with Blake's room.

By the time they reached the tub in Hanna's room, Hanna was fully dressed, with her hair pulled back in its usual severe topknot.

"Did you find out anything?" she asked Blake as they watched Bandy and his friend pick up the tub and leave the room with it.

Blake shook his head. "Not really, except that we probably have a description of the culprit."

"Oh?"

"Those two got some outside help," and he pointed to Bandy and Geezer who were just disappearing through the doorway into the hall. "Only it seems their helper's suddenly disappeared."

"Surely they know his name?"

"He introduced himself as Willie, only I doubt that's his real name, and the handyman said he's never seen the man before and hasn't seen him since."

"How marvelous." She took a deep breath, then strolled over to the window and looked out, staring at the dim lights, few and far between in the small frontier town.

Somewhere out there was a man who was trying to kill her, and she had absolutely no clue as to why.

"So what do we do now?" she asked, turning to face Blake.

He shrugged. "Isn't much we can do, I'm afraid, except really keep our eyes open the rest of the trip." He headed for the door. "Hope you don't mind. I think we should get an early start in the morning so I'll probably be pounding on your door before sunup."

"I'd better let Mrs. Brady know."

"No need, I've already told her." His gaze traveled from her clean scrubbed face to the toes of her kid shoes, then moved back up slowly until he was looking directly into her pale lavender eyes. "Make sure you lock your door after I leave," he said, his voice suddenly deeper. "I'd hate for our man to sneak back here to see if his slithering friend did its job."

"Don't worry, it'll be locked." Her eyes fixed on his in an invisible embrace she couldn't seem to shake.

Blake had his shirt on now, but it wasn't hard at all for her to remember the way he'd looked without it, and as she stared into his strangely golden eyes there were other things she remembered, as well. Things she had no right to remember. Feeling a flush getting ready to flood through her, she pursed her lips stubbornly, fighting against it, and finally managed to wrench her eyes from his gaze. Walking over to the dresser, she picked up the key where she'd set it earlier, then turned toward Blake.

"Now, if you don't mind I am rather tired," she said, hoping he wouldn't see the warm flush that was already tingling her ears. "And you did say we'd be getting up early."

"Don't mind at all," he answered. "You have a good night," and without another word, Blake left her room, closing the door firmly behind him, waiting until he heard her key turn in the lock before returning to his own room across the hall.

Hanna set the key on the dresser, then stood for a minute staring at her nightclothes, still laid out on the bed. Blake had made sure there were no more uninvited guests in the room and she was grateful. Yet the idea that there'd been one in there in the first place still troubled her. Well, there was nothing more she could do about it tonight, and pulling down the shade on the window, she reached up, unbuttoning her blouse. Tonight was going to be a long night, and a restless one, she was sure of it.

The sun was barely streaking the sky the next morning as the old buckboard pulled away from the Chez Pari Hotel and headed out of Hubbard Creek. As usual, Hanna was sitting beside Blake while Elizabeth sat on her chair in the back watching his horse trot along behind.

Blake had replenished their supplies just before leaving and Hanna looked over at him now. He'd told her while they were putting things in the wagon that they should reach Hangtown in another couple of days. She was glad, because after last night, she wasn't quite as self-assured around him as she had been at the start of the trip and it was a feeling she didn't like.

"Something the matter?" Blake asked as he glanced over, realizing she'd been eyeing him furtively.

"Not at all," she answered, her voice once more prim and proper as she quickly straightened, her eyes on the dusty road ahead of them. "I was just thinking that it's good we'll be there soon, then maybe I'll be able to find out just what all this nonsense with bullets and snakes is all about."

"That's all that's bothering you?"

"Should there be something else, Mr. Morgan?" she asked and she turned from the road and looked right at him, appearing to be in complete control of her emotions again.

He took a deep breath and half smiled, then flicked the reins, urging the horses a little faster. There was a knowing look in his eye as he said, "I guess not if you say so," and he watched her tilt her head defiantly and turn away from his scrutiny, her eyes once more fixed steadfastly on the horizon.

It was midafternoon three days later when they finally rode into Hangtown and Hanna sat on the seat staring at everything, her head shaking slightly in disbelief. "This is a town?" she asked, her gaze moving from one building to another, taking in the haphazard structures.

It was almost as bad as Fort Worth although there did seem to be several hotels. One building that had a sign over it stating the Hangtown Herald stuck out from most of the others because it was brand new and freshly painted, as was one other building a few doors away.

Blake reined their buckboard up in front of the new building farther down the street, then pulled the horses to a halt.

"That lawyer you're looking for has offices in there," he said, motioning with his hand toward the fairly new building that was painted yellow with white trim.

Hanna stared at it apprehensively, her gaze settling on the signs over the door. Milton Gibbs, Attorney at Law was on one sign, and below it was a sign that read Land Office—Deeds and Parcels. There was also another sign to the right of the other two that read Government Assayer.

"Which is he?" Hanna asked.

Blake smiled, amused. "All three."

"That's ridiculous."

"Not out here." He gestured toward the rest of the town. The feed store doubled as a blacksmith, the boot maker was also a gunsmith, and the general store sold everything from hats and food to hardware supplies. Only a small bank, saloon and the sheriff's office didn't do double duty at something or other. "Out here the more you can do, the better. Even old Doc Weatherby runs a pharmacy when he isn't pulling teeth, taking out bullets and healing sick cattle."

"He takes care of people and animals both?"

"Hey, he's a doctor, that's all that matters."

Hanna turned and looked at Elizabeth, who was already standing in the back of the buckboard, stretching to get out the kinks.

"I'm sorry, Mrs. Brady," she said, "I was hoping the place would be a little more civilized."

Elizabeth grinned. "You worry too much, Hanna." She took a quick appraisal of the town. "As long as there are people here there must be something worth staying for. Besides, we won't be living in town anyway, will we? I thought we'd be staying at the ranch."

"But if the town's this bad, what will the ranch be like?"

Elizabeth wasn't about to be discouraged. "Well, we'll never know unless you go inside and find out, will we?" she said. With that Blake got down, then helped both women alight.

Hanna felt self-conscious as Blake opened the door for her and she stepped into the small waiting room, listening to the little bell over the door as it announced their arrival. She'd have felt better if she could have cleaned up some first, but as Mrs. Brady reminded her, the sooner they got to the ranch, the better. Hanna reached up and tucked a stray hair beneath the wide-brimmed straw hat she was wearing. She'd discovered only a few days into the journey that she couldn't hold up the parasol all day long, and the little hats she'd brought from Boston did nothing to keep the sun out. So she had bought a big straw hat at a store in one of the towns they'd been through, but it had been made for a man, not a woman, and looked rather out of place on her.

"Maybe he's not in," she murmured halfheartedly, then tensed as she heard a man's voice call from the other room.

"I'll be right with you!"

"You ever met Mr. Gibbs?" she asked Blake.

"Nope. I've seen him a couple of times when I was passing through, but never had the chance to chew the fat with him."

Hanna was ready to ask Blake when he'd been here last when the door to one of the inner offices opened and a tall, thin man with dark fringed hair on each side of a balding pate stepped through it. He had piercing blue eyes, a rather thin pinched nose and one of his front teeth was gold capped.

"Yes, sir, and what might I do for you folks?" he asked, looking directly at Blake.

Blake backed off. "It's not for me, it's for Miss Winters here," he said.

Milton Gibbs's eyes widened in recognition. "Miss Winters, ah, yes." His gaze settled on her white hair beneath the hat. "I should have realized, I'm sorry. Come in, come in, I'm glad you finally arrived," and he gestured to one of the doors that had Attorney written on it.

Hanna didn't ask them, but Blake and Elizabeth followed her right into the lawyer's office.

"Excuse me, but..." Milton Gibbs looked at Hanna expectantly, then gestured toward Elizabeth and Blake. "This is rather private, you know."

"Oh, I'm sorry," she said, then introduced them to the barrister. "And I think as long as Mrs. Brady's going to live with me at the ranch, and Mr. Morgan's going to drive us there in the buckboard, that it'd be foolish for me not to include them," she went on. "Besides, according to your letter I should already know what's in the will. Reading it is just a formality, isn't it?"

Gibbs had to concede she was right, so after settling them all in chairs, reading the will and confirming that Hanna was the new owner of the White Wind Ranch as well as a small account at the local bank, the three of them left the lawyer's office.

Hanna stood just outside the door and stared across the dusty street to the weathered buildings of the quiet frontier town. Mr. Gibbs said it would probably take them another two hours to ride to the ranch in the old buckboard, and she wondered if maybe they hadn't ought to wait until tomorrow and spend the night in town so she could arrive at the ranch a little less weary and bedraggled. After all, it was close to three in the afternoon already.

Elizabeth, too, was looking over the town, only at the moment her gaze was on a man in front of the general store across the street. He was sitting on an old chair and leaning back on two legs so that he was resting against the wall near one of the display windows. It wasn't the way he was sitting on the chair that bothered her, it was the man himself. He fit exactly the description Blake Morgan had said the handyman at the Chez Pari in Hubbard Creek had given him of the man who'd helped set up the bath, and she felt the hair at the nape of her neck prickle.

"I'm not really sure," she said, answering Hanna's question. "It all depends."

"On what?"

"On whether that man across the way is who I think he is or not," and she saw both Hanna and Blake look in the direction she was looking.

Blake's eyes hardened and he inhaled sharply as fear settled in Hanna's eyes.

"My God," Hanna said, half whispering. "He fits the description perfectly."

"It may not be him," Blake cautioned her. "That description could fit half a dozen cowhands in Hangtown."

"But if it is him?"

"Then maybe you'd better not take a chance on staying in town tonight. From what's happened so far, it's evident someone didn't want you to get here at all, so maybe it'd be better to just keep on going."

Hanna thought over what he said, decided maybe he was right, and they climbed back onto the buckboard and headed southwest out of town following the directions given them by the lawyer.

The late afternoon sun was hot as they rode along, and Hanna wished she could have had time to change. Perspiration beaded her brow, and she could feel her clothes sticking to her.

At times they found themselves traveling through open prairies swept by hot gusty breezes that rippled across the pale grasses before losing themselves in the mesquite, sagebrush and greasewood. Later the road wound through rugged canyons hidden from the worst of the sun, and Hanna was amazed at the contrast.

They had been riding for almost two hours when Blake finally reined the buckboard off the main trail they'd been following and started down a narrow road that stretched out between two jagged cliffs dotted here and there with straggly cedar trees. The trees were hanging precariously to the sides of the rocky embankments that sloped down to the edge of the narrow road, and the rock formations nearly blotted out the deep blue sky.

Hanna felt dwarfed as she stared up at them, one hand on her hat to hold it on her head, the other hanging on to the side of the seat since the road was so uneven and bumpy.

Suddenly the crack of a rifle echoed, bouncing off the walls of the dry arroyo, and before Hanna could grasp what was happening, Blake, realizing the bullet had missed and whizzed right past Hanna's head, slapped the reins, yelled to the team and gave the horses their heads, moving the buckboard forward at breakneck speed.

Hanna wasn't just hanging on to the seat now, she was clutching it for dear life, and trying to hold onto her hat, too, as the buckboard flew down the road, dust billowing out behind it.

Another shot rang out, then another, and Elizabeth, who was hanging on as hard as Hanna, let her gaze move from one side to the other to see if she could spot where the culprit was. But they were going too fast, and there were any number of places where a person could hide up there in the rocks and never be seen from down here.

After what seemed like an eternity Hanna finally felt Blake pull back on the reins and the team begin to slow down. They'd put a good mile behind them in their mad dash, and now as the road skirted the towering cliffs, the rock formations eased off and gave way once more to rolling hills and flatter plains where an ambush would be harder to attempt.

Hanna leaned back against the seat and let out a sigh of relief as the buckboard slowly ground to a halt.

"Everybody all right?" Blake asked.

"If you could call being scared half to death all right, then I'm all right," Elizabeth said as she straightened in her chair after retrieving her parasol from the bed of the buckboard. "Hanna?"

Hanna was having a hard time finding her voice. Her heart was still in her throat and her hands were trembling.

"I think I'm all right," she answered, her voice tremulous, then she looked at Blake. "You don't suppose it was that little man with the mustache again, do you?"

"Hard to tell. Either him or one of his cronies, I suppose. Only there's no way we could ever prove it."

Hanna breathed in deeply, looking toward the road they'd just traveled. Well, someone knew they were coming, she thought, and she suddenly stiffened.

"Mr. Morgan, about how far do you think we are yet from where Mr. Gibbs said the ranch is?" she asked.

Blake shrugged. "Five, maybe six miles, why?"

"And do you think we have enough water in our water barrels for us to wash?"

"What do you have in mind?"

"I've decided that I think it'd be best if I arrived at the ranch in my best bib and tucker instead of looking like a fugitive from the poorhouse." She was slowly getting her self-assurance back. "If anyone out at the ranch is responsible for the attempts on my life, then the more respectability I command when I arrive the better. Don't you think?"

She glanced ahead, scanning the horizon, and her gaze rested on a grove of trees about a quarter mile away.

"If you'll just drive over to those trees... They should give us enough screen to wash and change clothes."

"What about our ambusher?" Elizabeth asked. "He could still be about."

Hanna smiled warmly as she looked at Blake. "Why, that's what we have Mr. Morgan for. You will stand guard, won't you? I mean ... you did say you'd make sure we got to the ranch in one piece."

Blake's topaz eyes crinkled at the corners as he studied her for a few seconds, contemplating. She was trying not to sound too frightened, but he could tell she was really shook up. Maybe she was right and it'd do good for her to show up in her prim and proper Boston clothes.

"I'd be glad to stand guard," he answered, heading for the grove of trees off to the left of the road.

It took a little over half an hour for Hanna and Elizabeth to wash the dirt from their faces and find something appropriate to wear. Elizabeth took no time at all deciding on the rust-colored poplin she'd worn when they'd left Abilene, Kansas, but Hanna was having a terrible time deciding.

Her best suit, the new purple one, had been ruined that first night out of Fort Worth and the only other two outfits she felt were good enough were a black linen suit she'd often worn to church on Sunday and a new red dress she'd bought just before leaving Boston. However, now that she looked it over, she realized that the purchase of the dress had really been a frivolous decision on her part. It was a bright scarlet faille with long sleeves, way too hot for the Texas heat. And the neckline in front was far too low for a respectable Boston teacher. Still, it just might be the thing to wear under the circumstances. She wanted to make the ranch hands think she was a strong person. The kind who could run a place like the White Wind.

Mr. Gibbs had told them that her brother's foreman, Jules Hayden, was running the place until she arrived, with help from an old Mexican housekeeper, and she was afraid he'd see right through her pretense of knowing exactly what being the owner of a ranch was all about.

"Wear the red one," Elizabeth urged her as she saw Hanna looking both of them over carefully.

"But the black's more appropriate," Hanna protested. "After all, I'm supposed to be in mourning over Henry."

"Are you?"

"Well . . ." Her face flushed. "I should be."

"Pshaw! Who cares way out here? Besides—" and Elizabeth popped her little yellow straw hat on her head as she talked "—you weren't all that close to him. Why, if he hadn't left you the place you wouldn't even have known he died."

"But that's no excuse."

"Aren't you ladies through yet?" Blake yelled from where he stood on higher ground watching the road and the woods at the same time. "It's gonna be dark before we even get there if you don't hurry."

"The red," Elizabeth urged again, and this time Hanna capitulated.

After putting the dress on, she let her hair down, brushed the tangles out, twisted it into its usual knot then put on a small red faille hat she'd bought to go with the dress. It had a narrow rolled brim with sheer veiling stretched over it, and the veiling was made into a bow at the back where it covered the knot of Hanna's twisted hair. The whole outfit was a bit fancy, but Hanna agreed with Elizabeth that it made her appear to be more a woman of the world, rather than a former teacher from a private girls' school.

"We're ready," she called out to Blake, who was some twenty yards away. A few minutes later when he joined them Hanna was certain she saw surprise in his eyes when his gaze fell on her clothes.

The dress was rumpled from having been stuffed into the trunk, but she was going to have to ignore that. The important thing was that she felt different in it. More forceful and commanding. Besides, as far as anyone at the ranch was concerned the wrinkles could be the effects of the long journey she'd been on.

Satisfied she'd made the right decision, she ignored the strange way Blake was looking at her and grabbed her handbag off the wagon bed of the buckboard where she'd set it earlier. "Shall we?"

After helping both ladies on board again, Blake grabbed the reins and drove the buckboard onto the narrow road, and they continued on their way.

Half an hour later they had just come over the top of a rolling hill when Blake suddenly pulled back on the reins and pointed up ahead.

"There it is," he said, squinting in the late afternoon sun.

Hanna reached up, shading her eyes as Elizabeth stood and peered over their shoulders.

The land stretched out before them like a pale golden green carpet, broken here and there by a bush, some rocks, and nearer the house, a number of trees.

But it was the house itself that commanded their attention. Hanna had thought it would be a wooden structure much like the ranches she'd seen closer to town. Instead it was made of adobe. The whole place was spread out like a small village with the main house in the center and the smaller buildings scattered here and there as if for fortification while wood and stone fences cut back and forth separating different areas.

Beyond the ranch, in the distance, the vast land was cut by a meandering river that flowed down from the deep purple hills in the background. The rugged tops of the hills were golden now from the setting sun as it fell closer to meet the horizon.

"But where are the cattle?" Hanna asked Blake, her gaze resting on what appeared to be a few horses in a corral to the left of one of the larger buildings. "Mr. Gibbs said there should be close to a thousand of them."

"Out on the range. They're probably in the middle of roundup."

"Roundup?"

He glanced at her. "I see you have more to learn about ranching than I thought."

Hanna's mouth pursed stubbornly. "And I'll learn it, too," she said then sighed. "Well, I suppose we might as well get on with the inevitable."

Taking his cue from her, Blake clicked to the horses and they continued on.

Up ahead at the ranch house, the housekeeper, Maria, stood upstairs in the master bedroom staring out a set of double doors at the buckboard as it ambled down the lane toward the gates of White Wind. She was tired and weary, the thought of visitors at this time of day bringing only irritation. Well, she wasn't going to ask them to stay for supper, that's for sure. Bad enough she had to put up with Jules Hayden ordering her around.

Opening one of the doors a little wider, she leaned her ample body against the frame and squinted, hoping to see better, but the sun was already too far below the horizon and whoever was in the buckboard was too shadowed to distinguish at this distance.

It was probably just some people who'd lost their way. Well, she'd set them on the right track again. Stepping back, she closed the doors behind her, then straightened, her dark eyes intense as she strolled from the master bedroom and made her way down the hall to the winding stone steps that descended to the parlor.

For eight years she'd worked for Hank Winters, and before that, since she was a young girl, for the de Vera family. These walls, every stone and board of this house were home to her. At fifty-three she'd been widowed twice, raised two sons and knew she'd no doubt die here. Ever since that lawyer in town had told Jules that Hank's sister was coming to take over, she'd been on edge.

What if the woman decided to sell the place? Or worse yet, what if she tried to run it herself and threw them all out?

She stood at the foot of the stairs gazing about the main room of the hacienda. It fairly reeked of masculinity, from the colorful woven rugs scattered about the wood floors to the heavy ornate furniture. Hank Winters had combined some of the furniture left by Antonio de Vera's widow with more familiar American ranch furnishings, but without any frills.

Leaving the stairs, she strolled to the fireplace and stood staring at the clock that graced the mantel. It was the one thing that really looked out of place. It was a ship's clock, and Hank had told her he'd bought it when he'd been on a visit to Galveston, some years back.

She'd often wondered about it, but had never had the courage to ask him. Hank Winters was the type of man who didn't answer questions easily. Especially if those questions might shed some light on anything in his past. That's why Maria had been surprised to learn that he'd had a sister living somewhere in the east.

Suddenly she frowned as she heard the rattle of horses and grinding wheels as the buckboard she'd seen approaching pulled up near the front veranda. *Madre de Dios,* she suddenly thought, what if it was

Señorita Winters? But then she'd arrive in a carriage, not a buckboard, wouldn't she?

Reaching up to smooth back her dark hair that was gently streaked with gray, she straightened the apron that covered her plain blue cotton dress and headed for the front door.

Outside, Hanna's stomach was fluttering wildly as Blake maneuvered the buckboard as close as he could to the veranda of the large adobe house, its red tiled roof a contrasting background for the bright flowering vines that climbed up to the second floor balcony. Her gaze shifted from the roof back down to the veranda that stretched the full length of the place.

Directly in the middle of the veranda was a huge open wooden door with windows on both sides of it. The plump figure of a Mexican woman suddenly appeared on the threshold, and Hanna remembered Milton Gibbs telling her about the housekeeper. He said her name was Maria Rodriguez and that she was half Comanche Indian, half Mexican.

Except for the woman in the doorway, there didn't seem to be anyone about. Hanna continued to stare at the woman, but it was too close to dusk and the veranda was too shaded for her to get a really good look.

"Something you want?" Maria called out in heavily accented English.

It was Blake who answered. "Where's Mr. Hayden?"

The woman stepped out onto the veranda. "Who wants to know?"

"The new owner of White Wind."

The veranda was only two steps off the ground and the poles holding up its roof were made from natural tree trunks rather than planed wood. As Maria took another step closer, Hanna finally got a good look at her.

Maria's dark hair was pulled back severely in front, braided, then wound into a tiara across the top of her head with the hair in back falling loosely to her waist, and her eyes were as dark as her hair. It was easy to see she had been pretty in her youth with a generous mouth, high cheek bones, a slight slant to her eyes, and the broadness of her nose giving away her Indian ancestry. But now her looks had faded from time and work, and wrinkles creased the corners of her eyes while extra pounds rounded the flesh on her cheeks. At the moment she looked tired and rather unfriendly.

"Señorita Winters?" Maria asked as she stared at the young woman who was being helped from the seat on the buckboard by the stranger who'd spoken.

Hanna straightened, trying to smooth the creases in her dress, then held her head high hoping she looked self-assured and turned to face the housekeeper.

"You must be Maria?"

"*Sí.*" Maria's eyes raked over Hanna. The resemblance to Hank Winters was uncanny, even to the white hair and strange lavender eyes, yet Maria had expected a schoolteacher to be dressed much plainer. Hanna Winters looked like anything but a schoolteacher. But then she didn't look like she'd be capable of running a ranch, either, not with those soft-looking hands.

"I was not sure when you would be here," Maria went on. "Or I would have been prepared for your arrival. As it is, I must apologize for not giving you a better welcome.''

Blake was helping Elizabeth down from the back of the wagon, and Maria glanced toward them curiously.

"This is my dear friend, Mrs. Brady,'' Hanna said when they had joined her. "And Mr. Morgan has been kind enough to bring us here all the way from Fort Worth.''

"For a price, no doubt,'' Maria said as she studied Blake with disdain. The man looked like any other drifter except for his eyes. They were too sharp, too alert and too intense, and Maria wasn't quite sure she liked him.

"Where is everyone?'' Blake asked.

"Out rounding up the cattle for the drive north, but Señor Hayden should return at any time. He and some of the men usually come home for supper.''

"In the meantime?''

"In the meantime I will have Paco tend to your things,'' she answered, and she walked over to the edge of the veranda, cupped her hand to her mouth and called out.

Seconds later a Mexican boy in his mid teens came running from the stables some hundred feet from the house. As he drew near he suddenly stopped abruptly, then walked the rest of the way when he saw there were guests. Maria quickly instructed him on what to do.

"I'll help him with the trunks,'' Blake said when he realized the boy was the only one coming. After introducing the youth as her grandson, Paco, to the new mistress of White Wind, Maria led Hanna and Elizabeth inside, while Blake stayed outside with the buckboard.

Hanna hadn't expected the house to be anything like it was. She'd expected worn bare floors and rough-hewn logs like most of the homesteads they'd seen since leaving Fort Worth. In some respects the adobe house was elegantly Spanish, with fancy bricks in the stone hearth and a carved mahogany mantel. Even the chandelier that hung from the ceiling in the living room had gilded candle holders, and gold-threaded drapes hung at the windows. But the rest of it was bold and plain.

It was cool inside away from the hot sun, and Hanna breathed a sigh of relief.

"I'm sorry, Señorita Winters, but I did not know you would have guests with you," Maria said once they were inside. "I have your room ready, but it will take time to change the sheets on the other beds."

Hanna reached up, removing her hat. "How many bedrooms are there?"

"Four. The master bedroom where your brother slept, and three others. I took the liberty of readying the master bedroom for you."

Hanna studied the woman curiously. "You do all the work here yourself?"

Maria smiled slightly, the first smile since they'd arrived. "Oh, my, no. Teresa and Dolores help. They are my sons' wives. Miguel and Sancho ride with Señor Jules and have worked with Señor Winters as long as I have."

"And how long is that?"

"Since he bought the hacienda from the widow de Vera eight years ago."

"I see." Hanna let her gaze move about the room. She was surprised to see that the staircase that gave access to the upper floors of the strange looking house was made of flat stone and wound around, disappearing somewhere behind the fireplace. The use of unplaned trees as banisters all but made a lie to the richness of the room's decorations.

Double doors opened on the far wall to the left of the fireplace, and Hanna strolled over to them and looked out into a courtyard with five-foot-high sunbaked walls, myriad flowers and a few shade trees. At one time it was probably a lovely place, but now the flowers needed weeding and the fountain that sat in the center of the garden was no longer spewing water. A few inches of stagnant water lay in the pool surrounding it. Evidently Henry hadn't cared all that much for flowers or gardens.

She turned to face the housekeeper. "I'm sorry we've inconvenienced you, Maria," she said. "But I did tell Mr. Gibbs I was bringing a friend. However, there's no need for you to make a fuss." She hesitated for a moment, then went on. "I am curious though. Mr. Gibbs said Mr. Hayden has been running the place. Does that mean he's been living here in the house?"

"Oh, *sí*. He even stayed here when Señor Winters was alive because he always ran things when the señor went away on one of his business trips."

Well, that's a surprise, thought Hanna. She had no idea her brother had had to travel anywhere on business. From what she'd always heard, cattlemen spent most of their time on their ranches.

She glanced toward the entrance hall behind Maria where Blake was helping the young Mexican boy with the trunks. For the next few minutes they were all busy as the trunks were taken upstairs and Maria showed Hanna her room.

It was a spacious room with a fireplace and doors leading out onto the balcony across the front of the house, but the furnishings were sparse and unfeminine. A patchwork quilt covered the four-poster bed while worn brocade drapes graced the windows.

Maria explained to them that Jules Hayden used the bedroom right at the top of the stairs, but that she'd get the other two rooms ready for Mrs. Brady and Blake.

"That won't be necessary," Blake informed her as he helped the Mexican boy set one of Hanna's trunks down at the foot of her bed. "I'll only be spending one night and I can sleep in the bunkhouse with the hands."

"Nonsense," Hanna said. "You'll sleep in the house. After all, if it weren't for you, I wouldn't even be here."

"It will be no harder to get two rooms ready than one," Maria added, turning toward the balcony doors as the sounds of horses and riders drifted up from below. "Señor Hayden is back," she informed them, closing the doors. A few seconds later a man's gruff voice rang through the quiet house and Hanna heard the front door downstairs slam shut.

So, Mr. Hayden thinks he owns the place, Hanna thought as Maria hurried from the room, her skirts flying, while the rest of them followed slowly behind.

Hanna was almost at the foot of the stairs, but Maria was already halfway across the parlor when Jules Hayden, slapping his hat against his knee to rid it of trail dust, stepped into the room.

"Who the hell left that buckboard—" were the only words that left his mouth, then his eyes suddenly came to rest on Hanna, her bright red dress standing out like a beacon against the creamy adobe walls.

Visibly shaken, he froze at first, then slowly straightened, still holding his hat in his hand. His eyes narrowed curiously, and the big heavy mustache on his upper lip twitched slightly.

"It's Señorita Winters," Maria explained quickly. "She just arrived a few minutes ago so I'm afraid your supper will be a little delayed tonight, Señor Hayden."

Jules stared hard at the woman who was staring back at him. He'd expected Hank's sister to be a quiet mousy individual, but it was apparent by the clothes she had on that Hanna Winters wasn't what most people would consider a typical Boston spinster.

His slate gray eyes, set beneath heavy brows, filtered over her from head to toe.

"I'd have been here sooner, Mr. Hayden," Hanna said, her voice pitched a little too high to be natural. "But I'm afraid your countryside makes traveling a rather fortuitous adventure."

Yep, she's a schoolteacher, Jules thought, as he listened to her answer. "You could've just sold the place and not come at all," he responded, caring little whether he insulted her or not.

"And missed out on all this." She gestured about the room. "I must say the whole trip's been quite fascinating so far." She glanced over at Elizabeth. "But here, let me introduce my friends," and she introduced Mrs. Brady and Blake.

While she was introducing them, Hanna studied Jules Hayden. He was a large man. Perhaps in his mid fifties. Big and rough, and with an air of authority she wasn't quite sure she liked. As a foreman he'd have to be able to handle himself with the hired hands, but she had a distinct feeling he probably took little advice from anyone, and was more used to giving orders than taking them. A strange man for her brother to hire.

When all the introductions were over, she addressed him again, her hat still in her hand. "Tell me, Mr. Hayden, just how long did you work for my brother?" she asked.

He hesitated, his eyes moving briskly from his perusal of Blake to Hanna. "Since he bought the place eight years ago."

"And you've stayed here in the house all that time?"

"Well, no, ma'am," he answered, his voice still showing his irritation at her arrival. "Hank had me move in here about a year after I made foreman, when he started making those business trips back east."

"Oh?"

"Said he wanted someone to watch over the place while he was gone and I could do it better from in here than the bunkhouse."

"Well, under the circumstances, Mr. Hayden, since I don't intend to be going away on any business trips, and since it just wouldn't be appropriate for two unattached women to be living here under the same roof with a single gentleman, I think perhaps it'd be best if tomorrow morning you started moving your things back to the bunkhouse, don't you?''

His jaw clenched angrily. "To hell I will. I'm the foreman here."

"That's right, the foreman, not the owner. I happen to be the owner, Mr. Hayden. Or have you forgotten?''

His eyes were blazing as he stared at her. "Hank'd turn over in his grave if he knew you was throwing me out."

"I'm not throwing you out, sir," she reminded him. "I'm merely delegating you to the bunkhouse where you belong. If you don't like the arrangement, then I'm sorry. But if you intend to stay at White Wind and continue being foreman, I'm afraid it's the way things are going to have to be."

Jules's eyes hardened as Hanna looked over toward the door, to where the housekeeper was standing.

"Now, I presume since we weren't expected, Maria, it's going to take you awhile to put together enough food for a meal, am I right?" She saw the hesitancy in Maria's eyes. "But if you'd be so kind. Anything will do. The simpler, the better."

"Señor Hayden already ordered roast beef for him and the men before he left this morning, *señorita,*" Maria answered and Hanna looked surprised.

"The men?"

"*Sí.*" Maria glanced over at Jules. "Since Señor Hank's death, Señor Hayden has had the two señors, Miles and Caracas, staying at the house here with him."

"Pete and José are my two best hands," Jules cut in. "There wasn't nothin' wrong with 'em stayin' here."

"Well, there is now." Hanna was peeved and she looked at Maria. "Is that why the other two rooms aren't ready, Maria?"

Maria nodded. *"Sí."* And she eyed Jules apprehensively. "But I would not let them near your room, *señorita*. That I insisted on."

Hanna smiled triumphantly. "Thank you, Maria. You did well." She turned once more to Jules, who was still fuming over this new turn of events. "As for your men, Mr. Hayden, I don't even want them to wait until morning," she continued, and her lavender eyes sparked dangerously. "I want their things out of here now, and they can take their meals in the bunkhouse with the rest of the men, too. I presume you do have a cook for the bunkhouse, don't you?"

"Heck's out on the range with the men."

"Then I suggest you tell your men to get started back toward the range, Mr. Hayden, and maybe they can get there before the food's all gone. For tonight, however, I'll concede to let you share our table, but as for tomorrow and the rest of your time here at White Wind you will eat and sleep in the bunkhouse with the rest of the hired help, is that understood?"

"Oh, it's understood," he answered, his voice seething with rage. His hat went back on his head. "Hell, after all I did for Hank, and this is the thanks I get." He started for the front hall, then turned abruptly to face her again. "And you can keep your damn roast beef, too. I wouldn't eat at the same table with you if you paid me.'' Turning again toward the hall, he left the room and seconds later the front door slammed shut.

Blake glanced over at Hanna expecting to at least see her a bit shaken up by her foreman's angry departure, but instead she looked pleased with herself.

''Well, now, that was a stupid thing to do,'' he said as he continued watching her. ''You know you just made yourself an enemy, don't you?''

''What do you mean, just made an enemy? The man showed his true colors the minute he opened his mouth. Didn't you hear what he said about my not coming? I wouldn't be at all surprised to find out that he was the one who tried to have me killed before I even got here.''

Maria's eyes widened. ''Someone tried to kill you?'' she asked.

Hanna took a deep breath. ''It's all right, Maria. They didn't succeed and I'm here,'' she answered. ''Now, since it seems Mr. Hayden has decided he doesn't care for roast beef after all, I think the rest of us are hungry enough to take care of his share, too.''

''Oh, *sí,* yes, *señorita,*'' Maria said hurriedly, and without another word, she left the room.

''Blake's right, Hanna,'' Elizabeth said as soon as Maria was gone. ''You don't know a thing about running this place and you're going to need Jules Hayden.''

Hanna wasn't about to be dissuaded. ''For what? To live in this house? He still has his job. I haven't fired him. All I did was let him know that I'm the boss around here, not him.''

"Bully for you," Blake answered. "You've proved your point, all right, only now I'd love to see what happens when you discover there's more to ranching than buying and selling a few cattle."

"I'll learn."

"Oh, yeah, you'll learn, all right. But I'll bet you aren't going to learn from Jules Hayden, or any of the other hands on the White Wind."

Elizabeth moved over from the fireplace where she'd been standing. "I'm afraid he's right, Hanna," she said. "And I have a distinct feeling you're going to be awfully sorry you made the man angry."

"Well, *I* don't think I will." Hanna's head went up defiantly. "After all, as you said before we left Boston, Mrs. Brady, ranching has got to be easier than riding herd on a bunch of spoiled young rich girls all day. Now, since Maria doesn't seem to have dinner ready, I think I'll go upstairs and see if I can find something a little cooler and more comfortable to slip into," and she turned toward the stairs. "You coming?" she asked Elizabeth.

Elizabeth stared at her for a second, then shrugged. "Might as well," she answered. "I'm afraid Maria looks like the kind who'd resent interference in the kitchen," and she followed after Hanna.

Blake watched them go, a worried look on his face. Whether Hanna Winters knew it or not, Blake was certain that her callous treatment of Jules Hayden had ended any hopes she might have had for succeeding at White Wind. Although in a way he didn't blame her. There was something about Hayden he didn't like, either, only he still thought she could have been a little more tactful. Shaking his head, he turned and went outside to find someone who could tell him where to put the buckboard that was still sitting in front of the veranda.

Chapter Four

Hanna stirred in the big four-poster bed. It had been an exceptionally hot night and she'd lost the nightcap off her head some time during her sleep. As she stirred, she suddenly realized that the hairpins had also come loose and her hair was tangled all over the pillow.

Opening her eyes, she stared at the ceiling for a few minutes, then turned toward the open double doors. A fly buzzed her nose and she brushed it away.

Already the sun was streaming into the room and she guessed that it must be late. She'd instructed everyone not to let her sleep past eight o'clock, but suspected they may not have taken her at her word.

Throwing back the covers, she sat up and stared toward the open doors, her thoughts suddenly reaching back to last night and her arrival.

Now that she'd had time to think it over, she began to wonder if maybe Blake and Mrs. Brady hadn't been right. Perhaps she had been a bit presumptuous in her treatment of Jules Hayden. But then just the thought of the high-handed way he'd taken over after Henry's death irritated her. She'd been thankful he'd been in charge of things in her absence, but having some of his men move in was unforgivable. He wasn't just making sure everything was still running smoothly, and she had to make sure he knew his high-handed tactics wouldn't be tolerated.

Stretching lazily, she stood up and walked toward the doors just in time to hear voices coming from the veranda below.

"Is that the last of it?" Jules was asking someone, and a man's voice she didn't recognize answered.

"Yeah."

"Good, then see that you put it with the rest of my stuff out at the bunkhouse and I'll meet you at the barn as soon as I get those supplies Heck wanted from Maria."

"I still think you shoulda told her off," the other man said. "If Hank was alive, he'da told her."

"Well, he ain't, and that's that. Now, we still got a job to do long as we're takin' her money, so get with it."

Hanna was curious. Grabbing her wrapper, she slipped it on and stepped onto the balcony to see if she could get a glimpse of what they were doing. Not wanting to be seen, she eased up close to the railing, then peeked over just as a man left the veranda carrying a couple of large boxes and some men's clothes over his arm.

"Your foreman's carrying out your orders and moving out," Blake said from behind her, and Hanna whirled. She'd forgotten that there was also a door onto the balcony at the end of the upstairs hall near the room he'd stayed in last night.

"Oh, you startled me."

"Sorry." He sauntered toward her and she clutched the neckline of her wrap together. He was already dressed for the day.

"You're not ready to leave?" she asked.

He straightened, then stared off toward the road they'd ridden in on yesterday.

"I was thinking about it." He looked at Hanna. "But then I haven't been paid my fifteen dollars yet, remember?"

"Oh, dear." Her hands clenched the wrapper more tightly, and she suddenly remembered that her hair was hanging loose, too, and she flushed. "If you'll wait here I'll get it for you. It's just in my room," and she started toward the double doors.

"Hanna?"

She stopped, staring at him curiously. It was unusual for him to call her Hanna.

"Yes?"

"Are you absolutely sure you're going to be able to make it out here on your own?" he asked.

She laughed self-consciously. "You don't think I will?"

His eyes darkened. "I don't think you realize what you're up against."

She continued to stare at him, her eyes narrowing slightly. "You mean because someone tried to kill me?"

"Hell, that's only part of it." He straightened, realizing again how vulnerable she looked when her hair was down like this. For some reason that old saying about letting your hair down really seemed to apply to Hanna Winters. Still, he went on. "You don't even know how to ride a horse, let alone saddle one. And you haven't the faintest notion of what a cattle drive is. I doubt you even know how to tell a cow from a bull, do you?"

The flush on her face deepened. "I told you, I can learn."

"Who's going to teach you?"

"I'll teach myself."

He exhaled, shaking his head. "Are all Bostonians as stubborn as you?"

"I'm not stubborn. I'm being practical. Henry learned. I will, too. I'm not stupid, you know."

"Oh, I know you're not stupid. But I think this time, Hanna Winters, you're biting off more than you can chew."

"I'll be the judge of that."

His eyes bored into hers and he knew that all the reasoning in the world wasn't going to make her change her mind. Besides, he didn't really want her to, what he really wanted her to do was ask him to stay. Yet, knowing her the way he'd gotten to since leaving Fort Worth, he knew damn well she wasn't about to let him influence her. He had hinted around enough about it last night and she hadn't taken the bait. If he stayed, the offer would have to come from him.

"For what it's worth, I can hang around awhile if you think you'll need me," he finally said, giving in.

Hanna looked puzzled. "Why would you do a thing like that?"

He shrugged. "Maybe I'm getting addlepated. But hell, at least I could teach you to ride a horse. That's something."

Hanna's eyes turned a deep amethyst as she contemplated his offer. He was right. Even if he knew nothing about ranching, he did know a lot about horses. But then that would be giving in and admitting that he and Mrs. Brady had been right.

"I don't think so," she finally said. "But thanks for the offer. Now let me get that money for you," and she continued on into her bedroom.

A short while later she stood on the upstairs balcony and watched Blake Morgan ride away from the ranch, her insides in a turmoil. He'd told her he'd hang around town for a few days just in case she changed her mind, but she'd assured him she wouldn't. In a way she'd wanted him to stay. It had been nice having someone to depend on other than herself or Mrs. Brady. As much as she hated to admit it, having him around had been a godsend.

That was just the problem. She was getting too used to having him around and she didn't like it. Especially after what happened in that little town. What was its name? Hubbard Creek. And even this morning out here on the balcony. She'd swear he'd been staring at her the same way he'd stared at her that night when he'd kissed her, and she couldn't have that.

No, this was the best way. She'd make it on her own or not at all. As he rode toward the horizon, slowly becoming a small speck in the distance, then vanished completely, a sudden feeling of loss swept over her and she shuddered.

This was ridiculous, she told herself quickly, and turning to take in the ranch grounds for a few seconds, she straightened stubbornly. Then, filled with determination not to give in, she headed for the doors to her room.

An hour later she was outside standing by the corral at the back looking over the horses with Elizabeth standing beside her. Hanna was wearing a plain brown skirt and white blouse, with the old hat on her head she'd worn during most of their trip from Fort Worth, and Elizabeth had put on a dark blue cotton dress she'd often worn at the boardinghouse, her hair covered with a big old straw hat Maria had confiscated for her from the house.

"You really should go through Henry's things, you know," Elizabeth said as she watched the horses flicking their tails vigorously, trying to keep off the flies.

Hanna made a face. "Why? They'll be there tonight. Right now I want to learn a little bit about what's going on around here."

"From whom?"

Hanna looked around. Not a soul was in sight. "Well..." Suddenly she spotted Maria's grandson Paco heading for the house from the barn. "Paco can show me," she answered. "Surely he knows something," and she called the boy over.

Paco was tall for thirteen with dark flashing eyes, beautiful white teeth and one of the warmest smiles Hanna had ever seen on a boy. His parents were Sancho and Dolores and they lived in a small adobe house way over the other side of the main house, with Miguel and Teresa's place right next door.

Paco was the oldest of Maria's grandchildren, and it was his job to feed the chickens, curry the horses and take care of the little things that went wrong while the men were out on the range.

Hanna watched him approach. Most of the Mexicans she'd seen since arriving in Texas wore what could be called typical Mexican garb, but not Paco. He wore the same loose-fitting white shirt, but it was tucked into tight-fitting buckskin pants while heeled boots covered his feet, and around his waist was a narrow gun belt. Not as fancy as the one Blake Morgan or Jules Hayden wore, but the six-shooter in it looked just as deadly.

Beneath his straw hat, his dark eyes studied Hanna curiously as he joined her. "You called me, *señorita?*" he asked.

Hanna swallowed, a bit embarrassed. "Why, yes, I did, Paco. You know how to ride a horse, don't you?"

"No, *señorita,* I never learned," he said then grinned impishly. "*Sí,* yes, I can ride a horse. As good as any other hand on the place."

"That's what I thought." Hanna was pleased with herself. "And do you think you could teach me to ride, too?" she asked.

Paco frowned. "Me? Teach you?"

"Yes, you." She straightened some, tilting her hat back a bit to see his face better because she had to look up at him. "Since it's a necessity that I learn how to ride and you're the only one who seems to be around."

"But I never taught anyone before. And besides, you probably don't even have any clothes for riding."

"He's right," Elizabeth cut in. "You don't own a riding habit, Hanna."

"Don't let that worry you, *señora,* no one rides sidesaddle out here." Paco grinned again. "That'd be a sure sign of a greenhorn."

"Then what would I have to wear?" Hanna asked.

Paco glanced down at her skirt. "Well, you could wear a pair of Hank's old pants, I suppose, but they'd be sort of big on you. But you sure couldn't ride in that getup."

"Then if I can find something to wear, you'll teach me?" she asked.

Paco thought it over for a few minutes. "All right, *sí,* I will teach you," he finally answered and Elizabeth shook her head.

"You're making a mistake, Hanna, you know that, don't you? You're going to end up with a broken arm or leg or even your neck."

Hanna glanced at Mrs. Brady, her eyes filled with determination. "Well, it's my neck. Now, why don't you come back to the house with me and help me find something to put on?"

Elizabeth sighed while Hanna told Paco to meet her by the horses again in about ten minutes, then the two of them headed toward the house where Hanna confiscated a pair of Henry's old pants Maria was getting ready to throw out, and a pair of boots that had been Paco's before his feet had gotten too big for them. Maria had been saving them for one of her other grandsons.

Hanna's shirt was really one of her blouses with the ruffles cut off and the sleeves rolled up, then because the pants were too big she cut down one of Henry's belts to hold them up.

"Well, you look right smart," Paco said a short while later when she joined him near the gates of the corral. "Now, which horse do you want to ride?"

Hanna's eyebrows raised and she looked over the top rail of the fence to where the horses were still moving around, nudging each other and trying to keep in the shade of an old sycamore tree.

There were five horses. Two looked like they'd be used more for pulling buggies, but the other three were fairly sleek looking.

"Which one's yours?" she asked.

"He's saddled in the barn already."

"Oh." She looked the animals over carefully. "How about that pretty little black one?" she asked, pointing to a beautiful gelding that had begun to prance about gracefully, the morning sun glistening off his shiny coat.

"Him?" Paco asked. "I don't know, *señorita*. He hasn't been broke too long."

"Does he belong to one of the hands?"

"He was Señor Hank's horse. Rather, Señor Hank was training him. Bought him down near El Paso last fall and was plannin' to train him for cutting."

"Cutting?"

"*Sí*. A good cutting horse is worth his weight in gold."

"What's a cutting horse?"

"They're trained to cut cattle out of a herd."

"Well, since Henry isn't here anymore, then I think I'll just use the horse for riding instead of cutting. She can be ridden, can't she?"

"She's a he, *señorita*," Paco corrected her. "Only he's a gelding."

"I thought you said he was a cutting horse?"

Madre de Dios, Paco thought as he stared at his new boss, and this one I promised to teach how to ride? I must be loco. Trying to be patient, he straightened authoritatively.

"A gelding is a horse who can no longer be used as a stud, *señorita*," he explained briefly.

She frowned. "Oh, and what's a stud?"

He inhaled, his face flushing slightly. Caramba, this señorita knows absolutely nothing. Now he knew he was loco.

"A stud is used for breeding."

Suddenly recognition lit her eyes. "Oh, you mean he can't . . . Oh dear, the poor thing."

"No, *señorita,* he can't," Paco answered. "But he's not a poor thing. He's quite content, and by gelding him one doesn't have to worry about him forgetting his work and taking off after some mare. Now—" and he hoped he'd explained sufficiently "—the first thing you have to learn is to catch him so you can saddle him."

Her hand flew to her throat. "You want *me* to catch him?"

"You want to learn how to ride?"

"Ride, yes, not chase horses."

"Well, one of the essentials for learning how to ride is learning how to catch the horse first. After all, you can't ride a horse you don't have."

Hanna felt her heart sink. Paco was right. What good would it do to know how to sit on a horse if no one was around to catch and saddle him for her?

"All right, if I have to I have to," she answered, and for the next twenty minutes Paco helped Hanna try to lose her fear of the animal until she was finally able to slip a halter on him and lead him to the barn.

Until now Hanna had never had any dealings at all with horses except to watch others drive them and saddle them, and as she entered the barn and turned to smooth her hand over the animal's hard head and down onto its velvety nose, she was amazed at how docile the horse seemed. Paco had warned her, however, that just because a horse looked and acted gentle one minute didn't mean he couldn't turn into a bucking maniac the next. He'd also informed her that the horse's name was Lucifer.

"Well, I'll have no truck with the devil," Hanna had told him. "So I'll just call him Lucy."

Paco had shaken his head, but Hanna didn't care. As she petted the horse's nose, she glanced at the Mexican boy who was trying to find a saddle she could use and smiled.

"See, he didn't mind being called Lucy at all, do you, Lucy?" she asked the horse, and as if in answer, the horse suddenly lifted his head and snorted, whinnying softly.

It took Hanna almost an hour to learn the technique of saddling the gelding. The first time on her own she forgot the saddle blanket. Then she got the headstall and curb bit on inside out. A few minutes later she had the cinch all fastened down before realizing it was twisted.

But eventually, three times in a row she managed to get it on right, and Paco was pleased.

"Now, let's see you get on," he said as soon as she got through fastening the cinch right for the fourth time all by herself.

Hanna stared at the horse. He seemed so much bigger up close than he had in the corral. After taking hold of the reins first as Paco had instructed her to do earlier, she put her foot in what he'd called the stirrup just like she'd seen men do since she'd arrived in the west, then grabbed the saddle horn and pulled herself up. Once in the saddle, she straightened proudly and looked at Paco.

"Well, teacher, do I pass?" she asked.

Paco smiled. "For a lady who didn't know the front end of a horse from the rear, you did just fine, *señorita*. But now the hard part starts," and he walked over to where his horse was saddled, mounted and rode toward her. "Now you will really learn how to ride."

For the rest of the morning, Hanna was kept busy putting Lucifer through his paces. First they rode all around the main house, then between the different outbuildings while Paco got her used to the reins.

As soon as he felt she'd mastered it enough, they left the ranch behind and headed for the river that flowed near the hills. By the time they rode into the ranch just before lunchtime, Hanna was not only pleased with herself, but pleased with Paco as a teacher. But she was also more sore than she'd ever dreamed.

A look of agony crossed her face as she unsaddled Lucifer, set him out to graze in the corral and headed toward the house. Her legs hurt, her back hurt, and oh, how her rear end hurt. She wouldn't be surprised to discover she'd turned her buttocks into one big blister, and Paco insisted she'd have to go out again tomorrow. Well, she'd just see when morning came again.

Elizabeth was coming down the hall from the kitchen as Hanna came in the front door, and she stared at Hanna curiously.

"You look terrible," she said her eyes steady on Hanna's face.

"Please, Mrs. Brady." Hanna sighed wearily. "I feel like one big sore."

"I told you, you should have taken things more slowly."

"You can't take riding more slowly. Either you learn or you don't."

"Is that what Maria's grandson told you?"

"No. It's what I've told myself." She straightened, trying to relax her legs a little more. "So how was your morning?"

"Well." Elizabeth looked pleased. "Maria and I've come to an understanding. She and her daughters-in-law will continue to take care of the house, only they'll let me help once in a while, too. After all, I didn't come out here to just sit on my fanny."

Hanna started for the parlor with Elizabeth in tow. "You could learn how to ride."

"At my age?" Elizabeth was mortified. "Good heavens, I'd probably end up ruining the horse."

"Nonsense. It really isn't that bad. In fact—" she grinned "—it's really kind of fun sitting up there with the world at your feet."

Elizabeth glanced toward Hanna's rear end. "You look like you were having fun."

"Don't be silly. Once I get used to it, it won't be this bad. Now, let me get changed and get something to eat, then I'll go through Henry's things. After all, if I'm going to run this place I'd better learn how to take care of everything," and she headed for the stairs while Elizabeth went toward the kitchen to help with lunch.

After a light meal in the kitchen at the back of the house, Hanna, dressed again in a blouse and skirt, made her way to the library off the entrance hall where she assumed Henry kept all of his business records. She started going over the books only to discover that Blake Morgan was right. There was much more to ranching than just buying and selling a few cows.

Besides, they didn't call them cows. They were steers. There was one ledger to tally the steers in and another for hired help including every man on the payroll as well as Maria and her brood. There was even one ledger kept especially for household and ranch expenditures. However, it seemed as if nothing had been either entered or accounted for in any of the ledgers since Henry's death, and that had been over two months ago. It was the first of June already.

"Maria?" she called when she heard a noise in the hall.

"Sí," Maria answered, sticking her head in the door, a dust rag in her hands.

"Mr. Gibbs said the foreman's been taking care of things since my brother's death. If so, why hasn't he written anything in these ledgers?" she asked.

Maria shrugged. "I know nothing about them, Señorita Winters. All I know is that he say Maria do this, Maria do that, I am in charge now, Maria, and I do it because if I don't he yell at me very loud."

Hanna frowned. "But he hasn't entered even one tally of any kind. Not even a record of the household expenditures since Henry's death."

"I know *nada,* señorita. Perhaps you should ask him."

"Oh, fine, and he's out on the range someplace hunting for cows." Hanna inhaled angrily, then addressed the housekeeper again. "By the way, Maria,

Mr. Gibbs said my brother died from an accidental gunshot wound. Were you here when it happened?"

Maria shook her head. "No, *señorita*. It didn't happen here. Señor Hank was on his way back from one of his business trips and was taking a shortcut home when it happened. He said he'd stopped for the night, rested his rifle against a tree and it fell and discharged."

"I was led to believe the accident happened here."

"Oh, no." Maria was adamant about it. "I was here when he arrived home with blood all over his clothes, and he died here. But it did not happen here. If it had happened here we could have removed the bullet in time, but it was at least three, maybe four days in him and by that time there was nothing we could do."

Hanna stared at the Mexican woman thoughtfully. "Why didn't he stop somewhere and have someone along the way take it out for him?"

"Like I say, he take a shortcut home over the range. There was nowhere to go for help."

"I see." Hanna said she understood, but she didn't, really. Why would a man who was as familiar with guns as Henry seemed to be be so careless with a rifle? And why would he ride cross-country instead of taking the roads where there would be houses and towns where people could help him if he had any trouble? It didn't make sense.

"Were you with him when he died?"

"*Sí*. Dolores and me. We were tending to his wound."

"Tell me, Maria. He wrote me a letter. Did he write it before he took his trip or after he came home?"

Maria's eyes narrowed slightly. "He write it after he get home. When he knew he would die. He tell me to get him pen and paper so he could do what he should have done long ago, then he sent Paco for Mr. Gibbs."

"Then Mr. Gibbs did speak to him before he died?"

"Ah, *sí*. And Mr. Gibbs make the will right out here. That's when we all learn that Señor Hank have a sister."

"You mean he'd never mentioned me before?"

"No, *señorita*. Señor Hank never mention any family so we think he has none."

It figures, thought Hanna. When Henry had walked out he had left the past behind.

"Well, that explains some things," she said. "But it still doesn't explain why Mr. Hayden hasn't taken care of the books since Henry's death."

"Maybe because he don't know how?" Maria offered. "Señor Hank always do those things himself."

"But he went away on business trips and left Mr. Hayden in charge. What if something had come up?"

"Nothing ever did. Besides, if worse came to worst Paco can cipher some and write a few words in English."

Oh, great. Hanna had forgotten that many of the people this far out on the frontier had few opportunities for schooling.

"How did Paco learn?"

"Señor Hank showed him. He and the boy were pretty close since Señor Hank have no family of his own."

This, too, was a revelation for Hanna. No wonder Paco seemed to be so at home with the horses and the ranch. Well, there wasn't much she could do now except try to study the ledgers and pick up where Henry had left off.

"Thank you, Maria, that's all," she said, and Maria left, heading for the parlor to give it its daily dusting.

It was late when Hanna finally settled into bed after her first full day on the ranch. She had not only started an in-depth inventory of Henry's books, but had taken a quick tour of all the outbuildings surrounding what Maria called the hacienda and met all of Maria's family except for her two sons who were still out on the range somewhere with the rest of the ranch hands.

Dolores and Sancho had three younger boys besides Paco, nine, seven and two, and a little girl of five, while Miguel and Teresa had two girls, five and six, and a baby boy a little over a year old. Every one of the children had the same dark hair and dark eyes as Paco.

As Hanna settled into the big four-poster bed, turning onto her side to relieve some of the pain from her first day on horseback, she thought over everything she'd learned today.

Mrs. Brady had said it'd be a marvelous adventure. It was an adventure, all right, only she wasn't sure just how marvelous it was going to be.

While they'd been riding Paco had explained to her what a roundup was, why they had it, and why it was so important to the ranch.

"Without the sale of the herd up north, there would be no money to keep the place going," he'd told her, and it all seemed so ironic. They needed the cattle to pay for the land, and yet, if they didn't have so many cattle, they wouldn't need so much land.

But then, as Paco said, "Even without the cattle the land was worth having," and after riding through it most of the morning, Hanna had been inclined to believe him.

Still, there was a lot to do, and as she closed her eyes, trying to get to sleep, she hoped she could handle it.

For the next few days Hanna continued to go over Henry's ledgers when she wasn't riding Lucifer, then finally one morning she met Paco by the corral and broke the news to him that she wanted to ride out onto the range to see for herself what a roundup was all about.

They hadn't seen a thing of Jules Hayden since the evening of their arrival and both Elizabeth and Hanna were a little uneasy about it.

"After all, he could have taken off with your whole herd by now," Elizabeth told her that morning at breakfast, and Hanna was inclined to agree with her even though Paco had told them it would be hard to change the running W brand, which was two Ws intertwined.

Paco was a little hesitant about taking her at first, but once they were riding his reluctance seemed all but forgotten. The day was beautiful, the sky a deeper blue than Hanna had ever seen, and even Lucifer seemed to be prancing a little more lively as they rode away from the hacienda, heading beyond the river toward the hills that signaled the start of the grazing land for the White Wind Ranch.

They'd been riding for a little over an hour when suddenly Paco reined up, his head tilted into the soft morning breeze, his nostrils flaring slightly as he breathed in.

"What is it?" Hanna asked, her eyes intent on his face, and she pulled Lucifer to a halt beside him.

His dark eyes narrowed thoughtfully. "Something is wrong," he answered.

Hanna was perplexed as she stared ahead toward a ridge he told her overlooked a grassy plain where the men usually camped and set up their corrals and branding fires.

"What is it?"

"Smoke."

"Smoke?"

Hanna frowned. "But I thought you said they used fires for the branding."

"*Sí*, but smoke from the branding would not carry this far. Besides, the smell is different."

He spurred his pinto forward and she quickly followed, then just before reaching the top of the ridge she saw it. Gray wisps, streaking into the blue sky, followed by dark swirls that drifted high like scattered storm clouds.

Finally reaching the edge of the cliff, they reined up abruptly and stared hard at the scene below.

To their right were a number of corrals with churning cattle, yelling and bawling, their nostrils already catching the scent of the danger they were in, with the rest of the camp, the chuck wagon, branding fires and tents some of the men stayed in sitting between the corrals and a grass fire that was about half a mile away and being fought by every hand the White Wind had.

"But how?" Hanna asked as her gaze took in the frantic panorama below. "And why?"

Paco's eyes narrowed. "Perhaps someone doesn't want your men to make the drive, *señorita.*"

Hanna frowned. He could be right. Killing her hadn't worked, so maybe whoever was doing it decided to try a new tactic. Without the money from the cattle drive the White Wind would be hard-pressed to keep afloat, according to what she had found in Henry's books.

"Well, let's not sit here speculating, let's go see if we can help," she said. "Now, how do we get down there from here?" Minutes later they were winding their way hurriedly down a trail a short way from the top of the ridge toward the plains below.

The heat was intense. Sweat poured off Jules Hayden as he straightened for a second, taking a gulp of fresh air, and spotted the two riders heading toward them from the ridge above. Wiping the dirt from his face and squinting, he cursed softly to himself as he realized who it was. "Damn ornery woman." He spat, then coughed, choking a bit as a whiff of smoke curled into his face.

"I think we're makin' it, boss!" one of the men yelled from behind him, and Jules nodded.

"Keep with it!" he yelled. Pulling his gaze away from the two riders, he went back to beating the flames with the blanket he'd been using and thanked God it wasn't a windy day. If it had been, they wouldn't have had a chance of stopping the fire's progress. As it was, he could already see breaks in the walls of flame.

Hanna spotted Hayden as soon as they reached the foot of the cliff. She rode toward him and reined up some hundred feet away.

"Can we help?" she shouted.

He glanced back, his eyes intense, jaw set stubbornly. "You can get the hell out of here!" he yelled. "What are you trying to do, get yourself killed?"

Men were strung out all along the fire line and Hanna glanced around her, realizing they were starting to get the thing under control.

"How'd it start?" she asked.

Hayden sneered. "Now, how the hell should I know? The grass is dry, there's people around." He stopped talking long enough to step over and help one of the men put out a burst of flames that had reignited, then he straightened again, looking at her. "Look, why don't you and the boy just head back to where you came from and let us handle this?"

"Because I thought maybe we could be of some help." She whirled Lucifer around, then motioned for Paco to follow her and rode to the chuck wagon.

By the time the two of them dismounted, tied their horses to the hitch rail and ran to join the men fighting the fire, the ranch hands had managed to pretty well contain it to one area. However, there were pockets that were still out of control here and there.

They were beating on it with blankets, canvas tarps, anything that could be used.

"You want to be useful, go get some shovels and start digging," Jules yelled when he saw Hanna and Paco were empty-handed.

"Digging?" Hanna questioned.

His eyes hardened. "That's right, lady, digging," and he pointed a short distance away. "If you two can get a dirt break dug about three or four feet wide and some twenty feet from where those flames are roaring the worst, it should slow them down if they make it that far. Meanwhile we'll try to keep it from even reaching the break, but if we can't do it, at least we can get it stopped there."

Hanna had never hefted a shovel before in her whole life, but not wanting to let the foreman think she was stupid, she grabbed Paco's arm and they ran to the chuck wagon. Grabbing a couple of shovels they found inside, they ran to where Hayden had told them to start digging.

The ground was harder than Hanna had thought it would be, but in spite of that, it wasn't long before they had a three-foot-wide break started. However, the faster they dug, the faster the fire came, and finally Jules ran up, grabbed the shovel from her inexperienced hands and began to dig furiously.

Smoke was swirling all about them now, sparks flying in the air. Every time the fire touched a mesquite tree or dry greasewood bush a new spurt of flames would sizzle and crack, until finally after almost a half hour of digging and slapping at them, the flames reached the fire break.

Hanna had grabbed Jules's blanket from him when he'd taken away her shovel, and now she let it drop at her feet as she watched the flames reach the dirt, have nowhere to go, then start to die out while at the edges of the break some of the hands still slapped at occasional sparks.

Reaching up, Hanna pushed her hat so that it fell to her back, hanging by the strings round her neck, then she brushed a few strands of hair from her sweaty forehead.

Her hands were black, she imagined her face was, too, and all she could smell was the pungent odor from the burnt grass and small trees. The place was a charred mess.

Thank God, she thought a few minutes later as she watched one of the men put out the last flickering flames and call down the line of men that the fire was out. There were fifteen hands besides Hayden on the White Wind payroll and every one of them including the cook had been fighting the flames.

"So all right, how did it start?" she asked again as she turned from the blackened ground that was still smoldering and smoking in places and looked at Jules.

The big man snorted, his mustache twitching nervously as it had that night in the parlor when she'd first met him.

"Like I said before, I don't have no idea how it started. All's I know is someone yelled fire, and we all came runnin'."

"And if the fire had gotten too close to the cows?"

"They're not cows, ma'am, they're cattle," he corrected her. "And if the fire had got to 'em we'da had to let 'em all loose, they'da scattered and we'da been startin' the tally all over again."

"I see."

"No, I don't think you do see. We was gettin' along just fine out here till a few days back when you showed up. But since then we've had the small water hole over at the north range get full of some kinda black smelly stuff that makes the cattle sick, two of the men quit cause they said they weren't gonna work for no greenhorn, and now this.''

"Someone quit?"

"Yeah, Ranklin and Morris."

"That means we've only got thirteen left besides you."

"And we were short of hands as it was."

"Why?" she asked and he looked at her funny.

"Why what?"

"Why were you short of hands? Why didn't Henry hire more men if they were needed?"

"You looked at his books, you tell me."

Jules stared at this strange woman who'd ridden into his life. All these years he'd thought for sure Hank would leave the place to him if anything ever happened. After all, they'd been close friends for so long. Granted, he'd never said he would, but with him not having any kin... Well, that had been wishful thinking on his part, he knew that now. Still, it just didn't seem fair and he didn't like it. He knew the place like the back of his hand and now this woman was going to make a mess of it all. He was sure of it.

"Why didn't you ride in and tell me when those men quit?" she asked.

His head lifted haughtily. "Cause I knew you wouldn't care."

"Not care? My dear fellow, this ranch is mine now, lock, stock and barrel, and that includes the men to run it. I want to be informed of everything. Just because I don't think it's proper for you to stay at the house doesn't mean I'm not interested in what's going on, whether it's out here or at the ranch. Is that understood?''

Jules's mouth was rigid. ''Yes, ma'am.''

''Good. Now, since it looks like the men are pretty tired maybe you should give them the rest of the day off to recuperate, and I'll come back another day to learn how things are done.'' She turned to Paco. ''Will you get our horses please, Paco, and we'll let the men get things cleaned up?''

Jules stared at her while she waited for Paco to return with the horses. Her pale white hair was smudged with soot and ashes and there was dirt all over her face, but he really didn't see any of it. All he saw was the woman who stood between him and everything he'd ever dreamed of owning. A woman who didn't have the faintest notion of what it was like to ride herd on cattle with the icy rain pelting your face and the bitter wind clawing at your clothes. Or how it felt to plunge a branding iron into a roped calf and smell the burning hide as it marked the struggling critter. She'd never had to sweat under the stinking sun searching for strays, either, and being a woman she never would. Why, hell, he could tell she'd just learned how to ride.

''You came out here to see what we're doin'?'' he asked, surprised she even cared.

Hanna took a deep breath. ''I understand it goes with the job,'' and she looked quite pleased with herself. ''If I'm going to run things, I really should know what everything is all about, shouldn't I? I bet my brother never sat back at the ranch and let others run things.''

''No, ma'am, he didn't.'' Jules's face was a mask of anger. ''He could rope, brand, shoot. There weren't nobody could train a good cuttin' horse the way he could,'' and he glanced at Paco on his way over with their horses. Hanna knew why he'd said the last as her gaze fell on Lucifer.

"Well, he's going to be my horse now, Mr. Hayden,'' she said. "And who knows. Maybe before I'm through I'll also know how to train a cutting horse,'' and she reached out to take the reins from Paco.

Mounting quickly, she glanced at her filthy hands, then reached up and set her hat on her head, anxious to get to the ranch so she could clean up.

"And, oh, yes, don't worry, Mr. Hayden, I'll find two new men to replace those men who quit on you.'' Not bothering to say goodbye, she kicked Lucifer in the ribs and headed back the way she and Paco had come.

Jules watched her ride off, his hands clenched around the shovel he was still holding, his eyes narrowing viciously. Damn female, he thought, then remembered that it wasn't even noon yet.

"All right, you lumberin' jackasses, back to work,'' he yelled at the top of his lungs. "We still got cattle to brand and strays to bring in.'' Within minutes, the fire was quickly forgotten and things started to get back to normal. Jules was damned if he'd give the men the rest of the day off. They had too much to do as it was.

Hanna was frowning as she and Paco rode out of the hills behind the ranch, forded the river and made their way across the long stretch of spring grasses toward the barn.

"You've been quiet ever since we left the men at camp, *señorita*,'' Paco said, his young face troubled.

Hanna sighed. "I was trying to figure out, Paco. Why does Mr. Hayden seem to hate me so much? He hasn't said a civil word to me since I arrived."

"You don't know?"

"If I did would I be asking you?"

The boy's face flushed and he straightened in the saddle, guiding his pinto around a large rock. "Señor Hayden expected your brother to leave the ranch to him."

"To him?"

"*Sí, señorita.* They had been friends for years, and Señor Hayden was sure he would own the ranch some day. When he learned Señor Hank had left it to a sister back east somewhere, he went out and got drunk for two days. Oh, he was mean. Like a rattlesnake."

"Mean enough to kill for it?" she asked hesitantly.

Paco glanced over at her. "I do not know, *señorita.* Men have killed for less."

This was a new turn of events. She had told Blake that she wouldn't doubt that Hayden was the one who'd been trying to have her killed before she got here, but at the time it was just a passing thought.

Now, however, she wasn't quite so sure. Spurring her horse a little faster, she suddenly made up her mind as to who she was going to hire to replace the ones who quit. If he was still around town. As the noon sun drifted high overhead, she made up her mind that right now, with everything that had already happened, it was the best move she could make.

Half an hour after a late lunch with a soothing bath behind her, Hanna, with Paco at her side, left White Wind on Lucifer's back again, this time heading for Hangtown.

Mrs. Brady had taken in some of Henry's old pants for her and she was wearing a pair of his worn buckskins with one of her pink blouses. She had washed her hair and let Maria French braid it down the back to keep it from coming loose instead of wearing it in its usual topknot.

Henry's hats had been too big, though, so she had tried to clean up her own as best she could, but in spite of the fancy perfume she'd put on it, it still smelled from all the smoke.

Mrs. Brady stood on the veranda watching them start out, a worried look on her face. It was a long ride to town, and she'd warned Hanna it was a bad idea, only lately it seemed Hanna wasn't listening to warnings.

It was as if ownership of the White Wind had suddenly freed the young woman from the self-inflicted prison she had built around her emotions years ago, and she was suddenly realizing she was as human as anyone else. The only trouble was Elizabeth was having a hard time trying to figure out whether the change was good or bad.

One thing was for sure, Hanna seemed to be enjoying herself in spite of the rough treatment the land was giving her. After watching the two of them disappear in the distance, Elizabeth turned and went back into the house.

The streets of Hangtown were pretty well deserted when Paco and Hanna rode in.

"I figured as much, *señorita,*" Paco said. "The only men who are worth hiring are already out on the range working, and the rest are in the saloons."

Hanna figured he was probably right. Still, Blake had said he'd hang around for a few days. She rode up to the front of a run-down building with a sign that read Palace Hotel. It looked like anything but a palace. However, since there were only two hotels in town, she figured it would be as good a place to start as any.

After dismounting and telling Paco to wait for her, she went inside. The inside was as bad as the outside, with worn furniture in the lobby and a desk clerk who seemed irritated because she'd disturbed his afternoon nap.

"Yeah, sure, Mr. Morgan's stayin' here," he finally said when he was fully awake and realized what she was asking. "Only you ain't gonna find him up in his room. He spends most afternoons at the saloon."

"There are three saloons. Which one?" she asked.

He thought for a minute. "Don't rightly know. But most fellas like the Sundown this time of day now that Trudy's got more time for them."

"Trudy?"

"Yeah, with Hank gone she's able to spread herself around some now."

"You mean Hank Winters?"

"Yeah."

"Do you have any idea to whom you're talking?" she asked, looking at him indignantly.

He flushed. "Well, I think so, ma'am. Leastways I heard Hank's sister from back east had come to town and since you resemble Hank somewhat I assume you're her."

"And you still talk about my brother the way you just did?"

"Shucks, ma'am." The desk clerk looked puzzled. "All I said was..."

"I know what you said," Hanna retorted, her proper Bostonian morals surfacing. "Never mind that now. Just tell me where this disreputable place is."

"Two blocks down on the left," he answered.

Hanna thanked him, then left briskly, shoulders up and head held high.

At first she'd planned to go into the saloon by herself, but the closer she and Paco got, the more her resolve began to leave her. She'd never been in a saloon in her life. The closest thing to it had been walking into the trading post in Fort Worth, and she'd been decently dressed then, not wearing men's clothes as she was now.

In spite of the encouragement from Mrs. Brady, and insistence from Paco that she looked very respectable in Henry's old pants, Hanna felt exposed.

It hadn't bothered her too much out on the range earlier when they'd confronted Jules Hayden and been fighting the fire, but here in town with all the men's eyes on her, she wasn't at all sure she liked it.

There was no way to change things now, however, but at least she didn't have to face it alone. Making Paco promise to stay right beside her, she rode up to the hitch rail in front of the Sundown Saloon and dismounted.

The afternoon she, Mrs. Brady and Blake Morgan had arrived in Hangtown there had been piano music coming from one of the saloons, but this afternoon all was quiet. As Hanna and Paco stepped through the swinging doors, it took a few minutes for her eyes to get accustomed to the light.

She let her gaze sweep over things. The Sundown was exactly what she expected it to be, crudely built with gaming tables toward the back, a scarred bar to her right and a number of fancily painted girls lounging about looking for customers, who were rather few.

She glanced at the man behind the bar. He was tall and pleasant looking with broad shoulders, a large paunch in front and a face that resembled a bulldog's. His eyes were studying her as she stood just inside the door with Paco behind her.

Finished with her perusal of the bartender, Hanna drew her gaze from him and began to look about the room. She spotted Blake sitting near the back of the place talking to a redhead with the biggest brown eyes Hanna had ever seen.

The redhead's eyes were devouring Blake while they talked and for some reason Hanna felt a twinge of anger deep down inside. Maybe she shouldn't even ask him, she thought, but then he'd offered, hadn't he? Still, he did seem to be a drifter.

Shoving aside the strange new feelings that were starting to gnaw at her, Hanna reached up, set her hat more firmly on her head and began walking confidently toward where the couple sat.

"Well, looks like we got company," Trudy said as she pulled her eyes from Blake Morgan's intense gaze and looked directly into Hanna's unsmiling face.

Blake turned, then did a double take. He'd hoped Hanna would show up, but hadn't expected it to be here in the saloon. And the clothes she was wearing...

"Hanna?" he said as he stood up, pulling off his hat and staring at her awkwardly. "I mean, Miss Winters?"

"Hanna'll do," she answered, her own eyes dead center on the brassy redhead.

Hanna had to admit the woman was pretty in a cluttered sort of way. Her fiery red hair was adorned with jeweled hair clasps and piled atop her head, and the blue satin dress she wore was covered with bows, beads and braid, while the rouge on her cheeks and the dark makeup around her eyes were so overdone they looked ridiculous. The only thing about her that didn't look cheap and tawdry were her earrings. Hanna would swear they looked like real diamonds. They were pear-shaped and dangled below her earlobes catching little prisms of red and blue from her hair and clothing.

"I'm glad you decided not to leave yet," Hanna said as she drew her gaze from the redhead and looked at Blake. "I was wondering. Does your offer still stand?"

"You mean about staying at White Wind?"

She figured it would be best to explain. "Hayden informed me today that two men have quit, not wanting to work for what they called a greenhorn or tinhorn or whatever, so I'm going to need some replacements. I was hoping maybe you'd be one."

Inside, Blake was pleased as could be, yet he didn't want to sound too eager. "And just when I was beginning to enjoy the leisure time," he said, pretending reluctance. After seeing the annoyed look on Hanna's face he continued. "But for you, I'll be glad to give it up, how's that?"

Hanna dismissed his remark with a stern look. "You never did say how much you knew about ranching, though," she said as an afterthought. "Maybe it wouldn't even work."

Blake smiled more congenially. He didn't want her changing her mind now. "Oh, I know enough to get by. But you said you needed two men. Have you hired anyone else yet?"

She glanced around the place. She figured Paco was right. Except for Blake, most of the men in here didn't look like they'd be worth hiring. "Not yet," she answered. "But I imagine word'll get around."

She quit looking the room over and again her gaze settled on the redhead.

"Oh, excuse me," Blake said, "but I wasn't thinking. Miss Winters, let me introduce Miss . . . Trudy. Trudy, Miss Winters."

Trudy had been busy studying Hank's sister ever since she'd stepped into the saloon, and now she'd come to the conclusion that her first impression of the woman had been right. Hank's sister was a prude.

"Miss Winters," she acknowledged testily, then noticed the white hair beneath the hat Hanna had on. "I was wondering what Hank's sister would look like." She smiled a slow, lazy smile. "Hank and I were friends, you know."

"So I heard."

"Oh?"

"The clerk in the hotel hinted as much. Tell me, did he ever mention to you that he had a sister, or were you kept in the dark, too?"

"No one knew he had any family until Milt made that will out for him. Why?"

"I was just wondering if maybe you were another one who thought you were in line to become owner of the White Wind when Henry died."

"Well, you certainly don't beat around the bush, do you?"

"I discovered a long time ago that it doesn't do any good to dance around things, Miss . . . What did Mr. Morgan say your last name was?"

"He didn't."

"Well, anyway, I can be just as outspoken as the rest of the people around here so don't think just because I've never run a ranch before that I don't have any brains in my head. If Henry was your paramour that was his business. I don't have to make it mine. Now, if you'll excuse us."

She looked at Blake again, noticing the amused crinkles at the corners of his eyes.

"Are you ready?" she asked.

"You want me to come now?"

"Unless you've got somewhere else to go."

"No, sir, I mean ma'am. All I have to do is get my horse, go to the hotel, grab a couple things and we can be on our way."

"Good." She started to walk away, then turned to look at Trudy. "Oh, yes, goodbye, Miss . . . Trudy. I hope I haven't spoiled your afternoon." Turning once more toward the door, she strolled outside and waited at the hitch rail for Paco and Blake to catch up to her.

"You sure weren't very nice to her in there," Blake said as he walked over to help her onto her horse. "What did she ever do to you?"

"Nothing really," Hanna answered. "But since she was a friend of Henry's and it seems like all of Henry's friends thought they should have first grabs at White Wind, I thought I'd better put her straight right now before she tries to cause any trouble.''

"And you think she will?''

"Who knows, she may already have.'' Hanna grabbed Lucifer's reins, put her foot in the stirrup, then let Blake help her into the saddle. "After all, we still don't know who it was who tried to keep me from reaching Hangtown, do we? Now, where's your horse?''

"At the livery. I don't generally ride him around town.''

"Then let's get going. I'd like to get back to the ranch in time for supper.'' She nudged Lucifer in the ribs. "Come on, Lucy, let's go.''

Blake stared at her with a curious look on his face. "Lucy? Did I hear you call that horse Lucy?'' he asked as he walked along beside her.

"Certainly,'' she answered. "His name's Lucifer, but he doesn't mind the name Lucy at all. Do you, Lucy?'' and she patted Lucifer on the neck. "Now, let's go get your things.''

Blake headed for the hotel to pick up his belongings, fighting to keep a straight face.

Chapter Five

The first storm clouds Hanna had seen since reaching Texas were rolling in across the horizon. She wondered if they would become full-blown and bring some rain.

"Actually I had an ulterior motive for asking you to sign on," she said as they rode along, leaving Hangtown behind. "It isn't just that we need some replacements. I probably would have come after you anyway."

"Oh?" This was a surprise to Blake.

"You seem like an extremely intelligent man, Mr. Morgan," she went on, "and I've noticed that you let very few things get past you. That's why, when the fire started, I thought right away of you."

"Fire? What fire?" Blake asked.

Hanna proceeded to tell him about the range fire that morning, and how she was suspicious of Jules Hayden's actions.

"But if he started it?"

"That's just the trouble," she went on. "It'd be stupid for me to have him try to find out how it started if he's the culprit. I thought perhaps, since you're a neutral party in all this, you could find out what's really going on. The attempts on my life, the fire. If it had reached those cattle we'd have been in a horrible mess."

He frowned. "In other words you want me to play detective?"

She glanced ahead at Paco, whom she was certain was riding out of earshot. "I guess you could call it that," she said. "Only no one must know except you, me and Mrs. Brady."

"Elizabeth approves?"

"She more than approved. She didn't know why I hadn't taken you up on your offer to stay in the first place. But then she's a bit more tolerant of people than I am."

Blake eyed her curiously. "Now what's that supposed to mean?"

Hanna straightened in the saddle, trying to look as prim and proper as she could under the circumstances.

"Well, let's face it, Mr Morgan," she answered. "You are just a drifter. We know absolutely nothing about you except that you were willing to help us when we needed help, and you were most welcome to have around during the attempts on my life. But then, when it comes right down to it, you could even be a participant in those attempts. We have no way of knowing. After all, it was very convenient your being in that trading post at Fort Worth."

"If you feel that way, why did you hire me again?"

"I didn't say I felt that way. I said it could be a possibility."

"But you don't think it is."

"I'm hoping my instincts are right."

"Well, thank you anyway." Blake had to admit she was being more truthful about their relationship than he was. "There's only one thing bothers me about the arrangements out at White Wind," he said as they continued to keep abreast of each other. "If I'm going to be just one of the hands, how will I be able to get away from Hayden to let you know anything?"

She frowned. "I hadn't thought of that." Suddenly her eyes lit up. "I know," she said, and there was a lilt of satisfaction to her voice. "I'm going to make you Hayden's assistant."

"And just how will that help?"

"Because I'm going to tell Hayden that anytime he has anything I should know, or if I want him to know anything, I'll work through you."

Blake wasn't at all sure the foreman was going to like her new arrangement any more than he'd liked the last one.

"There's only one trouble with that."

"What's that?"

"I don't think I've ever heard of a ranch foreman having an assistant before. Desk clerks maybe and bank managers and such, but a ranch foreman?"

Hanna inhaled stubbornly. "Well there's always a first time for everything." She patted Lucifer's sleek neck, the feel of the horse beneath her becoming more familiar with each passing day. "I should know if anyone should. So will you do it?"

He smiled, trying not to look too pleased, yet wanting to let her know he'd go along with her in whatever she decided.

"Why not, it might be just what I've needed to put a little spice into my life." And for the rest of the ride, as long as Paco stayed out of earshot, they discussed some of the things Blake was to look for.

Early the next morning after spending the night alone in the bunkhouse, Blake headed for the hacienda where Hanna had told him she'd meet him for breakfast before taking him out to where the men were.

Suddenly he stopped to stare toward the veranda. A lone horse was tethered at the hitch rail, its rider talking to Hanna. Blake looked curiously at the man from the shade of an old oak tree.

He'd never seen the man before, but from what he could see at this distance the man fit the description they'd given him when he'd left the home office at Junction City, Kansas. Right down to his clothes.

He had on dark brown pants underneath bat-wing chaps, with a worn, faded blue shirt, and even his gun belt and boots looked like they'd seen better days, as did his black hat that sported a colorful braided band around the crown.

The stranger was holding the hat in his hand and Blake could see that his hair was a sandy red color, thick and unruly. His face was square-jawed with a dark red beard clipped to emphasize its squareness.

Blake started moving toward the house. He had to make sure. The man and Hanna heard the faint jingle of his spurs as he approached, and when they glanced toward him, Blake was certain that the stranger was the man he'd been warned about. Especially when he gazed into the man's eyes.

They were red-rimmed and bloodshot, the color of black coffee, with thick red brows that almost met above his hawklike nose.

"Well, good morning," Hanna said when Blake was almost to them.

Blake stopped for a second, then stepped onto the veranda.

"I've found my other replacement," she went on as he continued to study the man closely, and she gestured toward the new arrival. "Cullerton Burris, I'd like you to meet Mr. Morgan, the new assistant foreman."

Blake reached out and took the hand offered to him. "The name's Blake," he amended.

The stranger nodded. "And most people just call me Culler."

"Good." Blake straightened, dropping the man's hand. "Culler's easier to spit out."

He looked at Hanna. She was wearing her riding pants again this morning.

"You gonna ride out with us?" he asked.

"I figured to. After all, you don't even know where the men are."

"Paco could show me."

"But I doubt Mr. Hayden would take Paco's word for it that you're his new assistant." She set her mouth stubbornly. "I'd better go. Besides, Paco has other things to do today and won't be able to go with us."

"Then maybe we should get started." Blake glanced at the sky. It was well past sunup. "It's gonna be late morning by the time we get there."

"But you haven't eaten yet."

"I'll just go grab something from the kitchen and get our horses saddled." He turned to Culler. "You eat anything yet today?" he asked.

The man shook his head. "Nope, left town way before sunup."

"Then come along, I'm sure Maria'll find something for us." But instead of going into the house to reach the kitchen Blake walked the length of the veranda, stepped off it, then headed toward the back of the house, while Hanna stepped through the door.

That's strange, she thought as she stood just inside the entrance hall and heard the men at the back of the house in the kitchen, I wonder why Blake didn't just come in through the front? Oh, well, she guessed it wasn't really that important. Knowing she'd need her hat today, she headed for the stairs and her room.

The sun was hot, the sky pale without a cloud in it as the three of them set out for the camp. Hanna had only been there that one time with Paco, but the young Mexican had assured her that if she just kept to the main trail she'd have no trouble at all finding the camp.

She and Paco had taken a shortcut the day they had come, but today's route bypassed the ridge, taking about half an hour longer.

The storm clouds from the day before had passed right over without dropping any rain and Hanna was glad. She hated muck and mud. It was close to midmorning by the time the three rode into the busy camp and the first thing Hanna did was to locate Jules.

He was standing near the branding fire arguing with a man Hanna had never seen before, and the conversation was quite heated.

"To hell we have," Jules yelled, his voice ringing through the noisy camp. "Every maverick we've branded's been on White Wind range."

"Yeah, with a Box T cow nursin' it."

"You're a liar!"

"What's going on?" Hanna asked as she, Blake and Culler joined the foreman.

Jules's eyes were blazing. "This no good son of a bitch is accusin' us of brandin' calves that don't belong to us!"

Hanna looked surprised. "Have you?"

"No, ma'am, we sure haven't. Every calf we've rounded up was on White Wind range."

She looked at the man who had been arguing with Jules. He looked to be about the same age as Jules, but heavier. The stocky stranger was slightly shorter than the foreman and had a bushy gray mustache that hid thin, cruel lips. Even his dark blue eyes beneath their gray brows had a cold hardness to them as they studied Hanna. His left cheek had a big scar gouged out of it.

"May I ask who you might be?" she said, her head tilting defiantly.

The man's jaw clenched stubbornly. "The name's Terrell, Whitney Terrell. I own the Box T."

"And you think my men have been stealing your cattle?"

"I didn't say they was stealin' 'em. I said they was brandin' my strays."

"And Mr. Hayden's told you he hasn't, so that should be the end of it."

"Hey, look, lady..."

"The name's Winters, sir, Hanna Winters."

The man's eyes narrowed. "I guessed as much, only I don't care who the hell you are. I came over to tell your men to stay clear of the Box T and I mean it."

"Good heavens, Mr. Terrell." Hanna was mortified. "We've got ten thousand acres here, why on earth would we have to go near your Box T?"

"You may have ten thousand acres, lady," he challenged. "But you don't have ten thousand steers. All you got is the piddlin' few that made it through the winter, and I don't intend to lose anymore strays to you and your men."

Hanna looked at Jules. "Are you sure you didn't get some of his by mistake?"

"You callin' me a liar?"

"No, I'm just making sure."

"Well, we didn't." He straightened, his eyes intent on Hanna. "Whenever we found a cow with a calf we always made sure it was one of ours, or else we didn't bring it in."

"Oh, yeah, you can say that now." Terrell was fuming. "Sure, I don't have no way to prove otherwise once your brand's on 'em, but I'll warn you, Hayden, just like I warned Winters, I ain't gonna sit back and let you steal me blind."

This time Blake spoke up. "I think the conversation's over, Mr. Terrell," he said. "Leastways it is as far as we're concerned. Now, why don't you just mount up and ride out of here while you can still sit on a horse?"

Whitney Terrell stared hard at Blake, then looked at Hanna again, realizing she wasn't going to knuckle under. Sensing more than just hostility in the air, he shoved his hat tighter on his head, turned abruptly and headed toward his horse. Mounting the big gray stallion rather ungracefully, he rode off, leaving the four of them staring after him.

Finally Jules glanced at Blake. "What the hell are you doin' here?" he asked.

"I hired him," Hanna answered. "In fact, I hired Mr. Burris here, too. Only Mr. Morgan is to be your assistant."

"My assistant? What the hell you talkin' about? I don't need no assistant."

"Oh, don't you?" Her eyes narrowed. "Then why hasn't anything been entered in the books lately?"

"Hank always took care of the books."

"And Henry's dead, so you should have taken care of them." She looked at him skeptically. "You don't know how to write, do you, Mr. Hayden?"

"Hell, yeah, I can write. Just as good as anyone else. But them books is different. Besides, it ain't no foreman's job to do the figurin'."

"I agree with you there, and I didn't really hire Mr. Morgan to do the books, either. I hired him to be sort of a liaison between the two of us. After all, Mr. Hayden, it seems you're so busy out here with the cattle and all that you just don't have time to come and keep me posted on things." She looked at Blake. "That's where Mr. Morgan comes in."

Jules inhaled, nodding. "Oh, I see. In other words he's gonna be your errand boy and report back to you if I ain't doin' my job."

"I didn't say that."

"What she means," Blake cut in, "is that to save you from having to spend a lot of time needlessly running back and forth from here to the ranch, you can just give me any report you might have, and I'll do the runnin' for you, and in between times I can rope and brand as well as the next hand."

Jules stared at him. There was something about Blake he wasn't quite sure he liked. Maybe because the man seemed to be too easygoing. Most drifters were that way though. That's why they were drifting.

"Please, Mr. Hayden," Hanna added. "Hiring Mr. Morgan is no reflection on the way you perform your duties. It's merely a way for me to stay on top of things. After all, until I become a real working part of this ranch it's going to be rough for a while."

Jules eyed her skeptically. "What do you mean by a real working part?" he asked.

She smiled congenially. "Why do you think I came out yesterday, just to watch? If Henry could learn how to rope and brand steers, so can I."

Jules's jaw dropped.

"You're not serious," Blake said.

She frowned. "I certainly am." She glanced toward the area where the cattle were milling about and her gaze rested on a big bull.

"Well, I may not be able to throw one of those big things," she said, correcting herself. "But surely a little calf wouldn't be that hard to rope."

Jules and Blake exchanged quick glances with each other and the new man Culler.

"Well, it shouldn't," she insisted.

Blake shook his head. "Hanna, before you can even think of throwing a calf you have to learn how to handle a rope."

"So?"

"So it isn't that easy." He reached to his horse and grabbed the lariat from where it hung on the saddle. "Here," he said, handing it to her. "Let's see you rope that calf over there," and he pointed to a small heifer that was roaming around, grazing not far from the rest of the herd.

There wasn't any brand on the animal yet and it didn't seem to be paying much attention to what was going on around it.

Hanna's hands curved about the lariat and she looked down at it, a frown creasing her forehead. There was already a loop in one end and she fumbled around with it until she separated the loop from the rest of it.

"Go ahead," Blake urged her, knowing full well she didn't know what she was doing. "Rope the damn thing."

Hanna continued to stare at the rope, then glared at the calf, then back to the rope again.

Trying to forget that she had no idea what she was doing, she began to walk toward the calf, every muscle in her body tense. If she could just slip the rope around the thing's neck, she'd show them. Moving slowly, so as to not scare the heifer, she inched closer and closer. Then suddenly, as the animal realized Hanna was heading for her, she started to bolt. Quickly throwing the end of the rope that had the loop in it as hard as she could, Hanna was both surprised and a little shocked to see the loop sail through the air and go over the animal's head, slipping down onto its neck.

However, the animal was still bolting for it's freedom and as it did Hanna felt the rest of the rope grow taut, then start to slide from her hands. Grabbing the end of the rope as hard as she could, Hanna hung on, trying to pull and tug to keep the animal from breaking free, only the calf was too strong.

With one desperate lunge the heifer took off in the opposite direction, pulling Hanna off her feet and dragging her through the dust and dirt behind it.

"Let go!" Blake yelled.

But she couldn't let go. It was if she were glued to the rope. Dirt, rocks and all sorts of debris flew into her face, and she shut her eyes, trying to turn her head away as she scraped across the ground.

"Damn female!" Jules yelled at the top of his lungs, and he dashed forward, running after the calf that was moving every which way. Finally catching up to it, he grabbed it, threw it expertly to the ground, then slipped the lariat from around its neck and let the thing loose.

As soon as the heifer was prancing away on its own, Jules returned to Hanna while he dusted the dirt from his pants.

"Why the hell didn't you let go of the rope?" he asked.

Hanna was still on the ground trying to compose herself as she spit the gritty dirt from her mouth. Tears were close to the surface only she was determined not to let them show.

"I couldn't," she answered, then relaxed some, breathing deeply, and she looked at her hand, which still had the rope wound around it. It was red and sore where the rope had pulled and burned. Slowly, trying not to hurt her hand more, she began to unwind the lariat, then as the other men joined them, she stood up, brushing the dust from her clothes.

"So you proved your point, Mr. Morgan," she said and she handed him the lariat. "I may not be equipped to wrestle a bull, or even a calf, but there are other things I can learn." She glanced toward one of the fires where some hands were branding a calf. "It's just going to take time, that's all."

Blake wasn't at all surprised at her statement. "Then you're not giving up?"

"Certainly not." She retrieved her hat from where it had dropped to the back of her neck, set it on her head and walked toward her horse while the men followed. "I may not ever be able to throw a calf, as you refer to it. But I bet I can learn to cut one out of a herd. Especially with the right horse, like Lucy," she said and patted Lucifer on the side.

Blake shook his head. "Why don't you give it up, Hanna? Let us handle the animals and you stick to the books?"

"Because I just don't trust anyone else, Mr. Morgan," she answered. "Not after all that's happened. Now, go ahead, all of you, get back to work while I spend the rest of the morning watching," and Hanna took Lucifer's reins and led him over near where they were branding so she could get a better look.

For the next few hours, Hanna hung around the camp, taking everything in and marveling at the stamina of these men. Hector, the cook, referred to by the men as Heck, told her while she was eating lunch that one man could herd up to three hundred steers all by himself if he had to, and that sometimes it took two to three days to drive the strays down out of the hills.

The whole thing was fascinating to her, but by late afternoon she decided she'd better call it a day.

She'd seen Blake only twice since their arrival and now as she unhitched Lucifer from where she had him tethered and mounted, she took one last look around. Neither Blake nor Jules were in sight. She supposed they'd ridden out again for more strays.

"You can tell Mr. Hayden and Mr. Morgan that I've decided to head back to the ranch," she told Heck as she settled down onto the saddle. "I'll expect Mr. Morgan to check in with me back there at the end of the day.'"

Heck nodded. "Be careful, ma'am," he said through tobacco-stained teeth, his dark brown hair flying around his face. "It ain't always good to ride alone."

"Don't worry, I'll be fine," she assured him, and minutes later she was heading down the road that led to the hacienda.

The afternoon had grown exceptionally hot and as Hanna rode along, she unbuttoned the top button of her blouse to get a little more air. Her clothes were sticking to her, and since most of the road cut across open plains there was no place to find relief from the sun.

All the while she was riding along she kept thinking about the conversation between Jules and the rancher named Terrell. It was obvious the man was really upset, but to accuse Jules's men of rustling was a serious matter.

Jules Hayden was a strange man, and not any too likable, but a rustler? Besides, he wouldn't have any reason to rustle someone else's cattle for White Wind, since none of the profit from the ranch went into his pockets.

She frowned, then breathed a sigh of relief as the road she was following began to wind into the hills where there were some trees to offer shade.

She'd been riding for almost an hour when suddenly Lucifer balked, snorted, then threw back his head skittishly. "What the... What is it, Lucy?" she asked, and she reined the gelding to a halt and looked around.

Everything seemed quiet. In fact, it was almost too quiet. Not even the scrub jays or mockingbirds were making their usual chatter.

Just as she decided it was nothing and nudged Lucifer in the ribs, urging him forward again, a shot rang out from up ahead on the road, a bullet whizzed right past her head, and Hanna panicked.

Digging Lucifer hard in the ribs, she pulled the reins, veering off the trail to the left. They crashed into the woods, Hanna hoping whoever was firing at her wouldn't be able to follow her in among the trees.

Another shot rang out, and Hanna didn't even look back. Instead she plunged deeper into the trees, giving Lucifer his head and hanging on as hard as she could, her body bent over low in the saddle as the gelding maneuvered first this way, then that.

Hanna had been riding for almost ten minutes when she realized she hadn't heard any shots for a while, and she reined Lucifer to a slow walk, then brought him to a stop.

"Whoa, boy," she said, patting the sleek horse's neck. "I think maybe we might have lost them, what do you think?"

As she looked back on the trail she caught a vague movement of gray behind some rocks, another shot rang out and she took off again.

This time she didn't bring Lucifer to a stop until they had ridden out of the woods onto a grassy plain where it was impossible for anyone to follow her without her seeing them.

The woods was at least half a mile behind her now as she sat in the saddle and looked around. My God! Where was she? When she'd taken off she hadn't paid any attention to where she was going. Now, as she nudged Lucifer softly in the ribs and began to edge forward, looking all around her, she had absolutely no idea where she could be.

The terrain was level up ahead for quite a ways, then began to slope into hills again with trees dotting the landscape. The sun was to her right on the horizon and Hanna tried to work out her bearings.

She'd been heading toward the sun when she'd left the roundup, so that meant if she headed toward the sun now she'd be heading the same way. However, she had no idea how many miles she might have ridden while trying to get away from her assailant, but she figured she should at least be going in the right general direction.

Searching the edge of the woods and not seeing anything that gave her a hint that someone might still be behind her, she reined Lucifer partway around and moved off again, heading northwest, her eyes alert for anything out of the ordinary, her heart still uneasy over the attack.

An hour after she'd lost the gunman who'd fired on her, Hanna reined Lucifer to a stop at the top of a small knoll, hoping to catch sight of the ranch in the distance. She let out a disgusted sigh. There was nothing. Nothing except more rolling plains, hills and rocky ridges, although she did spot a water hole to her left with a sloping hill and a stand of cottonwoods behind it.

As she sat in the saddle and watched, her gaze moved to the sky. The sun had dropped considerably in the last half hour, and an uneasy restlessness seized her as she realized it was going to be dark soon.

Well, she wasn't going to let it bother her, she couldn't. The ranch had to be over the next few hills. Riding down from the ridge she let Lucifer get a drink from the watering hole and quenched her own thirst before starting out again.

A few hours later as she stared into the growing darkness that was descending on the small canyon she'd ridden into, Hanna finally had to admit defeat.

Tears stung her eyes, and she swallowed hard. "I'm sorry, Lucy," she said to the gelding as the howl of a coyote cut through the stillness around her, "but I'm afraid we're hopelessly lost." Looking at the strip of darkening sky between the cliffs, she started to pray.

Blake sat next to Jules, not far from the chuck wagon, and watched the older man finish lighting a cigarette, a habit Blake had just never picked up.

"I hear you had a fire," he said, his gaze studying the other man closely.

"Yup," Jules answered.

"Know how it started?"

"Nope."

"Did you try to find out?"

"Yup."

"Care if I try to find out?"

"Nope. But it won't do you any good." Jules took a long drag off his cigarette. "We brought a bunch of cattle across there early this morning and they probably trampled anythin' that might've been there into the ground. Besides—" he flicked away a few ashes "—I went over the place as close as I could and there wasn't a damn thing."

Blake looked pensive. "Anyone around that area just before it started?"

"Not that I could see, but then I wasn't expectin' it so I wasn't really lookin'." Jules eyed Blake curiously. "Is that why she hired you, to find out who started the fire?"

"Nope, but she was nice enough to give me a job and I thought maybe I might try to help her out some."

"Don't do me any favors."

Blake frowned. "Why don't you like the lady, Hayden?" he asked.

"You saw what she did, movin' in, taking over. Hell, it wouldn't have hurt lettin' me keep my room in the house."

"It'd hurt her." Blake knew that wasn't all that was bothering the man, yet went along with him. "You have to remember, she comes from a society that frowns on such things. To her it just didn't seem right. Anyway, if you don't like working for her, why don't you just quit? There's nothing keeping you here, is there?"

Jules's eyes darkened. "Maybe I like it here." He tossed his cigarette butt into Heck's cook fire and stood up. "Guess I'll go make sure everything's settled for the night with the main herd. You got that report I told you to give her?" he asked.

Blake nodded, patting his shirt pocket. "Right here. I'll be taking off soon as I check around a bit where that fire started."

He watched Jules stroll toward some of the men who were still branding strays, then stood up, hefting his gun belt more comfortably onto his hips. Turning away from the chuck wagon, he headed toward where the ground was dark with the ashes from the fire.

Jules was right, they'd brought a number of cattle across the area, all right, but there were still enough traces of the fire to figure out where it had started.

Blake covered the area slowly, his gaze glued to the ground for anything that might be out of place. The scent of charred grass and wood was still strong, and he wrinkled his nose at the pungent odor.

Suddenly, as he kicked a small clump of burned mesquite ashes aside with the toe of his heeled boot, he hesitated and frowned. Stooping, he reached out and slowly began sifting his fingers through the cold ashes. It took only a few minutes to find what he was looking for. He had just spotted the edge of the small metal object where it lay beneath the gray ashes, and now he fingered the heel chain curiously. It could have come off any set of spurs, only as far as he knew, none of the men from White Wind had mentioned losing theirs.

Tucking it into his shirt pocket, he stood up and started looking around more, but there was nothing else. Well, at least it was a start.

He glanced at the sky. It was already getting late and if he was going to get to the ranch and back before dark he'd better get going. Leaving the area of the fire behind, he made sure he still had the note in his pocket with Jules's tally report for the day on it, then headed over to where Diablo was tethered. Mounting the horse, he took one last look at the camp, then reined Diablo around and started toward the trail that led to the main house.

At the camp the men would keep branding right up until dark, but since Hanna wanted a daily report of how many strays were flushed out of the hills, Jules was more than willing to let him leave early to take it in.

It was well past six in the evening when Blake caught sight of the ranch house and spurred Diablo a little faster, hoping maybe Maria might have a few left-overs.

Heck's cooking was all right if you liked spicy goulash, which Blake didn't, and besides, Maria had been making doughnuts when they had arrived at the ranch last night and he hoped there would still be a few around.

Maneuvering Diablo through the gate, he dismounted and tethered him near the house, calling out as he headed for the open kitchen door.

"Maria?"

The kitchen was empty and he frowned. Where the hell was everybody?

"Hey, Maria, Elizabeth, Hanna!"

By now, he could hear a commotion in the hallway just beyond the kitchen, and seconds later the house-keeper and Elizabeth came in.

"It's about time," Elizabeth said as her gaze fell on Blake, then she frowned, looking behind him expectantly. "But where's Hanna? I suppose she's headed for the front door. Her and her propriety."

Blake scowled. "What do you mean, where's Hanna? She's here, isn't she?"

"Here? Hanna was with you."

"And she came home."

Elizabeth's face went white. "Oh, my goodness! When?"

"Hours ago. Heck said she left about four o'clock." Blake's face grew solemn, all thoughts of the food he'd been looking forward to gone. "You mean you haven't seen her?"

Elizabeth's dark eyes grew wary. "We thought she was still out on the range."

"Where's Paco?"

Maria was quick to speak up. "He and Dolores went into town for supplies and they haven't come back yet."

"Oh, great, then I'm going to have to go out on my own." He started for the door. "There's only one way she could have come. I'll go back and see if I can pick up her trail. She might have tried a shortcut and gotten herself lost."

"Oh, Lord!" Elizabeth was frantic.

"Don't worry," he said stopping just long enough to reassure her. "I've done some tracking in my day, and it shouldn't be hard to pick up her trail. Now you two just calm down. If she's out there, I'll find her."

Blake was really getting worried. He'd been riding for well over an hour, studying first one side of the

trail, then tracking along the other, trying to find
where Hanna might have turned off, and he hadn't
found anything.

Finally, as he moved to the right side of the narrow
wagon tracks and began searching the ground beneath the trees, his gaze fell on a set of hoof prints that
had left the trail. Stopping, he dismounted and knelt
down, studying them just long enough to determine
that they had to be Lucifer's and he glanced up catching sight of some broken branches on a bush a few feet
away.

He stood erect and, leading Diablo, began to follow the tracks into the woods. Again he stopped, surprise and concern on his face as he saw a telltale bullet
hole in an oak tree to his left.

Moving up to it, he took his knife from its sheath,
probed for the bullet, found it and slipped it into the
pocket with the heel chain before continuing on again.

Blake was really alarmed. It was obvious that
someone had taken another shot at Hanna. Picking up
his pace, he began to move faster, heading deeper into
the woods, still following the trail she'd left. If she was
out there he had to reach her before dark, that is if her
assailant hadn't reached her already.

Hanna's hands were trembling slightly as she reined
Lucifer up the narrow draw toward the low-lying hills.
The sun had dipped below the horizon ages ago and
still she'd seen no sign of anything that looked even
remotely familiar. Nor had she seen signs that anyone
else might be in the vicinity.

Night shadows were already beginning to creep into
the rock crevices and beneath the trees, and she felt her

stomach tighten apprehensively. Not only was she hopelessly lost, but she didn't even have a gun or any kind of weapon, and she had absolutely no idea how to build a fire.

She cringed at the thought of being out here alone. Another coyote howled off in the distance, and she drew Lucifer to a halt, startled, as a couple of stray steers broke from the underbrush to her right and took off at a run. Realizing she wasn't after them, they soon settled down to grazing. She squinted, trying to see if she could tell what their brand was, but it was too close to dark and they were too far away. Pushing her hat off her head, she ran her hands along the sides of her pale hair, tucking stray hairs into the braid here and there, and wiping the perspiration off.

While she did, she let her gaze move over the tree-lined hills up ahead and began to wonder. Which would be better? To settle down for the night beneath some tree, or move up to the top of the draw where she'd be able to see anyone or anything approaching and spend the night there? Whichever way she looked at it, it was apparent she was going to be out here alone, and the thought was frightening.

"Well, at least I've got you, Lucy," she said to the black gelding, and as if in answer, the horse snorted, tossing his head lightly.

Deciding it would probably be better to find a good spot at the side of the gully, Hanna nudged Lucifer in the ribs and reined him to the right, riding him up the embankment where she tried to pick out a likely spot.

The place she decided on was halfway up the sloping side of the draw where a small rock formation jutted out leaving an overhang. Reaching the spot, she dismounted and let out a sigh.

No food, no fire, no water. What a horrible mess. Well, she couldn't think of that now. She was going to have all she could do to keep herself from dying of fright, and she jumped back, terrified, as a gray lizard darted across her path and ducked into a pile of rocks.

Lucifer whinnied softly and she reached up, petting his velvety nose.

"I don't like this any more than you do, old fella," she said, trying to keep her knees from shaking. "But I just don't see where we have much of a choice, do you?"

She gazed again over the landscape, watching as an early evening star began to glow in the distance. She wanted to scream, only she knew no one would be close enough to hear. Instead, she sat down beneath the overhang and watched the night settling in all around her, the edge of fear slowly filling every nerve in her body while tears trickled down her cheeks.

It seemed like Hanna had been sitting there for hours already, when in reality it was only about twenty minutes. The tears had finally stopped when she'd resigned herself to what lay ahead, and now her resolve was to get through it. Glancing down, she studied the gully below. It was almost too dark to see, but if she squinted hard she could still just barely make out which dark objects were trees, and which were rocks, and...

Suddenly she froze as she looked back along the trail she'd ridden only a short time before. Something was moving, but then it could be those strays she'd bumped into earlier.

Straightening anxiously, she stood next to Lucifer, straining as hard as she could to make out what it was. As she kept her eyes on the trail, every sense alert, the distinct outline of a man vaguely silhouetted itself against the sloping sides of the ravine and the hair at the nape of her neck began to prickle while fear shot down her spine.

As the man drew closer she could see he was wearing a hat and leading his horse, with his gaze steady on the ground.

Her first thought was that it might be the man who'd tried to kill her, so she held her breath, hoping with all hope that it would be too dark for him to track her up the side of the draw. The man straightened, gazing about perplexed. As he reached up, took off his hat and wiped his brow, Hanna recognized the familiar stance and let out a sigh of relief.

"Blake," she murmured half to herself, half to the horse. "Thank God, it is!" She grabbed Lucifer's reins and began waving her arms as she started moving down the side of the ravine. "Blake! Mr. Morgan! Oh, my goodness," she yelled, the fear in her voice giving way to instant relief as she plummeted down the hill. "Where did you come from? How did you find me? Oh, my heavens, am I glad to see you!"

Blake's eyes still hadn't adjusted to the growing darkness around him and he stood transfixed while he watched Hanna stumbling down the rocky slope, leading Lucifer.

He'd figured he had to be getting closer to where she stopped for the night, but hadn't expected to find her this easily.

Hanna reached the bottom of the draw and for the first time since she'd spotted Blake, she hesitated, suddenly overcome with self-consciousness at the lack of decorum she'd shown by yelling and flailing her arms. She drew up short and stopped, then stood staring at him very primly.

"Oh, dear, I'm sorry for the outburst," she said, her voice breathless. "I didn't mean to frighten you."

Blake inhaled sharply, relieved that he'd found her in one piece. "Frighten me? Takes more than that to frighten me." He glanced toward the overhang. "But what the hell were you doing up there?"

"Why, I was watching. Isn't that what you said to do? Find a vantage point so no one could sneak up on me?"

Blake smiled at her logic and the fact that she remembered the casual remark he'd made while telling her about some of his more adventurous experiences.

"Are you all right?" he asked.

"I am now. I was so afraid I was going to have to spend the night out here all by myself. Just me and Lucy."

"Well, now you've got company."

"Company?" She was still holding Lucifer's reins and she looked around. "Aren't we going to go back to the ranch?"

"Not tonight." He shook his head. "Hanna, the ranch is almost twenty miles that way." He pointed off to his right beyond the ravine they were in. "There's no way we could possibly make it back there tonight in the dark.''

''You mean we have to stay out here alone, just the two of us?''

''Fraid so.''

''Oh.''

He stared at her, wishing he could see her better, because he could just about imagine the look on her face.

''Don't worry,'' he said, straightening as he looked toward the end of the ravine. ''If I remember right there's a line shack up ahead about a mile or so, and we should be able to at least make it there.''

Hanna was at a loss. There was nothing she could do except agree with him. Yet the thought of spending the night out here alone with him was almost as bad as spending it by herself. Especially right now. Because as she stared at his vague form in the darkness, she had to admit that she'd felt a strange surge of excitement when she'd first realized it was Blake making his way along the floor of the ravine and not someone else. An excitement she wasn't at all sure she wanted to feel, and it irritated her more than being lost had.

''What's a line shack?'' she asked.

''It's where the line riders stay, but with all of them in now for the roundup, we should have it all to ourselves. Come on.'' He reached out to help her mount Lucifer.

Hanna hesitated, but only for a second, then let him help her onto the black gelding.

As soon as she was in the saddle, he mounted Diablo, then nudged the Appaloosa forward and she followed close beside him.

Hanna glanced over at Blake as they rode up the ravine, and suddenly she became apprehensive.

"How do you know there's a line shack so close by?" she asked, a wary suspicion beginning to gnaw at her. After all, he'd told her when they'd first met that he'd never heard of the White Wind.

His voice was noncommittal when he answered. "Like I said, I've ridden through here a few times before."

"How many?"

"Who knows. I never bothered to keep count."

As they left the draw, Blake skirted the trees and headed for a ridge to the right about half a mile away. The going was slow in the dark, but the horses were surefooted, and a short time later they rode into a small clearing just north of the ridge. Hanna caught a faint glimpse of a water hole, with what was left of an old ramshackle building about twenty feet away from it.

There was no moon yet, but the sky was full of stars as Blake stared at the remains of the old shack.

"This is it?" she asked and he glanced over at her.

"How the hell was I to know something happened to it?" He gazed about, trying to figure out what to do first, then dismounted and walked over to help Hanna down, just as a coyote howled a short distance away.

He felt her shiver but didn't mention it. Instead, he said, "Well, let's go see what we can salvage," and he walked to what was left of the shack. "Looks like they've had a fire," he offered, and stepping inside, he began to search through the ashes.

The place had been one room with a fireplace at the far end. Now, all that was left were part of the walls, half a chair and some canned goods that had rolled far enough from the heat that they didn't explode. However, all the labels were burned off.

It was apparent by the fact that everything hadn't burned all the way that someone had tried to put it out and he wondered why Jules hadn't mentioned it. But then maybe Jules hadn't been told. Blake looked at Hanna, who was standing just outside the mess, not wanting to get any dirtier than she already was.

"My goodness, it's certainly a sight, isn't it?" she said as she took everything in including the charred remains of an old sagging bed.

"At least the location's better than that place you picked back there in the gully. Here we've got water." Blake walked over and began checking some of the cans that hadn't burned. "And food," he added. "Now all we have to do is make sure we don't bed down with any rattlers."

"Rattlesnakes?"

"You didn't think that one back in Hubbard Creek was the only one in Texas, did you?"

"I guess I'd completely forgotten." She frowned. "Oh, dear, and I've been walking around here not paying any attention at all. And I don't have a weapon with me even if I did see one."

"Not very smart of you, is it?" He walked to what was left of the fireplace and started poking around to see what pans might be usable. "But then I guess after being shot at again, anything was better than taking a chance on being hit.''

"How did you know someone shot at me?"

He reached into his pocket and took out the bullet. "I found this embedded in a tree back there where you left the trail. Did you see who it was?"

She shook her head. "No. But whoever it was didn't give up any too easily. I thought I'd lost them once, but hadn't. After that I just kept going as hard and fast as I could, then suddenly realized I was lost."

"I figured as much." He dropped the bullet into his shirt pocket. "I'm surprised they didn't keep following you, though. You left a trail any greenhorn could track."

"I did not." She looked indignant. "I covered my tracks just like you said."

"Oh, and how was that?"

"Once in a while I'd double back, and one time I broke a branch off a tree and brushed away the tracks. I even rode partway up some small streams a couple of times so they wouldn't know where to follow."

"And dislodged the slime on every rock in them. I know, I saw."

"Well, you said it worked for you."

"It does when you know how to do it." He left the fireplace and joined her outside the burned-out shack. "When you go back, you don't go back on the same trail you've been riding," he said. "And when you wipe out your horse's tracks you don't leave marks from your boot heels instead, and when you ride up or down the streams you pick some with sandy bottoms so there are no rocks to dislodge."

Hanna began to simmer inside. "Why didn't you tell me all that when you told me how you did it before?"

"Because I had no idea then you'd have to use the information one day. In any event, whoever was after you must not have been much of a tracker because it seems to have worked. I didn't run into another soul until I found you." Blake set down the things he'd salvaged from the burned-out line shack at the edge of the water hole and straightened, looking around. "For now, though, I suggest we get us some wood and get a fire going so we can see what we're doing." He headed toward some underbrush and Hanna followed.

Once the fire was lit, Blake washed the soot and ashes from the cans he'd found in the cabin and opened them with his hunting knife. One was tomatoes, another peaches. The third was beans. Along with some hardtack he had in his saddlebags, it looked like a feast to Hanna, who suddenly realized she hadn't eaten since noon and was starved.

"How do you think the line shack got burned?" she asked as they settled down to eat.

Blake thought for a minute. "Could have been anything. A hot coal from the fireplace, overturned lamp."

"What do you think?"

"I think it was set, and I think someone was inside when it was set, and just made it out."

"What makes you say that?"

"The way it burned. The fireplace is still pretty much intact. So is the floor near it, but the side wall where the door was is completely gutted, and there's an ax head laying near what was once a window as if someone chopped their way out.''

"But why would anyone set a line shack on fire?''

"Maybe for the same reason they want you dead, whatever that is. Either way, I don't like it.''

She eyed him curiously as she continued eating, savoring the taste of the tangy tomatoes and beans he'd mixed together and heated for them.

"Why did you happen to come after me?'' she asked.

He smiled. "Because Elizabeth was frantic. She thought you were still with me, and when I showed up at the ranch alone she nearly had apoplexy.''

"But why'd you come alone?''

"Because I didn't want a bunch of cowhands tramping through the woods and ruining the trail you might've left. Besides, I didn't think I needed any help.''

That's right, he hadn't needed any help. In fact, Blake Morgan seemed to have a strange knack for knowing the right thing to do at the right time, and how to do it. A fact that had bothered Hanna more than once already since meeting up with him.

"I forgot to ask you,'' she said, changing the subject. "Did you get a chance to find out anything about the grass fire yet?''

He reached into his shirt pocket and pulled out the heel chain. "I found this, but that's all.''

Hanna took it from him and began looking it over. "What is it?''

"It's a chain from a spur. It goes under the instep of the boot just in front of the heel to keep the spur from riding up. Maybe if we can find out who lost it, we'll find out who started the fire.''

She studied the small piece of silver chain. ''It could've belonged to one of our men.''

''Only it didn't.'' He reached out and took the chain from her. ''Fortunately, it's not just an ordinary chain. A chain like that had to have come off a set of fancy spurs and most of the men I've seen around Hangtown wear plain old work spurs including the hands at the ranch.''

''Like yours?''

He glanced down at his boots. ''Well, not exactly. I keep my rowels filed down, and I don't use jingle-bobs, but mine are a lot dressier than most.''

They were, too, she thought, and frowned. Blake's spurs were steel and etched with fancy drawings that were copied in the tooled leather of the spur strap. ''What are jinglebobs?'' she asked.

''Just fancy little doodads that hang near the rowel and jingle when a man walks to let folks know he's coming.''

''I take it you don't like folks to know you're coming.''

''That's right, and it's saved my life many a time, too.''

Her frown deepened and she stared at him hard. ''Just who are you really, Mr. Blake Morgan?'' she suddenly asked.

Blake managed to swallow a mouthful of beans without choking on them while purposely avoiding her eyes.

''What do you mean, who am I? I'm Blake Morgan, that's all.''

"No." She shook her head, her gaze still steady on him. "You're not *just* Blake Morgan... You're *the* Blake Morgan, and I want to know who you are, what you're doing here and why you seem to have made me your private concern."

Blake laughed, hoping to throw her off guard. There was no way he was going to tell her the truth. Not yet, not until he knew for certain just how involved she'd been with her brother.

"You make me sound like someone important," he said. "I told you. I'm just a drifter. Oh, I imagine I've been around a little more than most and been in a few more scrapes. But that's all there is to it."

Hanna's eyes narrowed thoughtfully. "I wish I could believe you."

"You can."

"How?"

"By trusting me. Now—" and he stood up "—hand me your dishes and we'll get them washed, then we should try to get some sleep."

After they'd cleaned up everything they had cooked with, Blake stepped over to Diablo and untied two blankets rolled up together.

"One for you and one for me," he said, handing her one of the blankets. Knowing she'd insist on sleeping by herself anyway, he didn't bring up any other sleeping arrangements. "There's a good spot over there." He motioned a few feet away with his head. "And I'll stretch out right here." He walked to the fire and spread out the blanket.

Hanna stared at him, watching him put the blanket as close to the fire as he could, yet far enough away so he wouldn't get too much heat, then she did the same with the blanket he'd given her.

"You sure we'll be all right here?" she asked. "We won't have to worry about snakes?"

"Rattlers don't like the fire," he answered.

She glanced about apprehensively. "I certainly hope not." She watched him retrieve the saddlebags from their horses to use as pillows, toss them onto the blankets, then drop to the ground and stretch out on one side of his blanket, curling the rest of it up around him. "But you didn't even take off your boots," she said.

"Why should I?"

"Wouldn't it be more comfortable?"

"Not really. I'm used to sleeping in them."

"Oh."

"You can take off yours, though, if you want to," he said. "It doesn't really matter. Only when you put them on again in the morning make sure you check inside to see if anything's crawled in them during the night."

"Like what?"

"Lizards, spiders . . ."

"I'll leave them on," Hanna said emphatically and lay down, trying to get comfortable on the blanket.

After stretching out, she pulled the edge of the blanket over her as Blake had done and tried to relax, only she couldn't. The ground was hard and so were the saddlebags, although they were better than nothing.

She was on her side, facing Blake, and she stared at him. His eyes were closed already and she wondered how he could sleep in such surroundings. At least

when they'd ridden all the way from Fort Worth, she
and Mrs. Brady had slept in the buckboard, which was
far more conducive to sleep than being right on the
ground.

She watched the flickering firelight play across
Blake's face, and again the gnawing suspicions she'd
felt earlier began to prick at her.

Not only was Blake sleeping with his boots on, but
his guns, too. Only his hat had been removed for the
night. Even then, it lay right above his head where he
could grab it quickly.

Her gaze moved across his face and she felt strange,
alien feelings inside as she watched him relaxed in
sleep. She had to admit he wasn't really bad looking in
a rugged sort of way, and there was just something
about him.

Now look, Hanna Winters, she said silently to herself, he's just a man like all the others, so forget all
those funny notions that have been trying to take root
in your brain ever since that night back in Hubbard
Creek. He's a loner, a drifter, and besides, he's a man,
and that's the worst part of all because he's probably
no different from any other man. He just seems nicer.
Suddenly for the first time in years she thought back
to that day shortly before her father's death when
she'd learned what men were truly like.

She'd been almost twenty-one at the time and so
much in love she'd blinded herself to the truth. Even
during the clandestine wedding ceremony with Armand she hadn't suspected a thing, and that night
she'd even given herself to her new husband with all
the passion that was in her. Now, as she thought back,
she almost felt guilty about lying during the annul-

ment proceedings a few days later when she'd sworn
the marriage hadn't been consummated. But it had
been the only thing she could do. She hadn't been
about to admit to the world that she'd been played for
a fool. That the man she'd eloped with had thought
her father was rich, and that when he'd found out
otherwise he'd walked out of her life the very day after the elopement.

The whole thing probably would have been a little
easier to take if her father hadn't died of a heart attack two days later, leaving her to face everything
alone. She had also learned that her father had been
encouraging her relationship with Armand because he
thought Armand was wealthy and he'd been hoping to
recoup some of his own losses with Armand's money.

How ironic, she thought as she lay staring at Blake
and remembering. Both men had thought the other
had money and had only been using her to gain that
money. Was Blake Morgan using her, too? But if he
was, for what purpose?

Well, she'd just have to keep her guard up and all
her faculties alert, because she wasn't about to be used
by any man ever again, and especially not one like
Blake Morgan.

Deciding she'd better take a cue from him and get
some sleep, she hunkered down a little farther into the
blanket, closed her eyes and started to drift off.

Hanna still wasn't fully asleep, although she'd been
lying quietly for some time now. She could hear the
crackling of the wood in the fire and the little night
sounds that accompanied it, but quite abruptly, the
blood began rushing to her head. Somehow Hanna

knew that something or someone was right behind her. Keeping as quiet as could be, she just lay there, not moving, hardly daring to breathe, and afraid to even open her eyes.

Then, as she held her breath, she suddenly felt something claw at the back of her head, a sniffing sound filled her ears and something cold and wet nuzzled her neck. Not even waiting to find out what it was, she let out a shriek, grabbed the edge of the blanket, pulling it with her, and half crawled, fighting the air as she lunged right at Blake, landing directly on top of him.

Blake sputtered, his arms flailing as he woke up, startled to find Hanna clutching at him like mad and trying to bury herself against him. Then, as his eyes began to focus and his vision cleared, he realized what was happening, and gazed off to the spot where she'd been sleeping just in time to see a raccoon running hell-bent for the trees.

Hanna was panting heavily, her whole body trembling. When she'd left her bed the raccoon's paw had inadvertently pulled the ribbon off the end of her braid, and her hair was starting to fall free and cascade onto her shoulders like a pale mist.

"Hey, slow down. It's all right, it was just a raccoon," he said trying to calm her down. He reached up, trying to extricate himself gently from her viselike grip.

Hanna gulped a terrified swallow, then slowly began to come to her senses at the calm reassurance of his voice. She'd had her eyes shut and her face buried in his shoulder, but now she drew her head back and looked at him.

"You're sure it was a raccoon?" she asked, her voice still tremulous and shaky.

"Positive." Blake was sitting up now and she was still cradled against him, his arms partially around her. "I saw him running away."

Hanna flushed as she looked into his eyes. "Well, it could have been a bear."

"It could have been. But it wasn't."

The fire was much lower now and Hanna's back was to it so he couldn't see her face too clearly, but he knew exactly the expression she'd have on it by the tone of her voice. In spite of everything, she was trying to be Miss Prim and Proper, only this time it wasn't working.

Maybe because the night was warm and the stars overhead compelling, or it could be the firelight casting a rosy glow over everything making it seem so different, but suddenly Blake realized Hanna was staring at him the same way she had that night in Hubbard Creek. He also realized he liked it. She reached up to straighten her hair.

"No, don't do that. I told you before your hair looks pretty like that," he said, and he reached up and brushed her hand aside. He touched her hair, lightly at first, before running his fingers through it as he finished unwinding the rest of the braid.

Hanna trembled. "It looks terrible."

"Don't be ridiculous, it's beautiful." He let its silky softness fall through his fingers. "Why do you always try to hide it like you do?"

She flushed. "I don't."

Blake breathed deeply as his hand left her hair to touch her face. He cupped his hand along her cheek, his sinewy fingers plying her flesh sensuously. My God, she looked so pretty and soft. He felt a stirring deep down inside.

"You do try to hide it, and you know you do, Hanna." His voice was low, husky, the intimacy of the night around them deepening its timbre. "Why don't you just try to be yourself for a change and forget about Boston and what's right and what isn't?"

"Blake..."

"Like right now. Part of you wants to pull away and fight the feelings the other part of you is beginning to enjoy."

Her blush deepened. "You're insane."

"Am I?" he swung her into his arms, then laid her gently onto the blanket beside him and bent down, his lips gliding along her throat to caress her earlobe. His breath warm against her ear, he whispered, "Then I like this insanity."

Hanna suddenly felt a surging fire begin to play along the nerves of her spine as he once more began to tease her flesh with his lips. She tried to fight the heady feeling that was overpowering her, only it was hopeless. It had been so long since she'd felt like this. So many years since she'd truly let herself feel, and even though it was frightening, it was fascinating to know that she wasn't really dead inside as she'd so often thought.

She closed her eyes, savoring the velvety warmth of his lips as they caressed her ear, her throat, then with a low groan that came from deep inside him, Blake's lips moved to her mouth and captured it with the same heat that had been there in Hubbard Creek. Only this time, she didn't pull away. Instead she moaned contentedly and surrendered to the fire and passion that were consuming her, savoring the feel of his lips and letting them taste the depth of her longing with an eagerness that was intoxicating.

"I told you you'd like it," Blake murmured. Reaching down, he slipped his hand beneath her shirt and began to stroke her breasts, bringing her whole body to life while his lips captured her mouth again.

Hanna couldn't even think anymore. All she knew was that her body had awakened from a forced slumber she'd imposed on it, and she felt as if the whole world had betrayed her, only she didn't care. All she could do was feel.

"Let me love you, Hanna," Blake whispered as he stretched his body the length of hers. "Don't make me stop now. Let me give you the world that you lost somewhere along the way." As he drew back for just a second and looked into her eyes, seeing the surrender there, he let out a soft sigh.

Not wanting to lose the moment, he kissed her again tenderly, and deftly loosened his gun belt, tossing it aside. Then he began to move his hands slowly down her body, kneading her flesh beneath her clothes until Hanna drew her clothes aside so he could reach her.

Blake inhaled sharply as she finally stretched out naked beside him, her body arched, waiting.

Her face was tanned from the sun, but the rest of her was like fine ivory, smooth and silky in the firelight. He divested himself of the last vestiges of clothing and lay down, still staring at her hungrily, his heart in his throat. All he wanted to do was lose himself inside her.

Gently, as if afraid to move for fear of shattering the illusion before him, he reached out, touched her taut flesh, then his arms curled about her waist and he pulled her hard against him.

The sensation was intoxicating and he heard her sigh a deep sigh as his lips captured the valley between her breasts, then cupped a nipple in his mouth.

Slowly, deliberately, his tongue circled it tenderly, then released it. He drew her head to him and kissed her full on the mouth.

By the time he covered her, entering her with a thrust that forged its way deep inside her, neither Blake nor Hanna cared anymore about anything or anyone but the ecstasy that was overwhelming them. Blake gave Hanna stroke after stroke, the pounding rhythm bringing her to a shuddering climax as he suddenly felt himself plunged into the very same fulfillment deep in his core.

A slight breeze ruffled the leaves on a tree overhead and Hanna opened her eyes, slowly becoming aware of her surroundings.

Oh, my God! What have I done? she wailed silently to herself, then realized exactly what she'd done as she felt the heat of Blake still inside her, the strangely unfamiliar feel of his flesh covering hers, and a sickening dread began to mingle with the throbbing heat that still filled her. She swallowed hard.

"Blake?" Her voice was barely a whisper. "Mr. Morgan, please... I shouldn't... We shouldn't... Mr. Morgan?"

Blake had been completely relaxed, breathing deeply, his body spent, and now slowly the life began to surge back into him and he lifted his head, looking at her.

"Hanna."

"Please . . . this should never have happened," she murmured, close to tears. "I should never have . . . Please, Mr. Morgan, do let me up. I'm so sorry."

"Sorry?" He frowned, yet began to ease himself from her. "What do you have to be sorry for?"

As he moved from her, she sat up quickly, trying to cover herself, and reached for her clothes, beginning to put them back on. "Because now you're going to think I'm a loose woman, and I'm not." Her face turned bright red. "In fact I don't really know what came over me. Good heavens!" She was back to Miss Prim and Proper again. "I've never ever done anything like this before. What must you think?"

"I think you're one hell of a woman," he answered as he reached for his own clothes. "Whether you like it or not."

"Well, I don't," she shot back. "And I want you to forget it, do you understand?"

"Like I forgot what happened back in Hubbard Creek?"

"Exactly." She finished dressing, then pulled on her boots. "After all, I'm not some barroom doxy, Mr. Morgan, and I assure you, what happened just now was as much a surprise to me as I know it was to you and it won't ever happen again, I assure you. Now—" and she picked up her blanket and set it right next to his "—I think we'd both better try to get some sleep again, don't you?"

"If you say so," he said. He was standing, and picked up his gun belt, fastening it on as he stared at her, realizing she was fighting with herself right now, and he didn't want to push. "But you've laid your blanket down right next to mine," he said, surprised at her action. Especially after what they'd just been through.

"I realize that," she answered. "But I'm sure it won't make any difference now, will it? Besides, I couldn't stand the thought of another raccoon maybe breathing down my neck again."

"Suit yourself," he said and once more dropped to the ground, then watched her settle down next to him.

The fire was still low and he glanced over, his eyes catching hers as he stretched out, resting his head on his saddlebags. At first he was sure he'd seen tears in her eyes, but now they'd been replaced with a passionate warmth that was frightening in its intensity.

"Good night," he whispered softly.

Hanna's gaze bored deep into his amber eyes and she felt a shiver run through her. He wasn't going to forget, and she knew he wasn't going to forget, but then she wasn't sure she would, either. Blake Morgan had awakened something in her tonight she'd never, ever wanted to feel again, and she wanted to hate him for it, yet knew she couldn't, and it was turning her whole world upside down. Well, she wasn't going to let it. Not if she could help it.

"Good night, Mr. Morgan," she answered. As she closed her eyes she prayed that when morning came she'd truly be able to forget tonight, but deep down, she knew she wouldn't.

Chapter Six

Dawn was just starting to break in the east as Blake slowly woke up to the feel of Hanna's warm body cuddled against him. Opening his eyes hesitantly, he stared at her head resting comfortably on his shoulder. She was sleeping as peacefully as could be, and he wasn't about to disturb her. At least not just yet.

She hadn't put her hair into its braid last night and it framed her face with soft waves, like a white cloud. Strange, he thought, she looked so young and vulnerable in sleep.

A frown creased his forehead as he remembered their lovemaking and suddenly he remembered something that shouldn't have been. Hanna Winters wasn't a virgin. Oh, she was tight, and inexperienced, and it was as if the whole thing was new to her. But damn it, he was sure it hadn't been the first time for her, and he wondered how and why.

The thought was intriguing because to know Hanna there had to be a good explanation for it. As he stared at her, the heat that had overwhelmed him last night started to surge to the surface again, and he knew if he didn't stop right now he was going to ache all day, and he didn't want that.

"Hanna?" he finally whispered, hoping not to scare her. "Hanna, wake up."

Hanna had been arguing with Blake in her dreams, although as she slowly opened her eyes and stared at him, she couldn't for the life of her remember what the argument they were having was about. But the animosity was still there.

"Oh, good heavens!" she exclaimed, reaching up to shove her hair away from her face as she pushed herself from him. "I didn't mean to do that, really. I'm sorry, Mr. Morgan."

"Hey, I didn't mind, not a bit. It's just that I think we'd better get up and get started or we'll have all the ranch hands out looking for us."

He watched her sit back on her blanket and try to shake the cobwebs from her brain and get fully awake. Dark shadows still filled the clearing and he knew the sun wouldn't clear the horizon for some time yet.

"I figure if we leave now, we might get back before they send out a search party," he went on.

Hanna blinked the sleep from her eyes, then stretched and began to stand up. She was a bit wobbly on her feet and not quite fully awake yet. She glanced at Blake, who still sat on his blanket smiling at her. "What are you laughing about?"

"I'm not laughing, I'm smiling," he answered. "I wish I knew what makes you tick."

Hanna's eyes hardened. "What's that supposed to mean?"

He stood, too, retrieved his hat, set it on his head, and began to gather up their blankets. "You're an enigma, Hanna Winters. You're prim and proper on the outside and all fire on the inside, only you hate for anyone to know it."

"That's absurd!"

"Is it?" His topaz eyes darkened passionately. "The woman I made love to last night isn't the same woman I'm looking at this morning."

"You were supposed to forget about last night."

"That's right, I was, wasn't I? Sorry about that, but things are hard to forget. Forgive me."

Her eyes narrowed dangerously and Blake caught the warning.

"I am forgiven, aren't I?" he added quickly.

Hanna felt a cold hardness begin to fill her as she fought against the charm of this man she wanted yet resented for what he could do to her.

"I guess you're forgiven," she answered, her voice revealing her reluctance. "At least for now. But don't ever bring it up again." She stood quietly looking around. "Are we going to eat before we go?"

"If you want."

"Not really. The sooner we get back the better. Besides, maybe Maria'll have something better than what's in those cans you confiscated."

"You mean you don't like my cooking?"

She gave him a disgusted look, yet couldn't help the slight smile that tried to conquer the corners of her mouth. "Are you ever serious?" she asked.

His face sobered. "Sure, try me."

She stared at him hard, wishing she could understand him. He seemed to take life so casually at times, but then no one had been shooting at him.

"Oh, never mind," she finally said and started toward the water to wash the sleep from her eyes.

She could feel Blake's gaze follow her all the way. She knelt down and splashed water in her face, and wasn't surprised when he was right there and offered her a clean bandanna from his saddlebags to wipe on when she straightened and stood up.

"If you want I'll braid your hair again for you," he said as she wiped her face dry. "My kid sister used to wear her hair like that and I had to help her when nobody else was around."

Hanna lowered the towel and frowned.

"You don't believe me?"

"I didn't say that."

"Then turn around."

Hanna wasn't going to at first, but just at that moment the morning breeze blew a stray hair into her face. She brushed it aside, then turned her back to him.

Blake reached into his pocket and pulled out a comb, then his hands captured the sides of her head and his fingers grasped the hair gently, but deftly. He began to comb the strands and braid them, working diligently to get it all in without pulling.

While he worked, Hanna was all too aware of the intimacy of the act, only she tried as hard as she could to ignore it. The worst part was that it didn't seem to be bothering Blake. He'd comb a few skeins of hair, shove the comb into his mouth while he intertwined them, then he would hum softly as if he didn't have a care in the world.

Finally he finished the braid in the back and held onto the end so it wouldn't loosen again.

"What did you have it fastened with?" he asked.

She pointed to where she'd been sleeping when the raccoon had disturbed her. "It's over there."

With Blake in tow holding the end of the braid, she moved to where she'd spread her blanket near the fire the night before, retrieved the small piece of rawhide the raccoon had pulled out and handed it to Blake. "There," he said when it was fastened tightly, and he stepped back to survey his work. "Not half-bad, if I do say so myself."

Hanna hesitated before turning around. For some reason the loss of his nearness bothered her. Fool! she told herself. Angry at her reaction, she straightened stubbornly and finally turned around.

"I imagine it'll do for now, thank you, Mr. Morgan," she said in her most dispassionate manner. "Now, do you think perhaps we might be ready to leave?"

Blake's eyes narrowed slightly at her cold rebuff. "Why not," he said, his voice sharp and caustic for a change. "We just might make it back to the ranch in time for breakfast." He turned and headed for their horses.

Hanna watched him walk away and sighed deeply. You just don't understand, Blake Morgan, she said to herself, you just don't understand, and stuffing the bandanna he'd given her into her hip pocket, she reached down to pick up her hat where she'd left it on the ground the night before and set it on her head, then followed after him.

The kitchen was warm from the fire Maria had started in the stove so she could make breakfast, only

Elizabeth didn't really notice as she sat at the table, her hands ringing a cup of coffee, her gaze on the door.

It was close to seven already and not a sign of Hanna or Blake yet. Either he hadn't found her and was still searching, or he'd found her too late to head for home, or... She hated to think of the alternative.

"I can fix you some corn cakes," Maria offered from where she stood near the sink.

Elizabeth shook her head. "I'm just not hungry, Maria."

She reached up, ran a hand through her graying hair, then nervously checked the buttons on the bodice of her light blue cotton frock, one of the dresses she'd bought purposely for their trip out. She'd always felt nice in blue. It reminded her of one of the dresses Daniel had liked her to wear. He always had been partial to blue.

Her dark eyes filled with anxiety as she suddenly heard the unmistakable sound of a fast rider approaching. However, before she could make it to the door at the other side of the kitchen, Jules was already over the threshold, his face as anxious as her thoughts.

"So all right, where is he?" he roared, anger showing in his eyes.

Elizabeth was taken aback. "I beg your pardon!"

"That no-account assistant Hank's sister foisted on me. He was supposed to report back last night and never showed up."

"Well, naturally not," Elizabeth said, her voice just as haughty as his was loud. "He's out looking for Hanna."

Jules frowned. "Hanna? You mean Miss Winters? Where the devil is she?"

"Well now, if we knew that he wouldn't have had to go looking, would he?" Suddenly Elizabeth's eyes softened as she realized the foreman had probably left the camp grounds without any breakfast, and he was a big man probably used to a hearty meal. "Now, instead of getting yourself all worked up, why don't you just come over here. Maria'll fix you something to eat, and I'll explain."

Jules wasn't sure he wanted to listen to any lame-brained excuses, yet there was something about the woman's sincerity that got to him.

"All right," he finally said, and headed for the table.

"Your hat, Mr Hayden?" Elizabeth reminded him.

"What about my hat?" Jules questioned.

"You could take it off since you've decided to stay."

Jules hesitated momentarily, then reached up, grabbed the hat and set it on the table as he sat down. "So, all right, what happened?" While Maria fixed his food, Elizabeth filled him in on Hanna's strange disappearance.

"What makes you think Morgan'll find her?" he asked when Elizabeth was finished.

"He said he's done tracking before."

"And probably a lot of other things, too," Jules added sullenly.

Elizabeth's eyes sparked. "Now don't you go running down Blake Morgan. If it weren't for him Hanna wouldn't even have made it this far. He saved her life more than once on the trail."

"Oh, hell, I know all about that."

"If you think you're annoying me by swearing, Mr. Hayden, you're sadly mistaken," Elizabeth said, her voice very matter-of-fact. "My late husband was quite adept at it, and could probably have taught you a few choice words."

Jules eyes narrowed as he stared at Elizabeth Brady, and suddenly it was as if he were seeing her for the first time.

He figured she had to be somewhere near fifty, give or take a few years, and she was nothing like Hanna Winters. There was none of the crisp demeanor that Hanna carried around with her, and the Brady woman's dark brown eyes held a decided twinkle in them that softened the sharpness of her features.

Actually, she was a rather striking woman, warm and friendly, and far more sure of herself than most of the women he'd met around Hangtown.

"Miss Winters didn't say. You a relative?" he asked.

"Just a friend." Elizabeth sighed as Maria came over and put a plate of food on the table in front of Jules. "But now I'm really starting to get worried. If they don't show up..."

She never finished the sentence as the distinct drumming of hoofbeats could be heard in the distance and they all stayed motionless, listening.

"They're back!" Elizabeth finally exclaimed as she heard the creak of leather and harness and hoped that it was Hanna and Blake reining their horses to a halt near the back hitching post.

Blake had spotted Jules's big bay mare long before they'd ridden into the ranch yard, and now as he reined up beside it he glanced at Hanna. On the way they'd talked everything over and decided not to tell anyone she'd been shot at. That the less people who knew, the better.

The roundup was almost over and Pete and some of the men would be leaving by the end of the week to drive the herd north to the railhead in Kansas. Jules wouldn't really be needing Blake to help anymore on the range, so they'd decided that Hanna was going to have him stay at the ranch so he'd be free to come and go as he pleased while he tried to find out what he could about the fire, the heel chain and the bullet he'd dug out of the tree.

"So what are you going to tell Hayden?" Blake asked as they sat on their horses.

Hanna frowned. "I have no idea." Her frown deepened. "Besides, I wonder what he's doing here."

"Well, it looks like we're about to find out," he said, as they turned toward the house in time to see Elizabeth hurry out the back door followed closely by Jules.

Hanna and Blake dismounted hesitantly and Elizabeth ran to Hanna.

"Oh, Lord, am I glad to see you," she cried and she grabbed Hanna in a big hug, then set her away from her and stood looking into her face. "What on earth happened anyway?"

Hanna tried not to look too embarrassed as she glanced at both Mrs. Brady and Jules.

"I'm afraid I tried to take a shortcut back to the ranch and got lost."

"What a dumb thing to do," Jules said, his usual outspoken self.

Hanna looked disgruntled. "I don't need your comments, Mr. Hayden," she snapped defensively.

Jules eyed Blake curiously. "Where'd you find her?"

"Near the northwest line shack." They'd also decided not to mention that the shack had been burned down unless Jules brought it up. "But it was too late to start back last night."

"You should've come and gotten some help."

"Didn't need any." Blake looked pleased with himself. "She left a trail any greenhorn could follow."

Hanna was indignant. "That's only Mr. Morgan's opinion. But at least I'm glad *he* was able to follow it." She reached up and took off her hat. "Now, if you all don't mind... We've been riding since before sunup and neither of us has had any breakfast."

As they started toward the house Hanna glanced at Jules. "What are you doing here, anyway?" she asked.

"Lookin' for Morgan. He was supposed to take some men down near the southern boundary this morning to find out why the boys there are takin' so long. When he didn't show up I had to send Pete."

He opened the door for her and everyone followed Hanna into the kitchen where Maria was already setting food on the table. They all sat down and started to eat.

Hanna looked across the table at the foreman. "What's wrong with sending Pete?" she asked. "Is that bad?"

"Hell, no, Pete can handle it all right, it's just that I was hopin' to use him someplace else."

"I see." She studied the man closely for a few minutes. He didn't seem to be quite as blustery this morning, and she wondered if maybe Mrs. Brady had something to do with it. Mrs. Brady did have a way when it came to taking a person down a peg and bringing out the good points. "Well, I'm afraid you're going to have to do without Mr. Morgan's help for a little while yet, Mr. Hayden," Hanna said, finally deciding what to tell him. "Because I'm going to be needing him here at the ranch and to get some things done for me in town. Since the drive's going to be starting soon anyway, and he won't be going, I can't see any real reason he can't stay right here and take orders directly from me, do you?"

"Well, don't that take all."

"Not really," she answered. "You see, we still haven't discovered who tried to kill me while I was on my way here, so I've decided it might be wise to have someone other than Paco around who can handle a gun, and Mr. Morgan assures me he can."

Jules stared at her hard. Something was up, he knew it, but what? Had another attempt been made on her life? If so, why didn't they just come right out and say so? A wave of frustration swept through him. They didn't trust him.

"If that's the way you want it," he said, and he stood up.

"Aren't you going to finish your breakfast?" Elizabeth asked as she realized he wasn't through eating yet.

He glanced at the few bites left on his plate. "I just ain't hungry no more," he answered, then looked again at Hanna. "Did you get that list of supplies Heck's gonna need for the drive?" he asked.

Hanna nodded. "Mr. Morgan gave it to me this morning."

"Good, then I'll be goin' and you can send Paco out with them as soon as you get them." Without saying another word, he grabbed his hat from the table and left.

After he'd left, Elizabeth turned to Hanna. "I don't think he liked your explanation about why you're keeping Blake at the ranch," she said.

Hanna sipped at her coffee. "He doesn't have to. I don't owe him anything except his wages."

"Come on now, Hanna." Elizabeth shook her head. "He was trying to be nice for a change."

"That's just the trouble." Hanna's eyes narrowed thoughtfully. "Like I said, I still don't know who's been taking potshots at me, and it could just be him."

"You don't believe that."

Hanna glanced at Blake, then at Mrs. Brady. "I didn't say anything when he was here on purpose, Mrs. Brady," she answered. "But I didn't just get lost. Someone took some more shots at me and I ran. By the time I got away Lucy and I were hopelessly lost."

Elizabeth shook her head. "Well, then, it couldn't have been Jules, because I distinctly remember him saying he was at the camp all yesterday afternoon."

Hanna frowned. "He wasn't there when I left."

"And he wasn't with me," Blake added. "He also has a Colt five-shot revolving carbine, and I'd bet my bottom dollar that's the gun this came from." He reached into his pocket and pulled out the bullet he'd dug out of the tree.

Elizabeth still wasn't convinced. "I still can't see him wanting you dead. Besides, you said you lost whoever was shooting at you. I have a feeling you'd have never lost Jules Hayden if he was on your trail."

"She's right there, Hanna." Blake had to agree. "Unless he had some reason for not going after you."

"Like having to get back to the camp before he was missed?"

Blake shrugged. "Could be."

"Well, I wasn't about to take the chance. Now if you'll both excuse me, I'm going to have Maria heat some water for a bath, then go up to my room and soak off some of the dust and dirt from the trail." She looked at Blake. "While you, Mr. Morgan, head for town and see what you can find."

She stood up.

"Oh, yes, and while you're there leave that list of supplies at the store and tell them Paco'll pick them up later on, either today or tomorrow."

"Will do," Blake answered. He watched her closely while she called to Maria at the sink to ask her to have Paco set up a tub in her room, then, finishing his own breakfast, he excused himself and left, saying goodbye as he went out the back door.

As he neared town, Culler glanced behind him with a frown. Good, no one was following. He'd managed to sneak away without being seen.

The foreman had told him to make sure there were no strays left out in the hills northeast of camp some thirty miles, and it had been easy to get away. Especially since Hayden told him to take his time so nothing was overlooked, even if he didn't make it back until tomorrow.

Culler cursed softly as he rode along. It was almost the middle of June already. Even though he'd known his partner Whitey had been playing at a masquerade all these years, he'd never thought the day would come when he'd have to track down just who Whitey really was and where he'd come from. He thought back to the first time he'd ever laid eyes on the man.

Unbeknownst to either of them they'd both been hiding in the same rock formation waiting to rob the Denver stage. When Whitey had ridden down into the Concord's path the same time he'd eased onto the trail from the other side, Culler had just about had heart failure.

He'd thought the other horseman was the law until he'd spotted the bandanna pulled tightly across his nose, but instead of arguing over which one was going to get the loot, they agreed it would be better to share and share alike instead of either of them eating the other's bullets.

Over the years that followed Whitey had made quite a name for himself as a lone bandit, and it was rare for Culler to work with him except when Whitey thought the job was too big for just one man.

Now Culler wished he hadn't been with Whitey on this last job because things sure as hell hadn't gone right. Wells Fargo not only had a description of him that some stupid woman on the stage who'd pulled down his bandanna had given them, but he'd come away without a dime to show there'd even been a holdup. And now, on top of that, he was sure Whitey was dead.

It had taken him months of painstaking work to find Whitey's other identity, and he still didn't have any proof. That's why he was headed for town. Now, if he could just lay his hands on that two hundred and fifty thousand dollars... But being able to do that was getting harder and harder with each passing day. Just the thought of that much money made his hands tighten on the reins, and he nudged his horse a little faster.

It was close to eleven in the morning when he finally rode into Hangtown and dismounted in front of the Sundown Saloon. The boys at camp had said Hank Winters was sweet on one of the girls who worked here, and Culler was hoping maybe she might have known the rancher better than anyone else.

He gazed about surreptitiously to make sure none of the White Wind crew had been sent to town for anything, then walked up to the swinging doors and stepped inside the place where he stood looking around.

According to the men, the woman he was looking for was a redhead named Trudy, and it took only seconds to spot her. She was the only redhead in the place and was sitting at one of the tables in the back all by herself wiling the time away in a game of solitaire.

He strolled over. "Your name Trudy?" he asked.

Trudy eyed Culler curiously, her gaze intent on his worn clothes and dark flashing eyes.

"Who wants to know?"

"The name's Culler, Culler Burris," he introduced himself. "And I think we had a mutual friend."

"Oh?"

"Yeah, Hank Winters."

"You knew Hank?"

"That's what I'm hoping to find out." He pulled up a chair and sat down. "You're Trudy then?"

"Yeah, I'm Trudy. So what's this all about?"

Trudy was wearing a deep rose satin dress with little black beads trimming the bodice. In her ears were the same diamond drop earrings she'd had on the night she'd met Hanna. The dress clashed with her hair, but she didn't seem to mind.

As he tipped his hat back, Culler happened to catch sight of the earrings, and he froze. He'd be damned if they weren't just the proof he'd been looking for.

He leaned forward, his voice lowering so only she could hear. "Them's pretty earrings you got there, Miss Trudy," he said, his eyes still glued to them. "Hank give them to you?"

She looked surprised. "How'd you know?"

"Like I said, I think he was a mutual friend."

Trudy was skeptical. "But Hank said I wasn't ever to tell anybody where I got them, so how do you know he gave them to me?"

"Because I was with him when he, shall we say, acquired them?" He took a furtive look around the room. The place was empty except for a handful of men and dance hall girls at the tables and bar. But it was more people than he wanted around. "Hey, look, can we go some place private and talk?" he asked.

"About Hank?"

"Yeah, about Hank."

Trudy stared at the stranger, then thought over her years with Hank Winters and the suspicions those years had aroused. She happened to remember a remark he'd made one time that had helped feed those suspicions. Now suddenly she wondered if maybe this sandy-haired man with the cold, hard eyes might supply the answers she was looking for.

"I got a room upstairs," she said and stood up. "You can pretend you're a customer."

Culler stood up, too. "Fair enough. Just so you don't expect to get paid."

She laughed. "All depends on how far the talking takes us." She started to walk away and Culler followed.

Once inside her room he stood leaning against the door.

Trudy watched him closely. The man was dangerous, she was sure of it, but then she was used to men like Culler Burris. Besides, she could be just as dangerous given the opportunity. That's why she'd changed her name six years before when she'd left St. Louis.

"So all right, you wanted to talk?" she said. "Talk."

He straightened and walked over to look out the only window in her room, then turned to face her.

"Just how much did you know about Henry Winters?" he finally asked.

"What do you mean, how much did I know?"

"Just what I said." His eyes flashed anxiously. "Did you know those earrings you're wearing once belonged to a wealthy lady from New York City who was traveling west by stage to meet her husband in Oregon?"

Trudy reached up slowly and touched one of the diamond teardrops. "You're joking."

"No, ma'am, I sure as hell ain't," he answered. "You see, I was with an outlaw named Whitey when we robbed that stage. Got away with a twenty-thousand-dollar payroll meant for the miners out in Nevada and a box of jewelry from that lady that'd make a jeweler's eyes jump right out of their sockets."

Trudy stared at him hard for a minute as if contemplating, then went over to the dresser, opened one of the drawers and took out a small wooden box. After lifting the lid, she held it out for Culler to see.

"You mean like these?" she asked.

Culler's eyes narrowed. They were there, all right. Every last piece. He and Whitey had divided the money and the jewelry evenly between them, and he'd sold his share of the jewelry off. It was obvious what Whitey had done with his. Now Culler knew his suspicions about Henry Winters had been right. Henry or Hank Winters and the outlaw he'd known as Whitey were one and the same.

"You know what this means, don't you?" he said to Trudy and to his surprise she smiled.

"I suspected it years ago. Especially when I saw one of those wanted posters over at the sheriff's office, and Hank's business trips always seemed to coincide with some big robbery somewhere."

"And you didn't turn him in?"

"Turn him in? Now why would I do a thing like that? After all, he never did anything wrong to me. Fact is, he treated me better'n I been treated for years."

"But there was a ten-thousand-dollar reward on his head, dead or alive."

Trudy looked thoughtful. "I see what you mean. Only I didn't really have any proof, now, did I? At least not until you showed up. Besides, it would've been his word against mine. And anyway, why would I want to do a fool thing like that when I think I'd just about talked him into marrying me and taking me away from all this?"

Culler sneered. "I thought you liked it here."

"I would have liked being Mrs. Henry Winters much better. Only it's too late now. I guess I can probably sell some of this stuff." She looked down at the jewelry she was still holding. "But it still won't take me as far as I want to go."

"Would half of two hundred and fifty thousand dollars?" he asked.

Her eyes narrowed shrewdly. "Half?"

"That's what I'll give you if you can help me find out where Hank stashed it before he died."

"Why do you need me?"

"Because maybe you'll be able to remember something that might help me find out where it is. Something Whitey said one time makes me think maybe the money's hidden away in the house somewhere, and I was hoping you could give me a clue. Did he ever mention anything over the years about where he might have put anything valuable?"

"Only the bank."

"No, it's got to be in the house somewhere. You sure you can't remember anything at all?"

Trudy tried to think. She'd been in the ranch house dozens of times. "Well, there is the wall safe in the master bedroom upstairs off the front balcony."

"Wall safe?"

"Yeah, it's behind a picture of a big sailing ship just over the fireplace."

"You're sure about this?"

"Of course I'm sure. The night he gave me these he got them out of it." She glanced down at the jewelry box she was still holding. "I never knew they were real, though. I thought they were just some of those fake jewels you hear people talk about."

"Well, they ain't fake," Culler told her. "And I bet that wall safe is right where the two hundred fifty thousand is, and I bet Hank's sister doesn't even know the safe is there."

"But how will you get into it?"

"Don't worry about that." He smiled, his mouth set determinedly. "It shouldn't be that hard to crack." He reached up, setting his hat more firmly on his head, getting ready to leave.

"Hey, do I still get my cut?" she called out as he headed for the door.

"Sure, baby, just as soon as I get mine." With that, he walked out, closing the door softly behind him, leaving Trudy staring after him.

"I just better," she whispered softly. "Because if I don't, Mr. Culler Burris, you're gonna wish you'd never set foot in Hangtown." She took another good hard look at the jewelry in her hands before putting it back in the drawer and heading downstairs to finish out the day.

Blake was frustrated. He'd been trying all morning to track down both the bullet and the heel chain, with no luck so far. He left the sheriff's office, strolled up to Diablo and got ready to mount the Appaloosa, then happened to glance down the street toward the Sundown just as Culler stepped out the front door.

Now what the hell was Culler doing at the Sundown this time of day? he asked himself, only there wasn't any answer. As far as he knew the man was supposed to be out on the range with Jules and the rest of the White Wind crew.

He watched Culler stop on the top step before setting foot in the street, then Culler looked around furtively. Blake was glad there was a sorrel between Culler and his Appaloosa because Diablo would stick out like a sore thumb in a town that was half-empty.

Apparently Culler was satisfied that he didn't see anyone he knew. He mounted up and rode out of town.

It wasn't until Culler was well out of sight that Blake untied the horse and led him down the street, tethering him in front of the Sundown Saloon.

It was well past noon when Blake finally unhitched Diablo, mounted up again and rode out of town, heading toward the ranch. Although his talk with Trudy hadn't been all that productive, he was sure deep down inside she was hiding something. And he was also sure that if he'd just told her who he really was and why he was in Texas he probably would have found out what it was she was hiding. Only now just wasn't the time.

Not yet, anyway. Besides, if anyone had a right to know, it was Hanna, and he couldn't even tell her yet. Spurring his horse a little harder, he left Hangtown behind.

* * *

Hanna was in the library when Blake arrived, and he knocked before stepping inside.

"So what did you learn?" she asked as he strolled over to the desk where she was sitting.

Her hair was in its tight knot again and she was wearing a plain gray dress with a little white collar and buttons to the waist that gave credence to her prim manners. He was sure she was wearing it mostly for defense against the emotions he knew were smoldering deep down inside her.

"I didn't learn a damn thing," he answered. "Except that half the population out here uses a Colt five-shot revolving carbine."

"The same caliber?"

"Yup. So there goes your Jules Hayden theory."

"And nothing about the chain?"

"Now that's another matter. There's only one place in town where a man could have a new chain put on a pair of spurs, only nobody's been in to have it done. Not yet anyway. However—" and he looked rather satisfied with himself "—the man there did tell me there's about four fellas in the area could wear spurs fancy enough to have silver chains, and one of them's a wizened-up fella sporting a mustache who works out at the Box T."

"Terrell's place? Good glory, why would he be trying to kill me? And why set the range on fire?"

He shrugged. "Your guess is as good as mine."

"No." She shook her head. "There has to be a better explanation. Maybe he only rides for Terrell, but works for someone else."

"Maybe." He glanced at all the ledgers on the desk in front of her. "Find anything interesting?" he asked.

She eyed him curiously. "Strange you should ask, but I did."

"Oh?" He sat on the edge of the desk. "What's that?"

Hanna didn't know exactly how to tell him. Well, the best way was usually the simplest.

"It's these books," she answered. "I'll be checking along going over all the figures just as carefully as I can and there doesn't seem to be any money for hardly anything, then farther on down the page the debts are paid off and the slate's wiped clean. And I've gone over everything trying to figure out just where the money came from. There's nothing. It's just there."

"You're sure?"

"Positive. Look." For the next few minutes she let him peruse her brother's books with her. Suddenly Blake knew he'd guessed right. The figures, the dates.

He glanced up from the books and looked at Hanna. Should he tell her or shouldn't he? The question had been haunting him all the way to the ranch, only now that he was faced with the actual telling, he couldn't do it. No, it was too soon. He still wasn't all that certain she was as innocent of her brother's affairs as she pretended to be.

"Maybe he just forgot to record some of the money that was coming in," he said.

She laughed. "Oh, he forgot it all right, until he had a use for it. But then I guess Henry never was much of a one for keeping money straight." She sat in the desk chair and looked at him, studying his face. "You had a worried look when you came in. What's the matter?'' she asked.

He stood up and walked to the window, looking out. "It's that other new hand you hired," he said, talking over his shoulder. "I thought he was supposed to be out on the range with the rest of the men.''

"He is.''

He turned to face her. "He wasn't when I saw him.''

"Where?''

"Coming out of the Sundown Saloon. Trudy said he'd stopped in for a beer, but she was lying.''

"How do you know?''

"I asked the bartender how long he'd been in the place and he said long enough to enjoy himself, if you get my meaning.''

Hanna flushed, knowing all too well what he meant. "Maybe she just didn't think it was any of your business.''

"Well, I'd say it's your business," he answered. "After all, you're putting the finishing touches on a roundup and you need all the men you can get out there, so I'd sure as hell find out why Jules is letting his men have free time in town when they should be working.''

"I'll talk to him about it," she answered, then stood up. "Now, I don't know about you, Mr. Morgan, but I'm in need of a cool drink. Would you care to join me?'' A few minutes later they were heading for the kitchen.

The moon had been up for almost an hour as Culler led his horse quietly across the White Wind ranch yard, talking soothingly to him all the way yet keeping his voice down. Once at the side of the veranda, he ground reined him, then looking about and searching the darkness to make sure no one was about, he stepped onto the veranda and checked the posts that held up the balcony. They were good and solid and, not being planed smooth, they were easy to climb, like trees.

He'd taken his spurs off and stuffed them into his saddlebags before reaching the ranch house, and now quietly and deftly he began to climb to the balcony. Trudy had said the safe was in the master bedroom in front, so he wouldn't have to go through the house.

Breathing deeply, he finally reached the railing around the balcony and pulled himself over the side. One glance toward the double doors Trudy said were in the master bedroom showed him they were open, and he tiptoed forward, holding his breath.

That's what he'd been afraid of. The moon was up full, and where it streamed into the room he could see Hanna Winters sound asleep in the big four-poster bed.

Flattening himself against the doorframe, he stood for a minute, trying to figure out his next step. His gaze moved from the sleeping woman to the walls of the room, then it stopped at the sight of the picture over the fireplace on the inside wall.

Well, first things first. Before he could crack the safe open, he'd have to take care of Miss Winters, and he reached down taking a knife from its sheath at his waist.

The curtains on the doors were heavy drapes with cording and very quickly he sliced through, cutting off a generous piece of the cord. This done he stepped gingerly into the quiet room, then looked about for something he could use as a gag. He could use the bandanna from around his neck, but was afraid someone might trace it to him.

Picking up a lady's petticoat off a chair, he used his knife again, cut a piece from it, then moved over to the bed. However, just as he did Hanna began to move and he hesitated again, holding his breath.

Hanna was restless. She'd been dreaming of Blake again, and arguing with him in her sleep as usual. Now, half awake and half asleep, she punched the pillow up more beneath her head and began to settle down again. Suddenly she turned her head sideways with her eyes open just enough to catch sight of a shadowy figure standing close to the bed. The figure was blocking the moonlight from coming in and she squinted.

"Blake?" she mumbled, hoping to hear an answer, but instead of hearing Blake's voice, she saw two hands shoot out. They grabbed her by the shoulders and tried to force her hands behind her. "Oh, no, you don't!" she screamed hysterically, and using all the strength she could muster, she began to fight and yell.

A hand went over her mouth and she bit into it, sinking her teeth deep.

"Damn!" Culler yelled, then tried again, only to feel her teeth sink into his arm this time.

He lashed out, his hand striking the side of her face, but the effort got him nowhere. In fact now he was getting mixed up in her covers, and still she hadn't quit yelling.

Suddenly realizing that he wasn't going to be able to subdue her, Culler let go of her as quickly as he could, just as the bedroom door opened and Elizabeth rushed in. He made a mad dash to the balcony, went over the rail and started shinnying down, almost falling onto his horse in his hurry to get away.

The last thing Elizabeth heard as she moved to the bed and grabbed Hanna in an effort to soothe and comfort her were the hoofbeats from Culler's horse as they faded into the night.

Chapter Seven

Elizabeth's hand shook as she lighted the lamp and sat down next to Hanna on the bed.

"Are you sure you're all right?" she asked.

Hanna reached up, took off her nightcap, then nodded. "I think so." She looked at Mrs. Brady. "This is ridiculous, Mrs. Brady," she said. "First they try to kill me, then they try to kidnap me. What on earth do they want?"

"I wish we knew." Elizabeth put an arm around her. "Do you think you'll be able to get back to sleep?"

"Hardly."

"How about if I go get Blake?"

"Blake? What for?"

"Well, with him in the house maybe you'd feel better. He can sleep in the bedroom where he slept the first night we were here."

Hanna shook her head. "That isn't proper and you know it."

"Proper, my foot. At this point, Hanna, who cares?" Elizabeth was tired of Hanna's firm stand on conventionality. "The important thing is that we can't let anything happen to you, and if that means having Blake move into the house, then that's what you're going to have to do.''

Hanna glanced at Mrs. Brady, knowing she was right. With Blake close by it was less likely that anyone would make another attempt to get to her.

"All right, but what do we tell him?"

"The truth." Elizabeth stood up. "He's the only one down at the bunkhouse, so I'll go get him.''

She started for the door.

"Wait!" Hanna yelled. "That man might have decided to come back. I'd better go with you." She stood up and shoved her feet into her slippers. Walking to the huge armoire on the far wall, she took out her wrapper and put it on, then began to tuck her hair into her lacy nightcap as she followed Elizabeth out the door.

The bunkhouse was some distance from the main house, and Blake stirred, opening his eyes. He'd awakened from a deep sleep minutes before, only he wasn't quite sure what had awakened him.

At first he thought he'd heard someone yell, but the sound had been so faint it was indistinguishable, and as he opened his eyes he thought maybe it was part of the dream he'd been having. Then, a few minutes later, he was certain he heard hoofbeats fading off in the distance.

Rubbing the sleep from his eyes, he shoved back the sheet that covered him and sat up, glancing out the window. The moon was still up and he figured it had to be late. Maybe two, three in the morning.

Just to make sure everything was all right, he grabbed his pants off the chair where he'd slung them, slipped into them, then took the Colt out of its holster and headed for the door.

He was almost to it when he heard strange scuffling noises coming from outside. Slowing his pace, he flattened himself against the side wall, inching slowly toward the door.

Outside Hanna and Elizabeth were hesitant.

"Maybe *you* should go in," Hanna said, her voice barely a whisper. "After all, what if he's uncovered? I wouldn't want to embarrass him."

"So why don't we just knock?"

"And scare him half to death?"

"He'll be just as scared if we sneak in and wake him up that way." Elizabeth sighed, exasperated with Hanna's worry about modesty. "All right, how about we open the door, then both of us call to him first, giving him a chance to wake up?"

"That sounds better."

Hanna reached for the door handle, turned it, started to open the door, then froze as she caught sight of the barrel of a gun in the moonlight as it came out from behind the door and Blake said, "Hold it right there."

She heard the hammer on the gun click. "Oh, my goodness!"

The door opened the rest of the way. "Hanna?" Blake couldn't believe his eyes as he gazed past Hanna. "Elizabeth?"

"For heaven's sake, don't shoot," Elizabeth cried as she and Hanna stepped away from the door.

Blake came the rest of the way outside.

"What the hell are you two doing here?" he asked.

Hanna exhaled, relieved. "We were trying to wake you up."

"Why?"

"Because someone tried to kidnap Hanna," Elizabeth explained and they told him about the horrifying experience.

"Do you know who it was?" he asked when they were finished.

Hanna shook her head. "No. But one thing I do know. The man reeked of tobacco, I could smell it. And he'd been drinking, too. I always did hate the smell of secondhand liquor."

Blake was amused at her description, but he didn't show it. "Then it could have been anybody." He stared at her curiously. "But why wake me now? It's all over with and you're both all right."

Hanna could feel herself flushing, only she knew it was too dark for him to see. "That's why we woke you. I'd like to stay in one piece, and Mrs. Brady suggested it might be best if you moved your things into the house with us. After all, it doesn't do much good to have a man on the premises for protection if he's so far away he can't even tell when he's needed. Mrs. Brady figures you can use the same room you stayed in before."

Blake stared at Hanna, the moonlight full on her face, and he felt a familiar warmth shoot through her. Even with her hair shoved into that silly lace nightcap she wore, she had a way of getting to him that he didn't like.

Still, moving into the house was just what he'd been hoping for. It would be much easier to search for the money if he had free access to the house. He wasn't quite so sure about being that close to Hanna all the time, though. After all, things had already gotten out of hand once. However, work came first, and he straightened, still staring at Hanna. "When do you want me to move in?"

"Tonight."

"You mean now?"

"I don't think Hanna will be able to sleep the rest of the night if you don't," Elizabeth said. "Nor will I."

Blake thought for a second, then shoved the gun into the front of his pants. "Just let me get some of my clothes and put my boots on."

As he turned and went into the bunkhouse the two women looked at each other, relieved.

Culler was furious the next afternoon when he rode into Hangtown. He'd reported to camp that morning herding some ten steers he'd managed to scare up out of the hills to make it look good, and Jules had sent him out again for more they might have overlooked. This time he was supposed to be up near one of the line shacks. Herding cattle, however, was the farthest thing from his mind at the moment.

He'd been smoking a cigarette as he rode along and he took the last drag off it, then tossed the butt onto the dusty street as he reined up in front of the Sundown just as he'd done the day before. This time, though, the determination on his face was all too visible.

"So, where's my money?" Trudy asked a few minutes later when he sat down next to her with his beer.

Culler's eyes darkened. "There ain't none," he answered. "And there won't be, either, unless I can figure out a way to get into that safe."

"I thought you said you could handle it?"

"Don't get smart."

"Hey look, Mr. Burris, or whatever the hell you said your name was, you promised me half of two hundred and fifty thousand and I've been lookin' forward to it, so you'd better come up with somethin'."

His gaze raked over her. "I think I have."

"What's that?"

"You any good at actin'?"

She looked at him dubiously. "How good?"

"Good enough to make the spinster from back east think you got a fractured hip, or at least a bad sprain?"

Now Trudy was really curious. "Just what are you getting at?"

For the next half hour Culler let Trudy in on the great scheme he'd thought up on the way in.

An hour after Culler rode out of town, Trudy also left, dressed in a blue poplin suit with a matching hat and driving a small buggy she'd rented at the livery stable. Her destination was the White Wind Ranch.

It was close to four o'clock when Trudy reined up in front of the veranda at the White Wind. She could feel the dust from the long buggy ride as she wiped her hand across her skirt, smoothing it, then glanced toward the house. God, she hoped Culler's idea worked. With a hundred and twenty five thousand she could get away from Hangtown for sure. Getting down, she fastened the reins to the hitching post and headed for the door.

Inside the hacienda, Hanna was just making her way down the winding stone steps to the parlor. She had changed from her riding clothes only a few minutes before, and was wearing her dark green bustled skirt and pale green blouse with the little pearl buttons. Most of her morning had been spent out on the range going over everything with Jules and making sure things were set for the start of the drive the next day. Now she was headed for the library to make sure the tally sheets were in order.

Jules told her that Pete Miles would be the trail boss this time, with José Caracas taking over if anything happened to Pete. According to Jules both men had been with Henry as long as Jules had, and Pete had been Henry's right-hand man on many a drive over the years.

During the past few days Hanna had hired three more new men to help on the drive while Blake and Culler would stay at the ranch with Jules and the other men who weren't going.

Actually there were only two hands who wouldn't be on the drive besides Blake, Culler and Jules—Maria's sons Miguel and Sancho. Jules explained to her that Hank had always kept what he called a skeleton crew at the ranch when they were away on a drive.

"You mean my brother went along, too?" Hanna had asked, and was surprised when Jules told her he'd been one of the best trail bosses in the cattle business.

When Hanna reached the bottom of the stairs she hesitated at the sound of knocking on the front door.

"Maria?"

The housekeeper didn't respond so Hanna shrugged and headed across the parlor toward the entrance hall. A few seconds later she swung the door open and stood face-to-face with the young woman she'd met some days before at the Sundown Saloon.

"Trudy...isn't it?"

Trudy swallowed hard, trying to look convincing and yet not appear too pushy.

"I hope you don't mind, Miss Winters," Trudy said. "But I've been debating whether I should come or not." She hesitated. "Do you think maybe I could come in?"

Hanna hadn't expected this and was momentarily taken off guard. "Certainly, I guess I... Yes, do come in." She opened the door wider, then watched curiously as the woman she knew only as Trudy sailed into the entrance hall and quickly hurried into the parlor.

"You wanted to see me about something?" Hanna asked once they were both standing in the parlor.

Trudy tried not to act too self-conscious. "It's about the clock," she said and walked over to the mantel where the ship's clock sat among all the other knick-knacks. "You see, I know you probably don't think too much of my relationship with your brother, but Hank and I had been together for quite a long time, and he always said to me, 'Honey, if anything ever happens to me I want you to have that clock to remember me by.' So, well, you can see..."

"In other words, you came to ask me if I'd give you the ship's clock from the mantel?"

Trudy smiled, flushing self-consciously. "I guess you could say that."

"You came all the way out here just for that?" Hanna was amazed. "Why didn't you ask me for it that day when I was in the saloon?"

"Would you have given it to me?"

"What makes you think I'll give it to you now?"

"I'm not sure you will, but I had to ask."

"You mean because of Henry?"

"That's right. When you love someone it's nice to have something to remember them by."

"And since you can't have the ranch you figure the clock'll do, right?" Hanna walked over and looked at the old clock. It had evidently come from a clipper ship of some kind and had once been bolted down in some captain's cabin. "You mean my brother never gave you anything to remember him by over the years?"

"Well, he did give me these earrings." And Trudy reached up, fingering the diamond teardrops. "But jewelry just isn't the same."

Hanna stared hard at Trudy, wondering if she were really telling the truth or not. Especially since the old clock didn't seem like the kind of keepsake a saloon doxy would care to have around.

"You're sure it's the clock you want? Not maybe one of the pictures off the wall, or some other equally ridiculous item?"

"No, ma'am," Trudy answered quite firmly. "Only the clock."

Hanna inhaled, wishing she knew just what the woman was up to. "Well, I'll tell you now," she answered. "Right at the moment I'd rather not just hand the clock over, but give me a few days to think about it and I'll let you know. Will that be all right?"

Trudy's jaw clenched stubbornly. However, she tried not to let her anger show. When she'd first decided to ask for the clock it had been just a lark, a reason for her to be here. But now suddenly the clock had become a pawn between her and this white-haired sister of Hank's who thought she was too good to associate with someone who worked in a saloon. Trudy was more determined than ever now to not only leave with the hundred and twenty-five thousand dollars, but the clock, too.

"I can't expect more than that, I guess, can I?" she finally said, hoping Hanna couldn't read between the lines. "I'll be leaving then, and if you'll just send Paco or someone to town as soon as you decide."

She turned and started back to the entrance hall, and Hanna frowned, then followed after her.

Suddenly, just as Trudy reached the hall, her foot seemed to get tangled in something Hanna couldn't see, and Trudy went sprawling through the air, twisting sideways until she came to rest on the floor and up against a boot bench in the entrance hall, her face contorted with pain.

"Oh, my God! My back!" she shrieked helplessly, and Hanna was beside her in seconds.

"Heavens, are you all right?"

"I'm not sure." Trudy forced tears to her eyes. "I feel like something's broken."

"Broken?"

At that moment both Elizabeth and Maria came rushing down the hall into the entranceway.

"Good Lord, what happened?" Elizabeth asked.

Hanna glanced up at her. "Trudy fell."

"Trudy?"

"Henry's..." Hanna cleared her throat. "Henry's lady friend."

"Oh, you mean... Oh."

"She came to see if I'd let her have Henry's ship's clock off the mantel," Hanna explained. "But I told her I'd have to think it over. Now she thinks something's broken."

Elizabeth hurried over to the other side of Trudy and reached down, hoping to help her up.

"Ah, no, please, I can't get up," Trudy wailed and both Elizabeth and Hanna exchanged glances, then Hanna turned to Maria.

"Go get Mr. Morgan and send Paco for the doctor," she said to the housekeeper, and Maria practically flew out the front door.

She was back in no time at all with Blake. Trudy was still on the floor, wailing louder than ever.

"She thinks her hip's broken," Hanna said as she caught the surprised look on Blake's face. "I thought maybe you could carry her upstairs, then Maria's going to send Paco for a doctor."

"He's gone already," Blake answered and he walked over, took a good hard look at the teary-eyed dance hall girl, then reached down and started to lift her.

"Oh! Be careful. Oh, my God, I hurt!" Trudy yelled as he jostled her about so he could get a good grip on her to cradle her in his arms. With Hanna and Elizabeth following close behind, he carried her up the winding stone steps to the bedroom where the foreman once slept, and laid her down on the big wooden bed.

Trudy lay back gingerly, pretending she was in agony as Blake released her, then straightened.

"Are you comfortable enough?" he asked.

She nodded, sniffing as if holding back tears of pain. "I guess I'm as comfortable as I can be," she murmured, then looked at Hanna. "I'm so sorry, Miss Winters. I should have been more careful."

Hanna glanced at Trudy's feet. She couldn't for the life of her think what it was the woman could have fallen over. There was a small rug in the entrance hall, but Trudy hadn't even been near it when she tripped.

"It could happen to anyone," she said, trying to ease Trudy's embarrassment some. "It'll probably take a couple of hours for Paco to get back with the doctor, though, and in the meantime if you just stay quiet."

"Oh, I intend to. Besides, I couldn't move if I wanted. It's just too painful."

Hanna and Blake exchanged glances, then Hanna turned to Maria. "I'll let you play nursemaid, Maria," she said. "Unless you want one of your daughters-in-law to."

"No...no, they're working on supper, *señorita*. I will take the lady's shoes and stockings off and see that she's made comfortable until the doctor comes. You can all go on downstairs," she said, and she shooed them away from the room.

Hanna turned to Blake when they reached the parlor. "Well, what do you think?" she asked.

"About what?"

"Come on, Blake," Elizabeth said. "Look." She gestured toward the doorway where Trudy fell. "There's nothing there for her to trip on."

"Except maybe her own feet or the hem of her dress."

Hanna wasn't convinced. "If so, then she's the clumsiest woman I've ever known." Hanna shook her head. "It just doesn't make sense."

"Well, tell me then," he said. "Why would she fake it?"

"I don't know. But something just doesn't smell right, and why would she want that clock?"

"She wants the clock?"

"That's what she said. That's why she came all the way out here."

Blake walked over, picked up the clock and gave it a good once-over. There was a date on the back, March 8, 1832, and a name below the date. The Glouchester.

"Why'd she say she wanted it?" he asked as he set it down.

"She claims Henry told her she could have it."

"Did *you* tell her she could have it?"

"Heavens, no. I'm not giving anything of Henry's away until I find out why someone's trying to get rid of me."

"You think the clock might have something to do with it?" Elizabeth asked, joining in their conversation.

Hanna shrugged. "Who knows? But it seems awfully strange that that woman upstairs would drive all the way out here at this hour of the day all alone just to ask for it."

Blake had to agree, but since none of them could think of an ulterior motive, they finally decided to let things take their course and keep their eyes and ears open to anything Trudy might say or do.

Meanwhile upstairs in the bed where Blake had deposited her, Trudy lay quietly watching the Mexican woman leave the room. Unfortunately the housekeeper didn't shut the door behind her and Trudy swore softly to herself.

Damn! Now she didn't dare get up until nighttime or until she knew everyone had left the house. Well, she could do that, too. Culler said all of them were supposed to be out on the range tomorrow morning to watch the men start out on the drive north.

Now, if she could just put up a good enough act when the doctor got here so she'd be able to stay overnight she'd have the house all to herself in the morning and the combination to the safe should be in the library somewhere.

Resting her head more comfortably on the pillow, Trudy gazed about the room while she lay back and waited.

By the time Doc Weatherby left to go back to town that evening, supper at the White Wind was over, and everyone had congregated in the parlor to bid him goodbye and thank him for coming.

Trudy was still upstairs in the bed, however. Although the doctor said he couldn't find any broken bones, he did feel it would be best to have her rest for a few days. After all, a ride back to town in her condition could make matters worse if it was a bad hip strain or a hairline fracture.

Hanna watched Blake walk the doctor to the door, then she turned to Mrs. Brady. "Why do I have the distinct feeling that something's going on we should know about?'' she asked.

Elizabeth smiled. ''After all that's happened, dear, it's a wonder you're not suspicious of everything.'' She studied Hanna for a few minutes. Hanna had changed a great deal in just the few weeks they'd been at the ranch. She'd been rather quiet and unassuming before, but now it was as if she knew her word was law and she was using it for all she was worth.

Elizabeth strolled toward the front window and stared out. Doc Weatherby was riding out, all right, but someone else was riding in, and she frowned.

''Looks like we've got company,'' she said.

Hanna walked over to stand beside her. ''My heavens, I wonder what he's doing here?''

''Who is it?''

''Mr. Terrell from the Box T Ranch. I met him one day out at the camp when he was accusing the men of rustling.''

''Rustling?'' Elizabeth looked surprised.

''Well, not really rustling, but he did say they were branding stray calves that belonged to the Box T.''

''Then I wonder what he's doing here?''

''I have no idea.''

They watched Whitney Terrell dismount, tie his horse to the hitching rail, then greet Blake. Minutes later Blake was ushering him into the parlor.

''You remember Mr. Terrell?'' he asked Hanna, then turned to Elizabeth. ''And this is Miss Winters's companion and friend, Mrs. Brady. Mr. Terrell owns a ranch nearby, Elizabeth,'' he explained to her. ''Said he had a proposition for Hanna if she'll listen.''

"I'll listen to anything," Hanna answered, "but that doesn't mean I'll act on it." Her lavender eyes were hostile. "Go right ahead, Mr. Terrell."

"First of all, I owe you an apology," Terrell said, hoping to sound friendlier than he felt inside. "I didn't mean to be so ornery the day we met, but when a man's losing cattle, he sort of takes it out on those around him."

"You said you had a proposition?"

Whit stared at Hank Winters's sister. He'd expected a mousy woman, typical spinster material, and Hanna Winters was neither mousy nor a typical spinster.

"I'd like to buy the place off you," he said and she saw his eyes darken anxiously. "I gave your brother the same offer shortly before he left on his business trip and he was going to give me an answer just as soon as he got back. Said he'd probably take me up on it, too."

"You're a liar, Mr. Terrell," Hanna said, without even taking time to think over what the man said. "My brother was alive when he got back to the ranch, and if he had any idea of selling it he would have let me know instead of leaving it to me and telling me to take care of it. So you can just take your proposition and leave."

"Well, you certainly aren't any friendlier than your brother was, are you?"

"Not when it comes to people who think I'm some ignorant woman without a brain in my head." Her chin lifted haughtily. "You should have known I wouldn't sell. If I'd wanted to sell I'd have never come out here and tried to run the place. Now, if you don't mind . . . We can be neighborly and ask you to join us for coffee and some refreshments if you'd like, but as far as selling goes, don't underestimate me, sir. I intend to make White Wind a paying ranch if it takes me the rest of my life.''

Whit Terrell's face was red with frustration, and his eyes grew cold. ''No thanks,'' he said, refusing her offer of coffee. ''I can get coffee at home, but you be mindful, Miss Winters, it takes more than wishful thinking to run a ranch this size. It takes damn hard work and I doubt you're cut out for it. Don't worry, when the time's right, you'll sell, or go to your grave wishing you had.''

''Is that a threat?''

''Take it for anything you want, but just remember, I warned you.'' Crushing his hat back on his head, he started to walk out.

Blake was going to see him to the door.

''Don't bother,'' Whit said, his jaw set angrily. ''I know the way.'' Seconds later they heard the door slam shut, and the echo of hoofbeats as Terrell rode out of the ranch yard.

''Why do you always have to make enemies?'' Blake asked Hanna as soon as the hoofbeats faded in the distance. ''First Jules, now Terrell. Keep it up and you won't have anyone in the area on your side.''

She eyed him sharply. ''I didn't know we were taking sides.''

''You know what I mean.''

''He means that if you make a bunch of enemies,'' Elizabeth said, ''no one's going to care whether someone's trying to kill you or not.''

''I know what he means.''

"Then for heaven's sake, Hanna, quit acting like you're living on an island all by yourself. You need people out in this country." Elizabeth was infuriated with Hanna's attitude. "I know you're trying to be independent, but you're carrying it to absurdity."

"Well, thank you." Hanna wasn't any too pleased. "Now, if you two don't mind I have some things to go over in the library." She headed out toward the hall.

"I wish I understood her," Elizabeth said as she watched Hanna leave the parlor. "Back in Boston she was just as easy to get along with as anyone, but ever since arriving here, it's as if she's a different person."

Blake's eyes softened. "Maybe she is."

"I don't understand."

"It's simple," he said, his dark topaz eyes lingering on the doorway Hanna had just vacated. "Back in Boston her life was all laid out for her. The same thing every day. Out here every day's different. Black can be in different shades of gray and white is never spotless. She's been forced to take inventory of herself and what she is and I have a feeling she's frightened by what she's discovered."

"You think it's that simple?"

"I do."

"Tell me," Elizabeth asked. "Do you have any idea what's behind all this nonsense that's going on?"

"Not yet," he answered. "But as soon as I know one way or another I'll let you in on it. All right?"

"I guess it'll have to be."

"In the meantime, don't be too hard on her. See if you can round out the edges and maybe she'll still have some friends yet when this is all over."

Elizabeth smiled, then excused herself and went to the kitchen.

As soon as she'd left the room, Blake walked over, stood looking at the clock on the mantel for some time, then shrugged and headed for the door to go put the buggy Trudy had used to come in over at the barn and her horse in the corral with the others so neither would be in the way.

It was late. Everyone else was asleep already, but Hanna had been unable to sleep. For one thing it was hot. Too hot.

Throwing back the covers, she sat up on the edge of the bed, then finally stood up and stretched. There was a moon again tonight, and the sky was filled with stars as she walked over and stepped out onto the balcony, then looked up, marveling at how beautiful everything was.

Earlier in the evening she'd been going over the papers the lawyer had sent when she was in Boston, taking special care to read the letter from Henry carefully a few more times, only most of it still hadn't made any sense. She thought over it now. He told her to remember the east wing of the old house.

Heavens, they hadn't played in there since their grandmother was alive, and the place had been boarded up years before Henry took off.

Actually, Hanna had been only about nine or ten when her grandmother died and they'd just quit using the east wing. It was all so puzzling. Yet Henry's letter had been very precise. She'd never have to worry about money again if she'd just remember the days they'd spent in the east wing as children. The whole thing was frustrating.

Hanna hadn't bothered to put on her wrapper, and now she straightened, sighing as she felt a slight breeze catch the sleeve of her nightdress and rustle it. She turned her head into the breeze so she could catch the coolness on her face and froze as she saw Blake standing not ten feet away, leaning against the adobe wall of the house.

He had to have been standing there when she'd first stepped out because she certainly hadn't heard the hallway door open or shut. His feet were bare, as was his chest.

"I take it you couldn't sleep, either," he said, straightening and strolling toward her.

Hanna reached up self-consciously and tried to tuck a stray hair beneath her nightcap.

"I...didn't know you were out here," she exclaimed, embarrassed at being caught in her nightgown.

He smiled. "Don't worry, I won't bite."

"If you'd just said something..."

"I'm always restless. Especially at night."

He was standing less than a foot from her, and Hanna realized that her heart was pounding unmercifully. What was it about this man that bedeviled her so? She stared into his eyes. They were warm and vibrant, the look in them far too compelling to ignore and she swallowed hard as she saw the muscles on his chest tighten.

"I'd better leave you to yourself," she said.

He frowned. "Why?"

"Why?"

"Yes, why? I know you don't want to." Blake's gaze was steady on Hanna's face and slowly he reached up and began to take off her nightcap.

"No..."

"Shh...be still." His fingers caressed her cheek, then he slipped the lacy cap from her head, letting her hair tumble like a silvery cloud about her face. "There, that's what I like."

"But...this is wrong, and you're doing it again, Mr. Morgan...you know you are."

"What am I doing?"

"You know very well."

"You mean this?" he asked, and he leaned down, his lips caressing her neck just below the ear.

Finally he drew his head up again and stared into her eyes. "Is that what you mean?" he asked.

Hanna couldn't find her voice.

"Or is this what you mean?" he whispered, and this time he began to kiss her chin, her cheeks, her eyes, his lips teasing like the wings of a butterfly as they caressed her flesh, then finally captured her mouth. The kiss was long and sweet, filled with all the hunger Blake had been holding back the past few days.

Finally he drew his head away and glanced into her languid eyes. "Is that what you meant, Hanna? Is it?" he asked, his voice barely a whisper, the warmth of his breath invading her mouth.

Hanna's knees were weak, her head spinning, and she felt as if she'd explode. He wasn't supposed to be doing this, and she wasn't supposed to be liking it, and yet he was and she was and the whole thing was insane.

"Yes, that's what I meant," she finally managed to answer, her voice husky with emotion. "You were supposed to forget."

"I know. But how can a man forget? And you haven't forgotten, have you?"

"That's beside the point."

"No, that's the whole point. Hanna, we need each other," he said, his eyes boring into hers, and he felt her shiver. "Let me love you, Hanna. Let me make you live again. Don't turn away." With one last plea he kissed her again, then drew her close in his arms, picked her up, cradling her against him and began moving toward the doors to the master bedroom.

Neither of them spoke as Blake laid her on the bed and let his hands begin their exploration. Removing the nightdress from her damp body, he followed his hands with his lips until Hanna knew there was no turning back. He slipped the pants from his body and joined her on the bed. Sweat ran slick, the heat of the night mingling with the heat of their passion, only neither of them seemed to care as Blake's hands finished their teasing and he moved over her, then entered and the feel of his entry brought her loins to meet him, hot and demanding.

Over and over again Hanna let him love her, his body taking all she could give and giving back tenfold until suddenly Hanna cried softly, stifling the cry with her mouth pressed to his damp shoulder, then she felt him shake, his mouth searching for hers in his total surrender, and she drew her lips from his flesh to kiss him back.

"Mmm," he finally murmured against her lips, his voice husky and tremulous. "That was so good."

Hanna groaned again, her body still throbbing, his lips, still sipping at hers, bringing back the reality of what she'd again let him do. She'd promised herself it wouldn't happen again. Never again.

"Oh, dear," she murmured against his mouth, and he drew his head back.

"What do you mean, oh, dear?"

"Damn it, I've done it again."

There was a touch of agony in her voice and Blake frowned. He drew his head back and stared at her. "Is that so bad?"

"Good Lord, yes. Please, Mr. Morgan. I shouldn't be doing this."

His body was still against her, the perspiration like a lubricating oil, making them fit perfectly, and he marveled at how comfortable she felt beneath him.

"Then why are you?" he asked.

She looked at him and couldn't avoid his eyes, nor could she answer. The room was dark, but he was so close she could see him well enough to know that he wasn't mocking her.

"I don't know. I shouldn't... Oh, you're just..."

"No, you're just lovely, that's all. And you're not stern and cold like you pretend to be, and I think I'm falling in love with you."

"Don't say that." She sounded like loving her was the worst thing that could happen to him. "Men like you don't fall in love, and especially not with women like me."

He laughed softly. "What do you know about men like me?"

"Enough." Hanna stared into his ruggedly hand-some face, the feel of his flesh against her more wonderful than she ever thought anything could feel, and yet... "You're a drifter, a man who doesn't like commitment."

"Your words, not mine."

"You know I'm right."

He leaned down, licked the tip of her nipple, then straightened again to look into her eyes. "What if you aren't?"

Hanna could hardly talk. "What do you mean?"

"What if I was really falling in love with you. What would you do?"

She inhaled sharply and studied him closely. How strange it was to lie here like this beneath him, his body intimately coupled with hers, his hands still caressing her tenderly, and letting him do whatever he wanted with her while they talked. It seemed so natural even though it went against everything she'd planned for herself.

"I'd tell you you were crazy," she said. He started to kiss her again. "No," she said, and turned her head so he couldn't reach her mouth. "You'd better go, Blake. I'm sorry. I shouldn't have let myself get carried away like this, please."

Blake's stomach tightened savagely. She was doing it again. Refusing to take down the barriers she'd erected years ago, and he wished he knew why.

"If that's the way you want it," he said and he lifted himself from her, then headed to the chair where he began putting on his pants. "For now, anyway. But someday, Hanna, you and I are going to come to an agreement and you're going to have to face life head-on when it comes to love, and I hope you lose, because by your losing we're both going to win.'' Turning abruptly he quietly left the room.

Hanna watched him go, her heart in turmoil. She'd been hot before, but now she was suddenly cold, the cool night breeze sweeping across her sweaty body like a frosty snow.

She reached down and pulled the sheet over her naked body, but it didn't help. She wasn't cold physically, but emotionally. All the warmth had drained from her with Blake's going and she felt as empty and alone as she had the morning Armand had walked out on her.

She shivered, feeling the pain of Blake's going in every fiber of her being, and it was agony because her body still wanted him. Yet she also felt betrayed by him. He'd torn down the walls she'd erected around her feelings and it wasn't fair.

Another shiver ran through her and she pursed her mouth stubbornly. Why did she have to feel like this? Why did she have to feel at all? Why couldn't she just go on as before and ignore what he'd done to her? Yet she knew she couldn't.

Angry with herself, yet knowing that if she was going to sleep tonight something was going to have to be done, she threw the covers back once more, sat up, then moved to the chair where her wrapper lay.

Slipping it on, she moved gracefully toward the double doors, then realized Blake was still on the balcony. He hadn't gone into his room yet.

"Blake?" she whispered.

Blake whirled, surprised to see her standing there. She looked all soft and warm from their lovemaking, and yet there was a sadness about her eyes.

"Yes?"

"I'm sorry," she said, for something more to say, and she stepped closer until she was so close she could feel the warmth of his bare chest through the sheer wrap. "But I'm cold."

"Hanna?"

"Make me warm again, please," she pleaded, her voice breathless. "Make me feel again, please. I can't freeze until morning."

He sighed. "You're sure?"

"Tonight I am, yes."

"Tomorrow?"

"I don't want to think about tomorrow. All I know is I can't let you go, not tonight, not like this."

Blake sighed again. He didn't need any more coaxing—no man would. Responding to her plea like a drowning man gulping for air, he lifted her in his arms and headed for her bed once more.

This time, when the lovemaking was over, Hanna curled up against him, her body content for the first time in years, and she fell asleep. Now it was Blake's turn to lie awake staring at the ceiling and feeling guilty because he still hadn't told her why he was here.

How could he? How could a man go about telling the woman he'd just made love to that he wasn't sure he could trust her with anything except his heart? It was hours before he finally dropped off to sleep.

Chapter Eight

Hanna stirred in the big four-poster and slowly opened her eyes. The first thing she realized was that Blake's pillow was empty beside her, and suddenly she was cold again. As cold as she'd been last night when she'd gone to the balcony and begged him to stay with her.

Raising her head, she looked about the room. Not a sign of him. She glanced toward the double doors. It wasn't light enough out to really be able to see anything. She squinted toward the old grandfather clock on the far wall. My Lord, it was almost four o'clock already, and she'd wanted to get up early so she could see the drive start.

Hurrying from the bed, she rushed to the basin on the dry sink, poured some water from the pitcher and began to wash, her thoughts half on the cattle drive, half on Blake's whereabouts. A few minutes later, Blake stuck his head in at the double doors, just as she finished dressing.

"Are you almost ready?" he asked.

She whirled. He was dressed and she marveled at how good he looked to her this morning. She finished putting on her boots and stood up.

"I thought you'd left without me."

"You think I'd do a thing like that?" He was carrying his hat. "I had to get dressed, didn't I? Couldn't ride out with just my pants on."

Hanna knew she was blushing and tried to ignore it.

"Here, let me fix your hair," he said, and as he had the night they'd slept on the range together he braided her hair for her. When he was finished he turned her to face him.

"No regrets?" he asked, his hands caressing her shoulders beneath the white shirt she had on.

"You mean about last night?"

"Uh-huh."

"No regrets," she answered, and as she did, he bent down, kissed her full on the mouth, then grabbed her hand and pulled her toward the door.

"Come on, let's go see if Elizabeth's ready. She did say she was going to go, remember?" They headed for the door that led into the hall.

Jules had told them that the men had planned to start the drive shortly after sunup so they were going to have to ride hard.

Since Elizabeth had never seen a cattle drive and hadn't even been out on the range yet, Paco was going to drive her out in the buckboard while Hanna and Blake rode alongside.

Much to their surprise Elizabeth was in the kitchen waiting for them when they got downstairs.

"I didn't know you were so eager to go," Hanna said.

Elizabeth smiled. "I wouldn't miss it for the world. Maria said it's a stirring sight to see all those cattle and men."

Hanna glanced toward the parlor. "But what about Trudy? No one'll be here with her."

"I'll be here," Maria answered. "Now, don't you worry, I'll take good care of the señorita, you'll see."

Hanna was grateful for Maria. Maria had become a friend, and she was glad. She glanced at Blake. At least she hadn't made an enemy of Maria, she thought, and she was still thinking about Maria and her family as they rode out of the ranch yard heading for camp.

Upstairs in the bedroom Jules had once called his, the big bed was empty. Trudy had climbed out of it and was standing across the hall staring out one of the back windows watching Hanna Winters, Blake Morgan and the woman called Mrs. Brady leaving the ranch, with Paco accompanying them.

A frown creased her forehead. She'd been hoping the housekeeper would go, too, but no such luck. Well, she'd have to figure out something there. At least she'd been here often enough while Hank was alive that she knew Maria pretty well.

Suddenly a noise on the stairs brought her up short and she ran across the hall and leaped into the bed just in time, and since it was barely breaking dawn she pretended to be asleep yet.

Satisfied that Trudy was still sleeping, Maria made all the other beds, then went back downstairs to wait for her to wake up.

Dust swirled like smoke from a fire as Hanna and the others sat their horses at the top of the ridge and watched the cattle begin to surge forth, their low bawling filling the air with a whirlwind of noise. Jules had joined them beside the buckboard where Elizabeth and Paco sat.

Hanna could barely see Heck's chuck wagon up ahead as he led off, Pete close behind him. Jules explained that the trail boss always rode ahead to scout the trail while the rest of the men rotated positions in the main column. There were always two at the point, keeping the leaders in line, two swing riders making sure the center of the herd stayed together, and two at the flanks, with three men bringing up the drag to take care of strays and weaklings that didn't want to keep up. A wrangler was always somewhere near the men who rode drag, keeping the extra horses they'd brought in line since there was always a chance a man could lose a horse on the trail.

Pete had made sure they had enough extra horses for each man, and now, as he waved them all forward, Hanna watched with pride. These were her cattle, her men.

"You'd think you rode every one of them down and branded them yourself, the way you're acting," Elizabeth said as she looked at Hanna.

Hanna smiled, the first smile Elizabeth remembered seeing on her face in a long time. "I almost feel as if I have. Isn't it thrilling, Mrs. Brady?"

Elizabeth smiled back. "Good Lord, she loves it."

Blake was surprised, too. He'd never have guessed that Hanna would enjoy watching a bunch of bawling steers shoving each other around in the dust and dirt.

He sat his horse for some time, watching the others enjoying the spectacle. However, as he watched there was something that kept gnawing at the back of his mind and he couldn't quite forget it. It was the fact that Trudy was at the ranch all alone and Trudy had been Hank Winters's mistress. He wondered if maybe Trudy knew more about the money than he'd figured.

Was that why she'd pretended to hurt her hip? Because he was more certain now than ever that she had been faking last night. The thought had been eating away at him all morning long and now suddenly he decided he'd better do something about it, only he didn't want Hanna to know.

He glanced over to where Hanna sat. She was completely absorbed in watching the drive. He didn't want to just ride out, yet he could see no other way. If he let her know where he was going she might want to go with him, and he couldn't have that. Hell, maybe she wouldn't even miss him, he thought. Easing Diablo back a bit, he walked him off toward the trail that led to the ranch, then with the moving cattle covering the sound of his leaving he headed toward the road as fast as he could.

He'd been gone a good ten minutes when Hanna suddenly glanced behind her.

"Did you see Mr. Morgan?" she asked Jules, who was sitting on the buckboard with Elizabeth.

He shook his head.

"Mrs. Brady? Paco?"

"*Sí*," Paco answered. "I saw him head back toward the ranch a few minutes ago."

Hanna frowned. "Now why would he do a thing like that?"

Paco shrugged. "I don't know, *señorita*."

"Well, I intend to find out," Hanna said, then looked at Mrs. Brady. "Have Paco bring you back when you're ready," she said. "I'll see you at the house." Digging Lucifer in the ribs, she took off at a gallop, heading for home.

"Well, what's that all about?" Jules asked.

Elizabeth shook her head. "I have no idea, but whatever it is, it sure seems to have upset Hanna." She was frowning as she watched Hanna disappear in the distance.

Trudy was pleased. The housekeeper had brought her some breakfast, waited until she was finished with it, talked to her for a while about Hank, then said she was going to walk over to her son's house for a short time and she'd be back later. That meant Trudy finally would have the house all to herself.

As soon as Trudy was sure Maria had left, she climbed from the bed again and tiptoed downstairs to the library, sure she'd find the combination to the safe.

After searching thoroughly for what seemed like hours, she came up empty-handed. She closed the last drawer in the desk, then her jaw set stubbornly.

The bedroom. It had to be in the bedroom, probably somewhere near the safe. Lifting the skirt of her petticoat to make sure she didn't trip for real this time, she went to the window and peeked out to see if Maria was still with her daughter-in-law. She could see the woman playing with one of her grandchildren near the door of their home, so she headed for the stairs.

The house was so quiet it was unnerving, but Trudy tried to ignore it. After passing the room where she was supposed to be lying sick abed, she hurried to the master bedroom. The door was open, the room straightened. She stood for a minute in her bare feet gazing about, trying to figure out where Hank might have hidden the combination to the safe.

There was a small writing desk on the far wall next to a grandfather clock, and she moved toward it hurriedly. After all, she had no idea how long Maria was going to be gone. Lifting the lid, she began to go through the drawers.

There were some envelopes and papers, but no combination. Disgusted and upset, she was about ready to close the drawer when her gaze rested on the first few words of the letter that lay right on top. It read, "Dear Hanna, when you read this it will mean that I am dead."

Curious, she picked it up and began reading. She was almost finished when suddenly she heard a noise behind her and whirled.

"My God, you scared me," she said, her gaze resting on Blake Morgan where he stood in the doorway.

Blake's eyes were like simmering coals, his face livid as he stared at her. She was barefoot and wearing only her petticoat and chemise, but it wasn't her attire that bothered him, it was the fact that she was standing up without any trouble at all.

"Why?" he asked simply.

She knew what he meant. "Like I told Hank's sister. I want the clock and I figured I'd stay here until she gave in and gave it to me."

"That's why you're going through her things?" He stepped the rest of the way into the room, then saw the letter in her hand. "What's that?"

She laughed halfheartedly. "Oh, this? Nothing. It's nothing at all."

She'd been folding the letter while she talked because she hadn't gotten to read it all and thought maybe Hank had told his sister about the money, and now she lifted her hand and started to tuck it into the front of her chemise.

"Oh, no, you don't!" Blake yelled, and he lunged toward her, making a grab for the letter, only Trudy anticipated it and moved sideways, then ran to the other side of the bed.

"Get your hands off me," she screamed, but he paid her no mind.

"I said, give that here," he ordered her, but she only backed farther away.

"Never," she said, her hands trying to cover the spot between her breasts where she'd deposited the letter. As he grabbed for her, trying to pull her hands away and get the letter from her, both at the same time, they fell sideways, sprawling haphazardly onto the bed.

Trudy was beneath Blake now, her eyes narrowed, voice breathless as she called him every name she could think of, then suddenly she finally stopped yelling and submitted weakly to his brute force. Glad she'd finally given in, he reached into the front of her chemise and pulled out the letter just as they were interrupted by Hanna, who had stepped into the room only moments before.

"Well," was all Hanna could say. "Of all the..."
Trudy and Blake both stared at her, their eyes wide
with surprise. "You bastard, you," Hanna finally
blurted, her eyes brimming with rage. "You dirty
skunk. You couldn't even wait for the drive to finish
getting started so you could get back to her, could
you? And I thought you cared."

Blake had expected anything but this, and now, as
he stared at Hanna, then looked at Trudy's limp body
beneath him, her clothes rumpled and her hair all
askew, his heart fell to his feet as he realized what
Hanna must be thinking.

"And on my bed, too," Hanna went on. "You two-
timing Judas. You ... you ..."

Hoping to save the situation, Blake extricated himself quickly from the dance hall girl and stood up,
hoping to try to talk some sense into Hanna. He held
the letter out for her to see, unfolding it as he did.

"Don't jump to any wrong conclusions," he said,
his face flushing at the thought of what she was
thinking. "I was only trying to get this away from her,
that's all."

Hanna stared at the paper in his hand, only she was
so upset she didn't recognize it. "That's right, try to
talk your way out of it," she said, her eyes blazing
heatedly. "Just like every other man. Well, I'll tell
you, Blake Morgan, I hired you to protect this house,
and since you've been doing that job well enough, I
won't fire you, but that's the only job you'll do from
here on in, is that understood?"

Blake stared at her, his eyes hardening. He knew
very well what she meant.

"Well, is it?" she asked, once more the prim and proper Bostonian he'd gotten to know only too well.

He straightened his clothes as he watched her, then threw his shoulders back just as stubbornly. "It's perfectly clear," he answered.

"And as for you," Hanna said, looking past him to where Trudy had finally climbed from the bed and stood staring at them both. "Get out of this house, and I mean now, and I wouldn't give you anything of Henry's if you begged for it."

"Well!" Trudy tilted her head haughtily. "Just who do you think you are?"

"I happen to be the owner of this ranch, Miss... That's right, you don't use a last name, do you? I wonder why?"

Trudy's eyes narrowed.

"Well, that's neither here nor there. The important thing is that if you don't get your things on and leave right now, I'll have you thrown out bodily whether you're dressed or not, do you understand?" Hanna's eyes showed that she meant business.

"Don't worry, I'll leave, but you haven't heard the last of this," she said. "Hank owes me and I intend to collect." Picking up the skirt of her petticoat, she walked around the bed, swept past Blake and Hanna and left the room.

"I don't suppose I could talk some sense into you," Blake said as soon as Trudy had disappeared down the hall toward her room.

"Sense? My dear Mr. Morgan, I know what I saw and believe me it would take more than just a few words to try to explain it away."

"How about this?" he said and he held the letter out to her again.

"What about it?"

"Your house guest was trying to pilfer it."

"What is it?"

"Well, why the hell don't you take it and see?"

Hanna took the paper from him, then suddenly realized what it was. "She had this?"

"It was tucked down in the front of her chemise. What else did you think I was doing with her on the bed?"

Hanna felt the warmth creep into her face. "I don't believe you."

"Then believe whatever you like." He exhaled, disgusted. He was tired of this whole damn mess and he studied her face hesitantly. Maybe now was the time to tell her. Hell, maybe it would even help. Summoning all the courage he could muster, he took another deep breath, then said, "Remember back some time ago when you asked me who I really am?"

Hanna looked at him, frowning. "You said you were a drifter."

"Well, I'm sorry, I lied."

"I told you—"

"Just shut up and listen." He straightened, his topaz eyes taking on a hardness she'd never seen before. "My name *is* Blake Morgan. That part of it's the truth. But I'm not just a drifter, I'm a special investigator for Wells Fargo and I've been on the trail of an outlaw named Whitey for years now, and I think I've finally caught up with him."

"I don't understand."

"Hanna, your brother, Henry, wasn't just a rancher, he was an outlaw with a price on his head. Four days before he died he was wounded in a stage robbery that netted him and his partner two hundred and fifty thousand dollars."

Hanna shook her head. She just couldn't believe her ears. "You can't mean that. I know Henry wasn't an ideal human being, but a robber and a thief? No, there has to be some mistake."

"There isn't."

"How can you be sure?"

"Remember when you went over his books and found money popping up where it shouldn't be?"

She nodded. "Yes."

"Every time he ended up with money that wasn't accounted for it coincided with dates I have for robberies."

"But that doesn't mean it was Henry."

Blake studied her face. Was she only pretending she didn't know, or was she really innocent of the facts? If only he knew for sure. Well, he was going to have to assume she was pretending, and the thought hurt.

"Your brother got away with two hundred and fifty thousand dollars, Hanna, and my orders are to find that money."

"So that's why you were so available back in Fort Worth. And that's why you... That night when I got lost, and last night..."

He started to walk toward her, but she stepped back.

"Don't come near me, Blake Morgan," she said and her voice quavered unsteadily. "Just like my father and Armand, you're no different... You used me."

Her head lifted haughtily, her lavender eyes intense. "Well, it'll be the last time, I assure you."

"Hanna, I didn't."

"You did." She lifted her hands, covering her ears. "I don't want to hear it. I don't want to listen to any excuses."

Blake was prepared to argue the point, but as he stared at her, he realized it would probably be better to give her some time.

"I'll pack my things," he said and he turned, starting to head for the double doors. She pulled her hands from her ears and stopped him.

"Just where the hell do you think you're going?" she shot out, her voice harsh and caustic. "I haven't fired you yet, Mr. Morgan, so don't think you're going to get away that easily. I won't listen to any excuses from you, but I'm not firing you, either. So, if you're really who you say you are, you'll remember I hired you to find out who's trying to kill me, and you haven't found out yet, have you?"

"You know damn well I haven't."

"Then I suggest you do so before they succeed. Now, if you'll excuse me, I'm going to make sure that little tramp is gone." She turned and left the room.

Blake stared after her, a puzzled look on his face. He wondered if she was more upset over what she thought he'd been doing with Trudy, or the truth about her brother? Well, there was really no way for him to find out, not without the money, anyway. Taking the cue from her, he left the room, heading down the hall. He heard hoofbeats in the distance and figured Elizabeth and the others were coming back.

Maybe I should have told her about Culler, he thought, as he went by the bedroom where Trudy had been and saw it was empty. Then he shrugged. Hell, she probably wouldn't have believed him, anyway, and hitching his gun belt more comfortably onto his hip, he started down the winding stone steps toward the parlor.

Trudy was furious as she left the livery stable and headed for the Sundown Saloon. Not only didn't she have any money, but she'd been made to feel like a no-good tramp. Well, Miss High and Mighty would pay for that one, too.

Stepping into the saloon, she was just ready to tell the bartender to pour her a drink when she was brought up short by Culler's voice behind her.

"I see you came back empty-handed."

She whirled around. "Good Lord, do you have to sneak up on a person like that?"

"What happened?" he asked.

She snorted derisively. "Blake Morgan happened, that's who. Who the devil is he anyway?"

Culler frowned. "Far as I know he's a drifter."

"To hell he is. No drifter handles himself like Morgan. You sure you don't know anything about him?"

"No more than you."

"And that's another thing. Maria said someone's been trying to kill Hank's sister, and the other night when you tried to tie her up so you could get to the safe they thought you were the same fella who's been trying to get rid of her."

"You're kidding."

"Nope. Only that still doesn't help us. One way or another we've got to get into that house."

"We could kidnap the lady."

"How would that help?"

"Well—" and Culler smiled. "We could hold her until they turn over the money."

"And what if they don't know where the money is?"

"Then we tell them. Either way we can't miss."

Trudy stared at him, running the thought over in her head. Half of a quarter of a million dollars was worth taking the chance for, and yet... What if it didn't work? Oh, hell, she'd just have to take off again, that's all. Just like she did in St. Louis.

"All right, so how do we kidnap her?" she asked, and for the next couple of hours they retired to her room and went over their plans carefully.

Meanwhile out at the Box T two other people were talking over not the kidnapping of Hanna Winters, but something just as serious.

Whitney Terrell downed the contents of the glass of whiskey in his hand, his eyes already bloodshot from drinking.

"Damn the woman," he said, the scar on his cheek vivid in the late morning light. "She's got a charmed life."

Milton Gibbs sneered. "You should have followed her that day and finished her off."

Whit shook his head. "You know I ain't no good at trackin'. If I'd had Steele with me she'd have never gotten away."

Milt stood up from the big easy chair where he'd been sitting and strolled to the window.

"All right, now, look," he said, and he turned to face Terrell. "I told you I'd get her out here, now it's up to you. If you really want that land as bad as you say you do, you shouldn't be letting a few little setbacks get in your way."

"That's the trouble," Terrell said, his eyes studying the lawyer from Hangtown. "They ain't just little setbacks. She shoulda been dead weeks ago, but instead she's sittin' there just as big as life tellin' everybody she's running the place."

"And whose fault is that?"

"Okay, okay, so what do I do now?"

"Maybe since killing her hasn't seemed to work, you can coerce her into selling you the place."

"How's that?"

"She thinks a lot of that old lady she brought with her, right? So you kidnap the old lady, then tell Hanna Winters you'll kill the woman unless she sells."

"But that wouldn't be legal, would it?"

"Long as her signature's on the bill of sale it'd be legal and it'd be her word against yours if she tried to complain about it."

"I don't know." Terrell poured himself another drink as he looked about the parlor of his modest ranch house.

The Box T couldn't compare to the White Wind either in size or structure. Terrell had been here almost twelve years already and owned five thousand acres, but his dream had always been to make the place bigger by acquiring the White Wind. However, Señora de Vera had refused to sell it to him when her husband passed away, preferring to sell it to Winters instead, and Winters had been stubbornly refusing all offers since.

With his sister dead, though, it would have been easy to buy out the estate, and for a fraction of the price, too. Only Hanna Winters wasn't dead, and now he thought over the alternative Gibbs had just mentioned.

"All right, it just might work, at that," Terrell said, his hand clutching the refilled glass firmly. "I'll call in the men." Downing the whiskey he'd just poured, he headed for the door.

Elizabeth stood on the veranda and adjusted the small straw hat on her head. "Are you sure you don't want anything special from town?" she asked Hanna for the tenth time.

Hanna smiled. "Only the supplies I asked you to get."

"Not even a piece of licorice or hard candy?"

"All right, all right." Hanna remembered how she used to go to the museum on Saturday afternoons, then stop on the way home and buy a small box of hard candies that always lasted until the next Saturday. "But only a small amount, if they have any."

Elizabeth grinned. "I knew you'd give in. You always were partial to those little peppermint ones."

Hanna sighed. Mrs. Brady knew her only too well. "Just go so you'll get back at a decent hour," she said. "And tell Paco to drive slow, we don't need any more problems."

She watched Elizabeth head for the barn where Paco was hitching the team to the buckboard. Maria had added some of her own supplies to what Paco had brought out from town for the drive and now they had to be replenished.

Since Elizabeth had been wanting to get some things in town anyway, it was decided she'd go this time instead of Sancho's wife, Dolores.

Hanna continued to watch as Paco helped Mrs. Brady onto the buckboard and the wagon rumbled out the gates. Blake was off somewhere, she didn't much care where. She'd seen him ride away shortly after sunup, heading in the direction of town, and Jules had taken Miguel, Sancho and Culler with him to check on the line shacks and watering holes. Something he'd been neglecting to do during the roundup.

Hanna was glad no one was around except Maria and her daughter-in-law. Ever since Blake had told her of his suspicions about Henry, she'd been running the whole thing over in her head and coming up without any answers. Was that why he wrote in the letter that she'd never have to worry about money again? Because he had two hundred and fifty thousand dollars hidden somewhere on the ranch?

Was that what the little tramp from the saloon had been after? Maybe Henry had confided in her sometime over the years. Hanna had to find the answers, and there was only one place to start.

As soon as the buckboard was out of sight, she turned, went into the house and headed for the library.

An hour later, Hanna still didn't have any kind of definite proof, but her suspicions had grown considerably. According to Henry's books, whenever things got really bad and it looked like the ranch would go under, miraculously the bills were suddenly paid, and things went all right again.

Could Blake have been right? Hanna closed the ledger she'd been looking through, then leaned back in the chair. Blake said the outlaw had been known as Whitey, and Henry's hair had been white since he'd been in his early twenties, just like hers. And Maria said Henry had taken all those business trips.... Even Jules had verified that. But Henry? The thought was shocking, to say the least.

Of course, her father often used to tell them about how one of his ancestors had been a pirate years before. Maybe Henry had inherited his wild ways. She set the ledger aside just as Maria stuck her head in from the hallway.

"Excuse me, *señorita,* but Señor Culler wants to see you out back," she said, surprising Hanna.

"I thought he went with Jules."

"*Sí,* but he say you have to come. I guess something happened."

"Good heavens, what now?"

Hanna stood up, left the desk and headed toward the kitchen.

"What is it? What's the matter?" she asked as she confronted Culler at the back door.

The man shook his head. "Don't ask me, ma'am," he answered. "All's I know is the foreman said to come get you and said it was important. Said he's got somethin' to show you."

Hanna stared at him for a few minutes, then frowned. "You'll have to wait till I change first. I assume he's still out on the range somewhere?"

"Yes, ma'am, but I can lead you right to him."

"Fix Mr. Culler a cup of coffee while I change, Maria," Hanna said. "I'll be right down." She left Culler in the kitchen while she went upstairs to get into her riding clothes.

Some ten minutes later Maria stood at the open door of the kitchen and watched them ride off.

Big billowy clouds rolled across the deep blue sky and somewhere toward the side of the road a mockingbird could be heard. Paco clicked to the team, keeping them at a steady pace.

Elizabeth was humming softly. She and Paco were almost talked out already and there was still about an hour yet before they'd reach town.

They were riding along a stretch of road that went right through a copse of trees and Elizabeth glanced about, still marveling at the diversity of the land.

Boston was Boston. The countryside never changed. You were either at the seashore or inland, but it was all the same. Not here. Here the land changed from one mile to the next and one never got bored with the landscape. She was so glad she'd come with Hanna.

Suddenly she saw some riders emerging from the trees up ahead.

"Paco!"

"Shh, *señora,*" he said, his eyes steady on the road. "Don't say anything because I think we are about to be held up."

"Oh, my God!"

Elizabeth's stomach was twisting nervously as six riders, bandannas pulled up over their faces and guns drawn, cantered toward them. Paco didn't even have a chance to make a run for it.

"Hold it right there," one of the men said even though Paco was already bringing the team to a halt.

Paco's eyes narrowed. "We don't have no money, *señors*," he said. "It just the two of us and we're broke."

"Tell the old lady to get down," the man ordered.

Elizabeth fumed. "Who are you calling an old lady?"

"Shut up and get down," he repeated.

Elizabeth stared at him.

He rode his horse a little closer, then leveled his gun right at her.

"I said get down."

This time Elizabeth wasn't about to argue. With Paco's help she started to climb down. As soon as she was on the ground the man who'd told her to get down and who seemed to be the leader rode his horse next to her. Keeping the gun in his right hand, he slipped his foot from the stirrup.

"Put your foot in there and give me your hand," he said, motioning toward the empty stirrup.

"You mean you want me to get up on there?" Elizabeth looked at the horse.

"That's right, lady."

"Well, I won't."

"You will or I'll put a bullet between your eyes."

"Go right ahead," Elizabeth said. "It'd be better than riding up there with you."

"All right," the bandit answered, his hard cold eyes intent on her face. "If that's the way you want it, I'll put the bullet between the boy's eyes instead then." He turned his gun on Paco, who was still sitting on the seat wishing he could do something.

Elizabeth knew she was beaten. The man just might do it, and she couldn't have that on her conscience.

"All right, you win," she said.

She lifted her hand, put a foot in the stirrup and let him pull her up. She landed sitting sideways in front of him.

"Now, sit still," he said, and his arm went about her, holding her close. He motioned for the other men. "Let's go," he said as Paco watched, flabbergasted, unable to shoot for fear of what they might do to Elizabeth.

"Hey, wait, *señors*, why do you do this thing?" Paco yelled and the man holding Elizabeth reined up for a second and turned to face him, pushing the straw hat on Elizabeth's head away from his face so he could see better.

"Tell your boss she'll be hearing from us," he yelled, and before Paco could ask anything else they rode off, leaving him sitting in the middle of the road still holding the reins not knowing quite what to do.

Finally, getting over the shock and realizing he had to do something, Paco slapped the reins angrily, maneuvered the wagon around in the road, and headed back for the ranch at full speed leaving a trail of dust in his wake.

Hanna was getting leery. She and Culler had been riding for well over half an hour already and she was sure all they'd done was circle around, except for the trail they were heading up now.

They hadn't been on this trail before, and she could see a line shack ahead nestled at the side of a hill, half-hidden by some trees.

"Is that where we're headed?" she asked.

He nodded, then took a pocket watch out of his pocket and checked the time.

"Is something the matter?"

He shook his head. "Nope, just wanted to see how long it took."

The trail up to the cabin was a narrow one and he motioned for her to lead the way.

"Where's Jules? And where are their horses?" she asked as they neared the place and she realized there didn't seem to be a soul around.

"Just keep on goin'," Culler said from behind her, and this time Hanna turned and found herself staring into the barrel of the man's Colt aimed right at her.

She reined Lucifer to a halt and stared at Culler.

"Just what on earth do you think you're doing?" she asked.

He sneered. "What does it look like? Now keep moving."

"You'll regret this."

"I said keep moving."

Hanna looked into his eyes and suddenly felt a shiver run through her. The man was serious. Gently digging Lucifer in the ribs, she moved forward. Then, as she reached the front of the small cabin, the door suddenly opened and Trudy stepped out.

At first Hanna didn't recognize her because she was wearing men's clothes, and no makeup and had her hair down and tied back in a queue. But the face was undeniably Trudy's.

"You, too?" Hanna remarked as she pulled back on Lucifer's reins. "I might've known you'd hire someone to get what you want. It's the money, right?"

Trudy was surprised. "You know about the money?"

"I didn't yesterday, I do now."

"Well, well, then we won't have to explain, will we?" Trudy looked at Culler, who was still holding his gun on Hanna. "You're sure now that you weren't followed?" she asked.

"Positive." He addressed Hanna. "Now, get down."

Hanna just stared at him.

"I can put this bullet right where I want it, Miss High and Mighty," he said. "And that means I can cripple you, I don't have to kill you. So, like I said, get down."

Hanna knew better than to argue. Grabbing the saddle horn, she hefted her weight sideways and slid from Lucifer's back.

"Now, get inside," Culler told her as he, too, dismounted. With Trudy holding the door for her, Hanna walked into the place. It was one of the line shacks, all right, and she assumed Jules had been here, checked it out for supplies and gone already.

"I thought you were with Jules," she said as Culler and Trudy followed her inside.

Culler grinned. "I was, only I asked him if I could run an errand in town and he said yes." His grin hardened. "Now, all I got to do is figure out how to get word to everybody that you ain't comin' home and why."

"I don't understand."

Trudy stepped up, confronting her. "What don't you understand? It's simple, Miss Hoity-toity. Your brother brought two hundred and fifty thousand dollars back with him on his last supposed business trip, and we intend to have it."

Hanna frowned. "Then you knew about Henry?"

"I didn't, Culler here did. Fact is, he was his partner."

Hanna looked hard at Culler. "You knew my brother?"

"I knew a man named Whitey."

"But that doesn't mean he was my brother."

"Oh, he was your brother, all right." While Culler talked, he walked over, picked up a length of rope and began to tie Hanna's hands behind her back. "I've been trackin' him since March when we pulled the job, then had to split up."

"But that doesn't mean it was Henry."

"You want proof, the little lady here can give you proof. About five years ago Whitey and I robbed a stage up near Denver. Had a nice big payroll on it, but there was also an old lady on her way to meet her husband and she was wearin' enough jewelry to choke a horse. Even had a box of it in her trunk. Well, Whitey and I split the jewelry and I sold mine over the years, but he gave it to Trudy here. I recognized those earrings she was wearin' the minute I spotted her in the saloon 'cause I wanted them earrings, only he won out when we drew cards for 'em."

Hanna couldn't believe what she was hearing. Actually, she didn't want to believe it because that meant Blake had been telling the truth, at least part of the time.

"But why take me?" she asked.

"Because you're going to be our way of getting our hands on that money," he answered as he knotted the ropes tight, then sat her down and tied her to the chair.

He looked at Trudy. "You know how to write?"

"A little."

"Good. 'Cause you're gonna write the ransom note."

While Hanna watched, the two of them sat at the table and with Culler dictating, Trudy wrote out a note demanding the two hundred and fifty thousand for Hanna's return. It wasn't very nice, but it would be effective.

"But how do we get it to them?" Trudy asked as she finished.

That's one part of it Culler hadn't thought of.

"I'm not going to take it," she went on. "It'd be just my luck that old lady'd try to shoot me."

"Let me think," he said.

The room was quiet and Hanna watched them anxiously. Maybe they'd give up on the whole idea.

"I know," Culler finally said. "I'll go back to the house, wait till I can catch that Mexican housekeeper alone and give it to her. She won't dare do nothin' except give it to that old lady or even Morgan. Then I'll come back here and give them time to think it over." Straightening arrogantly, he walked out the door carrying the note with him while Hanna watched in dismay.

Chapter Nine

Blake was upset. Trudy hadn't been in town and no one seemed to know where she was. He was sure she'd known about Hank Winters, and he was also sure she could have told him something about where the money was hidden if Hanna hadn't made her leave.

He should have followed her right then and there, but he felt bad enough that Hanna thought there had been something between them. If he'd followed Trudy to town he'd never have been able to convince Hanna that he wasn't having an affair with the saloon girl.

Damn, where could she be? He reined up at the door to the hacienda, wondering what the buckboard was doing here. As far as he could remember, Paco and Elizabeth were supposed to be in town today. He'd been surprised when he hadn't run into them while he'd been looking for Trudy.

He glanced toward the door, then dismounted quickly as Paco ran out, yelling something in Spanish.

"Hey, slow down, boy," Blake said, and he caught Paco by the shoulders. "What is it? What's the matter?"

Paco was never so glad to see anyone before in his whole life.

"They have Señora Brady," he cried, his face mirroring his fear.

"They who?" Blake was at a loss.

"I don't know who, but some masked men stopped us on the way to town." He told Blake everything that had happened.

When he was through, Blake frowned. "But why would anyone kidnap Elizabeth? It doesn't make sense."

"They said the señorita would be hearing from them."

"Hanna?"

"*Sí.*"

"Where is she?"

"That's just it, Señor Morgan, she is not here, either. Abuelita said Señor Culler came and told her Señor Jules wanted her out on the range and she rode off with him."

"She left with Culler?" Blake swore. "Damn." He should have told her about Culler, but then maybe Jules really had wanted her.

He tensed as he heard riders approaching the back of the house.

"Come on, Paco, let's see if that's Hanna getting back." But when they made their way around back it was to see Jules, Sancho and Miguel riding in. Neither Hanna nor Culler were with them.

"Where's Hanna?" Blake asked.

Jules reined his chestnut up to the hitching rail and got down. "What do you mean, where's Hanna? The lady's here, ain't she?"

Blake's worst fears were starting to take root. "Maria said she took off with Culler well over an hour ago."

"Culler told me he had business in town and asked if he could take the rest of the day off. Said you wanted him to run an errand for you."

"Something's wrong, dead wrong."

Blake decided it was finally time he took a chance and confided in Jules.

"There's something you should know, Jules," he said, hoping the foreman would understand, and he quickly told him not only who he was, but why he was there.

"You mean you think Hank was this Whitey fella?" Jules was flabbergasted.

"Don't tell me you never suspected?" Blake eyed him curiously. "Where'd you think he got the money he always showed up with?"

"Oh, hell, Hank was a gambler. He could turn a card slick as the best of them and he'd always hinted that he got lucky in a poker game. Who was I to question it? But an outlaw?"

"Trudy's the proof," Blake replied. "And Culler, too. A lady on the last stage they robbed described Culler right down to the fancy braid on his hat."

Jules shook his head. "If that don't beat all. No wonder Hank never wanted me to learn the books."

"You'd have gotten suspicious." Blake looked around, his gaze lifting toward the riverbank near the hills. "But right now we got problems," he said, and he told Jules about Elizabeth, too.

The man's face grew livid. "What the hell!" he shouted. "Why the devil would anyone kidnap her?"

Blake wished he had an answer. "If I knew that it might help. But at least we know where to start looking." He frowned. "I thought if we try to track them from where she and Paco were waylaid we might be able to locate her."

"Go get your horse, Paco," Jules ordered him, anger firing him on. "And you, too, Morgan." His eyes darkened ominously. "If they hurt even one hair on that little lady's head there's gonna be hell to pay, you can be sure of that." He mounted again, yelling for Paco to hurry while he followed Blake around to the front of the house.

A few minutes later the three of them, with Miguel and Sancho following close at their heels, rode out the front gate at White Wind, hoping to find some trace of Elizabeth, while back beyond the river Culler was riding down out of the hills, confident he was going to end up a rich man before nightfall.

Elizabeth stared at the man who sat opposite her in the old house. At first she'd had no idea what was going on or where she was being taken, but as time passed and she'd listened to the men talk, things had suddenly started to fall into place.

The man who'd held the gun on her and made her ride his horse was the same man who'd tried to kill Hanna on the long trip from Fort Worth, she was sure of it. Not only did he fit the description, but he liked to run off at the mouth, too, and from some of the things he said it was easy to pinpoint him as the culprit.

However, it wasn't until they rode into the ranch yard at the Box T that Elizabeth realized who was behind it all. Now she sat on the sofa in the parlor, her eyes fixed on Whitney Terrell as if he were Satan himself.

"You know you'll never get away with this, don't you?" she said, hoping her voice sounded more convincing to him than it did to her.

He smiled. "And why won't I?"

"Because Blake Morgan won't let you."

"A drifter like him? Hey, my men are just as good with their guns. Only it won't come to that, I assure you."

Elizabeth reached up, adjusted her hat, then smoothed the skirt on her pink calico dress. A dress she'd made special since her arrival, so she didn't look so out of place in her trim Boston clothes.

"Just what are your plans?" she asked.

"Well, I'll tell you now, Mrs. Brady. That is your name, right? Anyway, the point is that I'm going to give Hanna Winters exactly one day and no more to sell the White Wind to me, lock, stock and barrel, including the cattle that are on their way to Kansas."

"And if she doesn't you'll kill me?"

His eyes narrowed. "You catch on quickly."

"But that's illegal." Elizabeth shook her head. "No court in the world would allow something like that."

"Out here, my dear lady, the only court is the law of the land and once Miss Winters's name is on a bill of sale it'd be just my word against hers, and with the family lawyer on my side."

"How much are you paying him?"

Whit studied the Brady woman closely. Milt said she'd been Hanna Winters's housekeeper before coming west with her, but it was obvious the woman wasn't stupid. In fact, she was even rather attractive for her age, but then, that was something he couldn't think about. Not now, anyway.

"I'm paying Gibbs enough," he answered and she looked puzzled.

"You mean you'd actually kill me?"

He was sipping at a glass of wine and she saw his eyes narrow. "Why not? You don't mean anything to me."

"But I'm a human being."

"So?"

It was incredible. The man was infuriating. No wonder Hanna had treated him the way she had that night he'd come calling. Hanna always did seem to have an uncanny way of judging people that was rarely wrong. Although she'd been wrong about Jules, that's for sure. Suddenly Elizabeth thought about Jules and the others and what they must be thinking, and if they even knew. If only she could get away.

She stood up.

"What do you think you're doing?" Whit asked.

She straightened. "I was hoping maybe you'd come to your senses and realize that you can't do this."

"Can't?" He set the glass of wine down, rose from the chair where he was sitting and called for one of his men.

"Yeah, boss?" Steele said as he looked in at the door. Steele was the man who'd brought her here.

"I'm afraid we're going to have to tie her up, Steele," Whit said. "I don't think she's going to be any too cooperative." Just at that moment, Elizabeth made a bolt for a side door that opened onto a porch out front, only the man named Steele caught her before she got there.

She stared into his wizened face, seeing the small mustache just as the handyman back in Hubbard Creek had described him. As he held her in a viselike grip, then began tying a rope around her wrists, Elizabeth knew that Whitney Terrell would do just as he said unless Hanna complied. A fear like none she'd ever known before suddenly flooded Elizabeth and for the first time since leaving Boston she suddenly wished she hadn't come to Texas.

Blake was restless as he studied the ground and kept the others back so he could pick up the trail. Paco said there'd been six of them, and that meant they should have left enough tracks.

Suddenly his eyes narrowed as they fixed steadfastly on the distinct hoofprints of six shod horses.

"Over here," he called, and with Blake leading the way, the five of them took off. However, they didn't go far. Unfortunately some half hour onto the trail a number of cattle had wandered across the area, and Blake lost the trail. Angry and disappointed when he couldn't find it again, they headed to the ranch to see if someone would get in touch with them.

Fortunately, they didn't have long to wait because as they rode in they were met at the door by Maria who was shouting in both Spanish and English, all at the same time, so excited she was almost hysterical.

"Now calm down, Maria," Blake said as he dismounted and led her into the parlor. "One word at a time, tell us what happened."

Maria rolled her eyes. "First of all, *señor,* the man named Culler was here and said to give you this." She handed him a note.

Blake frowned, then read it and his jaws tightened angrily.

"What is it?" Jules asked.

He inhaled. "Culler's holding Hanna until we give him the two hundred and fifty thousand dollars Hank stole as a ransom."

"You're not serious?"

"Dead serious."

"But you don't even know where it is, do you?"

"The note said it's in a safe behind a picture upstairs in the master bedroom. Come on." They all hurried up to Hanna's room where Blake stood staring at the picture of the ship named the *Glouchester.*

Reaching out, Blake took it down and they all gasped at the sight of the safe.

"But how do we open it?" Jules said. "None of us knew it was even there."

Blake stared at the safe curiously, then glanced at the picture in his hands, and suddenly he remembered something.

"Hey, wait a minute," he said, trying to think. "The clock."

Jules frowned. "What do you mean, the clock?"

Blake looked at Paco. "Get me the clock off the mantel, and hurry," he said.

Paco left and was back in minutes holding the clock out to Blake, who set the picture of the ship aside, then took the clock from him, turned it around and checked the back.

"March 8, 1832. They didn't even have clipper ships in 1832," he said. "And this is a picture of the *Glouchester*, and it says Glouchester on the back of the clock."

Reaching up, he began to work on the safe. "Three to the left," he murmured hurriedly, as his fingers moved nervously on the dial. "To eight, then one to the right to eight, then three to the left to two, and there." As he finished the last turn, the safe gave a click and he swung the door open.

To their surprise it was almost empty. All that was in it were a few assorted papers, a couple of pieces of jewelry and a great deal of dust, but no two hundred and fifty thousand dollars.

"Oh, great," Morgan said, his gaze sifting over the stuff. "We still don't know where the money is."

"But that's not all," Maria cut in, anxious to get the rest of it off her chest. "Another man, he came and he gave me this." She handed Blake another note.

This time after reading it he handed it to Jules who read it apprehensively.

"But damn it, we can't have Hanna sign a bill of sale when Hanna ain't here," Jules blustered furiously. "What the hell does Terrell think he's doing?"

"Don't you see?" Blake said, his thoughts running rampant as he tried to think of a way out. "Whoever has Hanna knows nothing about what happened to Elizabeth, and vice versa, and we're at a stalemate. We can't ransom Hanna because we still don't know where the money is, and we can't have Hanna sell to Terrell so he'll release Elizabeth because we don't know where Hanna is."

"Madre de Dios!" Maria said, shaking her head. "Then what will you do, *señors?"* she asked.

Jules straightened, his gaze going to the double doors where the shadows of night were starting to fall.

"I guess we're gonna have to take matters into our own hands, won't we, Morgan," he said, hefting his gun belt confidently. "After all, there are five of us and we're all pretty good shots."

"No," Blake said as he looked about the room. "Paco doesn't go. I want him to stay here in case Culler comes back so he can track him to where Hanna is. First we go after Elizabeth." Not even bothering to take time to eat, Jules, Sancho, Blake and Miguel left the ranch yard on horseback, their guns loaded as they headed cross-country for the Box T.

It was dark already as the four riders approached the Box T and Blake reined in, the others following suit.

"You know your way around?" he asked Jules.

Jules nodded. "I been here before."

"Good, then I'll let you lead the way in."

Seconds later they were off their horses and approaching the place on foot, leading their horses behind them.

Evidently Terrell kept a skeleton crew home during the cattle drives, too, Blake thought as he realized the place looked deserted. Blake knew he probably should have gone right to the sheriff, but since the sheriff knew who he really was already and had promised to keep mum about it, he no doubt wouldn't have too much trouble convincing him later that they had a reason for being here in case the lead started to fly.

Inside the house Elizabeth was furious. Not only had they tied her wrists, but her ankles, too, and they'd only untied them once when they'd accompanied her to the outhouse, then tied her back up again. They had moved her from the parlor to a pantry at the back of the house off the kitchen. She had lost her hat somewhere in the process, but that didn't seem to matter anymore.

The supper they'd given her hadn't been enough to keep an insect alive, let alone a woman, and it had smelled terrible. It had been a small bowl of chicken soup with some rice in it, but Elizabeth swore it had probably sat around in the heat for a day or two.

She shuddered at the thought that these men really meant what they said, and she wondered if she'd ever see Hanna again.

Outside, Blake looked at Jules. "I want you and the others to stay put," he said, his eyes narrowing in the darkness so he could see better. "I'm going to go on in and talk to Terrell."

"Talk to him?"

"That's right, talk. In the first place we have to see just how serious he is about what he's doing, and secondly maybe I can find out where they're holding her because I doubt they're serving her tea and crumpets."

Jules knew Morgan was right, and yet he didn't like it. He'd known for years that Terrell had been trying to get White Wind away from Hank, and Terrell had almost succeeded when he'd burned down the line shack with Hank in it last winter. Hank had gotten out alive, but they hadn't had enough proof Terrell was the one who started the fire so they hadn't been able to do anything about it. But this! And putting Elizabeth's life in jeopardy. Hell, she was exasperating at times, making him take off his hat when he came into the parlor, but at least she made a man feel like he was something special, and his jaw clenched angrily at the thought of what she was going through.

"All right. We'll wait for you here," he said. "But if I hear any gunplay I'm comin' the rest of the way in, and fast."

"You do that," Blake answered. Seconds later he was on his horse, leaving the others behind in the shadows near some of the outbuildings while he rode in alone to feel out Terrell and give the place the once-over.

He was some thirty feet from the front porch when a voice stopped him.

"You on the horse. That's as far as you go."

Blake reined Diablo to a halt. "I came because of the note," he yelled.

Now he could see the man who belonged to the voice. He was sitting on a chair on the porch, a rifle across his lap, silhouetted by the dim light coming from the window behind him.

"You stay right there," the man said, and Blake saw him ease out of the chair and go to the door. He stuck his head inside, said something Blake couldn't hear and a few minutes later, Whitney Terrell stepped onto the porch.

"Where's Miss Winters?" Terrell asked, his eyes scanning the empty darkness behind Morgan.

"The lady can't come."

"The hell she can't."

"We have to talk, Terrell," Blake said. "And I'd rather do it inside, unless you got some objections."

"Ain't nothin' to talk about. She read the note, that's all there is to it. I got the bill of sale all made out. Hell, it ain't like I'm takin' the place for nothin', she'll get money for it, all nice and legal like."

"You aren't takin' the place at all because Hanna Winters isn't there to sell it to you."

"What the devil you talkin' about?"

Terrell didn't like it, but he nodded reluctantly and Blake rode the rest of the way in.

A few minutes later as they stood in the parlor and Blake finished telling Terrell the predicament they were in, the man only laughed.

"You expect me to believe that?"

Blake was disgusted. "Whether you like it or not, it's the truth."

"Hey, look, Blake, or whatever your real name is, if you think I'm gonna believe Hank Winters was an outlaw named Whitey, you're sadly mistaken. That's about the dumbest excuse I've ever heard of." His eyes darkened, the scar on his cheek showing white in the flickering lights of the parlor. "Now, I'll give you until tomorrow morning and that's all. You bring Hanna Winters over here to sign those papers or her old landlady just disappears, is that understood?"

"How do I know she hasn't disappeared already?"

Terrell stared hard at Morgan for a minute, then looked at Steele, who'd ushered Blake in. "Go get the lady," he ordered him.

Elizabeth was hot and sweaty. The pantry was worse than any place she'd imagined. They'd just thrown her in here unceremoniously and she'd landed on a stack of burlap bags that smelled stale and musty. And she was thirsty, too.

It seemed like she'd been here forever. Leaning her head against the wall, she was just about ready to let out a yell to see if maybe somebody'd come and give her a drink, when the door opened and the man she knew only as Steele came in.

"Come on, lady, the boss wants you out front," he said, and he reached down, untied her ankles, then pulled her to her feet and began shoving her toward the door.

Elizabeth's legs were stiff from being in one position so long and she struggled to stand as straight as she could.

"You'll pay for this, you'll see," she said as he pushed her through the door and down the hall.

Suddenly she stopped and stared into the parlor, her gaze coming to rest on Blake.

"Thank God, Blake," she murmured half to the man pushing her, half to herself, only the minute she saw Blake's face she knew something was wrong.

"I'm sorry, Elizabeth," Blake said and he glanced to where another of Terrell's men was standing guard near the door with a gun. "But I'm afraid I haven't exactly come to rescue you. I just wanted to make sure you're safe until we can figure out what to do."

"Where's Hanna?" Elizabeth asked trying not to let Terrell see that her predicament was bothering her.

Blake looked disgruntled. "That's just the trouble, we don't know."

Terrell laughed. "He wants me to swallow some cock-and-bull story about Hank having been an outlaw, and a bunch of stolen money, said your lady friend's been kidnapped, too, don't that beat all?''

Elizabeth frowned, her dark eyes steady on Blake. ''What's he talking about?''

Blake had been studying Elizabeth since she'd come into the room. She looked tired and worn, the dirt and sweat putting years onto her already advanced age, and yet her eyes were sparking vibrantly. It was going to take more than Terrell's threats to do Elizabeth in. Yet he could tell the past few hours had taken their toll on her.

''First of all, are you all right?'' he asked.

''I'd be much better if this insane man would just come to his senses. Now, what's all this nonsense about Hanna?''

Blake told her what they were up against.

''And he doesn't believe you, right?'' she said, and she looked over at Whitney Terrell.

''Not only doesn't he not believe me, but he insists that if the bill of sale isn't signed by morning... Well, you know the rest.''

Elizabeth continued to stare at Terrell. ''It figures. Well—'' she straightened her head haughtily as if ignoring the fact that she was sentenced to die ''—if he's stupid enough to think you'd be lying I guess there isn't much you can do except try as hard as you can to find Hanna before morning.''

Blake winked at her, hoping she'd catch on. ''That's what I intend to do,'' he said. ''So just stay calm and say a few prayers, okay?''

Elizabeth nodded.

"Okay, take her back," said Terrell, and he motioned toward Steele. "I've heard enough of this nonsense."

"Back to the pantry, huh?" Elizabeth said, and Terrell cut her off.

"Shut up," he said. "Just make sure you tie her feet again, too. We don't need her walkin' off."

Steele gave his boss a nod, then pushed Elizabeth into the hall, moving her toward the kitchen.

"All right, Morgan," Terrell said as soon as Elizabeth was out of the room. "You've got until morning."

Blake's jaw set stubbornly. That's what you think, he said to himself, then he reached into his pocket and pulled out the heel chain, realizing now where it had to come from.

"Here, I think this belongs to one of your men," he said as he tossed it to Terrell.

Terrell caught it and smiled. "Hey, yeah, that's Steele's. Now where the hell did you find that?"

"Why'd you have him set the fire?" Blake asked.

Terrell sneered. "Because with her drive broke up she'd have had to sell," he answered. "There wouldn't have been no money to keep it going."

"You're a bastard, Terrell."

"I'm a businessman, Morgan."

Blake stared at him hard, then without saying another word, he turned and walked out.

Blake knew that Terrell was standing on the porch watching him ride away. He rode right past where the others were hiding until he knew he was out of sight of the house, then he quickly turned his Appaloosa around, left the main trail, and filtered through the trees and shadows to where the rest of the men waited.

"Jules?"

"Over here," the foreman said.

Blake dismounted, then moved quickly in the dark, checking his gun on the way, and when he reached Jules and the others he told them what they were up against.

"They haven't hurt her, have they?" Jules asked, and Blake reassured him that except for a bit of wear and tear, Elizabeth seemed fine.

"But there are two guns at the front that I could see and since they must be keeping her at the back of the house, there are probably more back there."

Jules thought for a minute. "Well, we know he's got at least six men with him," he said. "'Cause that's how many Paco said there were."

"All right," Blake said. "Now this is what we're going to do." And they made their plans.

A few minutes later, they moved forward. Blake had made Jules and the others take off their spurs and stuff them in their saddlebags because of the jingle-bobs, and now as they crept through the darkness, he was glad. They weren't making a sound.

Miguel and Sancho were to locate the men at the back while Jules moved in to get Elizabeth loose, and Blake was going to cover the front. As Blake made his way to a watering trough where he had a good bead on the front door, he smiled, amused at Jules's concern for Elizabeth. He was going to keep an eye on the two of them when this was all over.

Meanwhile at the back of the house, Jules was making his way along the side of the porch. From what he could see, only one man stood between him and the door. However, it was one man too many, and he'd have to eliminate him.

Easing himself forward as slowly as he could, he moved about an inch at a time, then stopped just to make sure. Finally he reached the corner of the porch. He stood for a minute, looking around, trying to figure out what to do next. Suddenly there was a single shout from the bunkhouse off to the right of the porch, and the man on the porch stood up.

"Carl? Joe?" the man yelled, but was greeted with nothing but silence.

Good, Sancho and Miguel evidently got their men.

"Keating?" the man yelled as he went up the steps into the kitchen. It was then Jules realized there was another man in the kitchen. He'd forgotten about that, and he'd also forgotten about the old Indian woman Terrell had as a housekeeper, since he wasn't married, and he began to wonder where she was. Well, he couldn't worry about that now. Anyway, he'd never known her to carry a gun.

He watched the men as Keating came out of the kitchen, then the two men left the porch and started toward the bunkhouse.

Now was his chance. Leaving the spot where he'd been standing, he started for the porch steps and was almost to them when suddenly the man named Keating must have sensed something and half turned.

"Damn!" Keating blurted anxiously, but by the time he had Jules in line with his six-shooter, Jules was already firing.

Keating went down and so did the other man. Jules didn't wait to see if there was anyone else. Taking the steps two at a time, he shoved the door open and yelled.

"Elizabeth?"

"In here," she called out and as he heard shots from out front this time, he paid no attention to the old Indian housekeeper who was cowering in the corner, and he made a lunge for the pantry.

Elizabeth was never so glad to see anyone in all her life as she was to see Jules. As soon as her hands were free, she looked at him and smiled with relief. "Well, it took you long enough to get here, Mr. Hayden," she said, the warmth in her eyes letting him know she was grateful. "Now I just hope we can get the rest of the way out of here alive."

"Don't worry about that," Blake interrupted from the door of the pantry. "Everything's well in hand."

"Terrell?" Elizabeth asked.

"Unfortunately, he's dead." Blake's gun was still in his hand and he holstered it. "He tried to get the drop on me."

"Oh, my." Elizabeth was still rubbing her wrists where Jules had cut the ropes. "What are you going to do?"

"About Terrell?" Blake's jaw set firmly. "Not much I can do except explain to the sheriff. Lucky that man Steele's still alive. He should be able to confirm everything that's happened here."

"So should she," Elizabeth said, and she pointed toward the old Indian woman still hiding in the corner.

It was some fifteen minutes later when Blake and Jules, with Elizabeth sitting in front of Jules on his horse, rode out of the Box T, leaving Miguel behind while Sancho rode into town for the sheriff.

"So now what?" Jules asked as they rode along.

"Now we see if Paco learned anything about where Culler's holding Hanna."

"And if he hasn't?"

"Then we wait until we hear from Culler." He spurred Diablo a little faster.

This time when they got back to the ranch Culler wasn't there, but Trudy was. Blake stared at her curiously as he stepped into the parlor where she was sitting waiting for them as if she owned the place.

"I thought you'd be in on this," Blake said, his eyes sifting over her.

She was wearing a riding skirt instead of the usual fancy dress and her hair was tied back, but the diamonds were still in her ears.

"So I'm ambitious," she said and she smiled triumphantly. "Now where's the money?"

"Didn't Maria tell you?"

"She gave me some stupid story about the safe being empty, but like I told her, it's the only place Hank could've had the money stashed."

"Well, it's not there."

"I don't believe you."

"You'd better," he said and his voice lowered viciously. "Because it's the truth."

"Then where'd he put it?"

Just then Elizabeth and Jules came in from the kitchen where Elizabeth had been getting her bearings after the long ride over from the Box T.

"Did you ever think that maybe he didn't have it?" she cut in. "You're all so sure Henry had the money when he got home. Maybe he wasn't this outlaw Whitey after all.''

"Oh, he was Whitey, all right," Blake assured her. "There's more than enough evidence to prove that."

"Then maybe he lost the money somewhere before he got home. That is possible, isn't it? After all, the man was shot, and from what Maria says he had a hole in him the size of an egg."

Blake looked at Trudy again. "She's right, you know. The money was probably never here in the first place."

"To hell it wasn't. I saw that letter Hank wrote to his sister. He said she'd never have to worry about money again. It's got to be here."

"Then you tell us where it is because that safe upstairs was empty."

She stood up. "So what do I tell Culler?"

"Tell him it won't work. That there's no way we can give him two hundred and fifty thousand dollars we don't have."

"He won't like it."

"I don't care what he likes. You just tell him. And tell him to release Hanna, too, because if he doesn't I'll see that he never lives to spend two hundred fifty thousand even if he should happen to come across it."

Trudy looked disgusted. "You think you're pretty smart, don't you?" She started to leave the room. "I'll tell him, but don't be surprised if he doesn't believe you." She walked out, heading for the kitchen and the back door.

"You aren't going to just let her go, are you?" Jules asked. "Hell, she can lead us to Miss Winters."

"I know," Blake answered. "Only I don't want her to know she's doing it." He waited until he heard Trudy reining her horse out of the ranch yard, then he looked at Jules. "Come on, let's go." He was reloading his gun as he, too, headed for the back door with Jules right behind him.

Hanna was weary and hungry. She'd had some bread and beans washed down with water hours before, but nothing since. In fact, she'd been alone in the cabin for the past half hour, although she knew Culler was sitting right outside the door.

She'd heard him whistling off and on, and occasionally the smoke from his cigarette would waft in through the cracks, but he hadn't come in from outside, not once in the last half hour.

He'd left one lone lamp lit in the cabin and Hanna looked around the place for the umpteenth time. There was still no way she could get out even if she were able to move. There was just one door, two windows, and barely enough room to call it a cabin.

There were two chairs in the place, and Culler had tied her to one. Her wrists hurt, as did her ankles, but it was her pride that was hurt more than anything else.

She'd come out here hoping to make a new life for herself and had botched things up horribly, and yet none of it had been her fault, really.

Henry! It was all Henry's fault, the whole thing. If he hadn't messed up his life things might have been different. Still, it was hard to imagine Henry robbing stages and banks. Yet that's exactly what Culler said Henry had done. Why, he'd even robbed a few trains, according to Culler. The thought was awesome.

She tried to remember back to when she and Henry were little. It seemed so long ago. Henry had always been the one to play pretend, and she'd been the more practical one.

Suddenly her thoughts wandered over the letter Henry had left her, and she began to remember something. Pretend, let's pretend. Why hadn't she thought of it before? It had to be the answer, and smiling smugly to herself, she suddenly relaxed. She was sure now that she knew where the money was.

Now that she remembered, the whole message in the letter seemed to fall into place. It was the only explanation. However, she certainly wasn't about to let Culler know she knew anything at all. The man was obsessed.

Her ears perked up at the sound of a horse outside. Then she heard talking and realized Trudy must be back. She couldn't hear everything that was being said, only an occasional word here and there. However, they sounded like they were arguing.

A few minutes later, the door opened and Culler strolled in. His face was livid, his eyes cold and vicious. Directly behind him was Trudy, and she didn't look any more pleased than he did.

"All right, Miss Winters, you want to play rough, we'll play rough," he said, his voice sharp and caustic. "Since it seems nobody at the house knows where the money is, that leaves only you."

"Me?" Hanna was astounded. "How would I know? I was in Boston when Henry stole that money."

"Well, I'll tell you," Trudy offered. "I got a good glimpse of that letter Hank wrote to you while you were in Boston, and in it he acted like you should know.''

"That doesn't mean I do." Hanna sighed. "Do you think if I knew where two hundred and fifty thousand dollars was that I'd be struggling to make ends meet at the ranch? Henry left me barely enough money to pay this month's wages. Good heavens, you must think I'm stupid."

"She's right, Culler," Trudy said.

Culler wasn't convinced and he stared at Hanna contemplating. "Just what did that letter say, Trudy?" he asked and Trudy tried to remember what she'd read during the few seconds she'd had it.

"For one thing it said if she remembered something about where they played when they were kids she'd never have to worry about money ever again."

Culler looked at Hanna. "And have you remembered?"

"Don't be ridiculous." Hanna was affecting her old prim and proper mannerisms to try to hide the fear that was growing inside her. "Henry might've thought he was giving me some sort of clue to where he'd hidden the stupid money, but I have absolutely no idea what he was talking about."

Culler's brown eyes narrowed, the heavy brows over them making them even more menacing. "I think you're lying," he said and he reached out, grabbed her hair and stared into her face. "Either you tell me what I want to know or I'm gonna start cutting," he said, and he drew a knife from a sheath in his gun belt and laid it across her cheek. "And when I'm through with you you'll wish you'd never heard of Texas or the White Wind."

Hanna's heart was in her throat, the fear turning her insides to jelly. It wasn't worth it and she knew it. No amount of money was worth being scarred for life. And yet even if she told him, there was no guarantee he wouldn't kill her anyway.

The knife moved harder against her flesh and tears came to her eyes.

"Well?" he taunted viciously.

She was just ready to tell him what he wanted to know when he looked at Trudy, who was watching the whole thing with apprehension.

"Did you hear somethin'?" he asked, his gaze suddenly darting from one window to the other.

She shook her head. "No."

"You sure you weren't followed?"

"I told you, I checked to make sure."

"You'd better be right." He turned his attention back to Hanna, his fingers twisting harder into her braid. Just as he started to open his mouth to say something, the door suddenly burst open and Blake stepped onto the threshold, gun in hand, with Jules right behind him.

"Okay, put it down, Culler," Blake spat out, his eyes boring into the outlaw's, his gun leveled on the man.

Culler froze. "I can still cut her, Morgan," he yelled.

"You do and you'll be wearing a bullet right between the eyes. Is that what you want?"

"I want the money."

"There is no money. I've come to the conclusion that Whitey lost it somewhere when he was trying to get home. Hell, it could be out on the range where he stashed it, God knows where.''

"Then why'd he write that letter to the lady here, telling her she'd never have to worry about money again?''

"Who knows. He probably buried it somewhere figuring she might know what he was talking about, but she doesn't. Now, lower the knife and back away.''

Culler stared hard at Blake. Morgan had the upper hand and he knew it, yet he hated to give up.

"What happens if I give in?'' he asked, his mouth twitching nervously.

Morgan straightened, his hand tightening on his Colt. "I take you into custody, you serve a few years for robbery, a couple for kidnapping, if the lady presses charges, and with good luck, you can be a free man again some day.''

"And if I don't?''

"You'll die with your boots on. Now, what'll it be?''

Culler glanced at Trudy. She had already given up, hands spread high with Jules's gun leveled on her, and slowly he realized he'd rather take his chances on being alive. His hand eased in Hanna's hair, and he released it, at the same time lowering the knife. Hanna let out a sigh of relief.

As soon as the knife left Hanna's cheek, Blake stepped forward, grabbed it out of Culler's hand and stuck it in the waistband on his pants, then forced Culler and Trudy into a corner so Jules could keep a drop on them while he untied Hanna.

"Am I glad to see you,'' she said as he knelt down and began untying her. "The man was crazy.''

"I know, but don't worry. It's all over now."

She pulled her hands around in front of her and tried flexing them to get the circulation back in them.

"How did you manage to follow Trudy without her seeing you?" she asked.

He reached out and helped her rub the circulation into her hands. "It comes with the territory. It's my job, remember?"

She looked into his topaz eyes and saw the truth resting there, and suddenly she thought of the money.

"What are you going to do now?" she asked.

He helped her to her feet. "What can I do? I know Henry was Whitey, and I know he had the money, but if I don't have it . . ." He shrugged.

For the first time in her life Hanna felt a strange sense of apprehension. She was sure she knew where the money was, and yet . . . Henry had died for that money. He'd wanted her to have it, and she did need it. Rather, the ranch needed it, she knew that.

Only it wasn't her money even if it was where she thought it might be. She should tell Blake where it was right now, only for some strange reason she couldn't.

Maybe it was because Blake had lied to her right from the start. Or maybe she was still smarting over his bedroom escapade with Trudy. Or maybe she, too, had a little larceny in her heart, just like Henry'd had. But for some reason she couldn't tell him. Not just now, not yet.

"So what happens?" she asked as she moved around some to get the circulation back in her legs after sitting down so long.

"We tie these two up, take them to the ranch and maybe the sheriff will be there to meet us," he an-

swered. With Jules helping they tied up Culler and
Trudy, found Hanna's horse outside where it had been
tethered with the others and headed for the ranch. On
the way Blake told her all about their earlier escapade
rescuing Elizabeth.

It was close to morning. Everything had been taken
care of, including the events at the Box T. The sheriff
was gone already, Jules and Elizabeth were in the
kitchen arguing over something inconsequential, and
Hanna was standing on the veranda staring toward the
horizon where dawn would soon be creeping into the
hills.

She still hadn't told Blake about where she thought
the money could be, and she didn't know why.
Reaching up, she brushed a few stray hairs back,
tucking them into the braid, which was really a mess
now.

"Why don't you just undo it?" Blake asked from
behind her.

She whirled around.

"You know I always like it when it's loose," he went
on, and stepping up to stand in front of her, he
reached out, slipping the leather tie from the end of
her hair, then using his fingers, he began to comb it
free until it lay like white clouds on her shoulders,
framing her face. "You're lovely, you know that," he
said. "But then I guess I've told you that before."

"Blake . . . please."

"No. You listen, and you listen good, Hanna Winters. I know you've been upset with me because I lied
to you about who I really am and why I was here, and
I'm sorry about that, but I had no choice. You'd never

have let me come with you if I'd told you the truth then. But I'm not lying to you now. I love you, Hanna. I've been trying to deny it, trying to tell myself you were just a passing fancy, but it isn't working and I know that."

Her lavender eyes filled with tears.

"Now, don't cry. I hate to see you cry."

"But you don't know. I want to trust you so badly, Blake, and yet..." She turned away and walked to the railing. "There's something you don't know about me."

"Go on."

"It was after Henry had gone. I wasn't quite twenty-one at the time. Oh, I'd had a few beaus, but nothing serious and then I met Armand. He was handsome and charming, quite the ladies' man. Actually, you might say he swept me off my feet. The courtship was short, not quite a month, but like so many gullible young women I thought I was in love." She turned. "Well, I eloped with Armand and we had one night of bliss that I thought was the start of a lifetime together, but it wasn't. The next morning when he discovered my father was penniless and in debt to his ears, Armand walked out on me and I haven't seen him since. He never even showed up for the annulment proceedings, and I've hated men ever since."

"Hate's a strong word."

"Well, then, let's say I've avoided men ever since, and then you came along, and now you've lied to me, too."

"But I'm not lying now."

"How do I know that? How do I know that you're not just saying this because you think I might know where the money really is? That by getting in my good graces you're hoping I'll tell you."

"Do you know where it is?"

She could feel her face flushing. "I don't know."

"What do you mean, you don't know?"

She stared at him apprehensively. "I just mean I don't know." She lifted her head stubbornly. "Besides, what if I did know? What then? I suppose you'd take the money and leave."

He shook his head. "You haven't heard a word I've said, have you?"

"What do you mean?"

"Hanna, didn't you hear me talking with Jules before? There's a ten-thousand-dollar reward for the person who finds that money."

"So what good would that do me? I'd still be alone."

"With ten thousand dollars you could buy Terrell's ranch, now that he's dead, and still have enough money left over to keep the place going until Pete and the men get back from the cattle drive. But the most important thing is that without the money standing between us, maybe we could have some sort of a future together."

"Us?"

"Yes, us. Now look, all that seems to be standing between us now is your fear that all I want you for is to find out where the money is. Well, if you give me the money, then if I stay, you know it's because I love you."

"And if you don't stay I'm out the money and you, as well."

"I guess that's the chance you'll have to take."

She stared at him, wanting him more than she'd ever wanted anyone or anything in her life. She was in love with him, really in love, and she knew it, and yet he'd lied to her ever since this whole thing began.

"All right," she finally said, taking her heart in her hands and throwing it at his feet. "I'm going to trust you just this once more, but if you blow that trust, Blake Morgan, if you trample on my heart, I'll never trust anyone ever again." She stepped past him and walked into the house.

Blake was frowning as he followed her into the parlor where a dim lamp cast shadows about the room. They could still hear Jules and Elizabeth in the kitchen, but it sounded like the argument was over, at least for now.

She walked to the fireplace, then stopped and stood staring at it apprehensively.

"What is it?" he asked.

She turned to face him. "Henry used to pretend a lot when we were kids," she said, her voice unsteady. "And one of the things he was fondest of pretending was that he was Robin Hood and stole from the rich to give to the poor, and he had a special place to keep his treasures, right in front of the fireplace."

She turned toward the hearth, dropped to the floor and began examining all the stones in the hearth one at a time.

Suddenly she stopped. "Here," she said, her fingers running along the side of a flat rock right in front. Blake dropped down beside her.

After a close examination Blake dug his fingers under the edge and began to lift. The stone moved easily, and within minutes it was shoved aside to reveal a deep hole. Down inside the hole, covered with dust and dirt, were four canvas bags with the words Wells Fargo written across them.

"Thank God," Blake whispered as he reached in and drew them out one at a time. Opening them quickly, he began to check their contents.

While he did, Hanna looked at him curiously, then, seeing him so absorbed in the money, she stood and walked to the double doors that led to the garden.

The first few rays of dawn were lightening the sky to the east and she felt a shiver run through her even though the night had been warm.

"Jules, come in here!" Blake shouted from behind her where he still knelt at the fireplace. A few minutes later she heard a babble of voices as Jules and Mrs. Brady both came in, only she paid no attention to what they were saying.

All she could think of was the fact that he had the money now. Blake had the money and there was no reason for him to stay any longer. She was sure she had seen it in his eyes when he'd read the words Wells Fargo on the canvas bags. It was over and she'd lost.

She leaned her head against the doorframe, pushed back her pale hair and felt tears sting her eyes. He was so absorbed in finding the money he'd forgotten she even existed, and the tears rolled down her cheeks.

Suddenly she was brought up short by his voice, close to her ear.

"Just what do you think you're doing?" he asked, his voice low.

She turned to face him. He was directly behind her, his tall frame filling her vision.

"Jules?" she asked, avoiding his eyes.

"I had him take the money to the library for safe-keeping, and Elizabeth went with him. Why?"

"I just wondered."

"What else have you wondered?"

"When you'll be leaving."

"When do you want me to leave?"

This time she couldn't avoid his eyes, and when she looked into them she trembled. "Whenever you like."

"And if I don't like?"

"I don't understand."

For the first time in his life Blake suddenly realized he'd really been telling the truth there on the veranda. He didn't want to leave, ever.

Reaching out, he took her by the shoulders. "Like I told you, Hanna Winters, you took a chance and won. I'm in love with you, don't you understand? It isn't the money that's kept me here, it was you. And it isn't the money that's going to keep me here, either, it's you. I want to teach you everything you need to know about taking care of a place like this, if you'll have me, and while I'm doing it I'll teach you everything you need to know about love, too."

Hanna couldn't believe her ears. "You really mean that?" she asked her heart suddenly filling and melting the cold icy feeling that had gripped her only moments ago. "You really mean you love me?"

"I really, really mean it," he said emphatically, and while the voices of Jules and Elizabeth filtered into the parlor as they argued over the best place to put the money for safe-keeping until it could be returned to Wells Fargo, Blake lifted Hanna into his arms and climbed the winding stone steps toward the master bedroom as the early morning sun bathed the ranch in its golden glow.

*   *   *   *   *

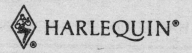

HARLEQUIN SUPERROMANCE®

A PLACE IN HER HEART...

Somewhere deep in the heart of every grown woman is the little girl she used to be....

In September, October and November 1992, the world of childhood and the world of love collide in six very special romance titles. Follow these six special heroines as they discover the sometimes heart-wrenching, always heartwarming joy of being a Big Sister.

Written by six of your favorite Superromance authors, these compelling and emotionally satisfying romantic stories will earn a place in your heart!

AVAILABLE WHEREVER
HARLEQUIN SUPERROMANCE
BOOKS ARE SOLD

HARLEQUIN®

I N T R I G U E®

A SPAULDING AND DARIEN MYSTERY

Amateur sleuths Jenny Spaulding and Peter Darien have set
the date for their wedding. But before they walk down the
aisle, love must pass a final test. This time, they won't have to
solve a murder, they'll have to prevent one—Jenny's.
Don't miss the chilling conclusion to the SPAULDING AND
DARIEN MYSTERY series in October. Watch for:

#197 WHEN SHE WAS BAD by Robin Francis

Look for the identifying series flash—A SPAULDING AND
DARIEN MYSTERY—and join Jenny and Peter for danger and
romance....

WELCOME TO

The quintessential small town, where everyone knows everybody else!

Finally, books that capture the pleasure of tuning in to your favorite TV show!

Join your friends at Tyler in the eighth book, BACHELOR'S PUZZLE by Ginger Chambers, available in October.

What do Tyler's librarian and a cosmopolitan architect have in common? What does the coroner's office have to reveal?

GREAT READING...GREAT SAVINGS... AND A FABULOUS FREE GIFT!

Each book set in Tyler is a self-contained love story; together, the twelve novels stitch the fabric of the community. You can't miss the Tyler books on the shelves because the covers honor the old American tradition of quilting; each cover depicts a patch of the large Tyler quilt!

And you can receive a FABULOUS GIFT, ABSOLUTELY FREE, by collecting proofs-of-purchase found in each Tyler book, *and* use our Tyler coupons to save on your next TYLER book purchase.
